I0716328

SUPERFICIAL

DIANE BILLAS

ALSO BY DIANE BILLAS

Does Love Always Win?

This is a work of fiction. All of the characters, organizations, and events portrayed in this novel are either products of the author's imagination or are used fictitiously.

Published in the United States by Creative James Media.

SUPERFICIAL. Copyright © 2024 by Diane Billas. All rights reserved. Printed in the United States of America. For information, address Creative James Media, 9150 Fort Smallwood Road, Pasadena, MD 21122.

www.creativejamesmedia.com

978-1-956183-33-7 (trade paperback)

First U.S. Edition 2024

To my son Luke,
I can't wait for you to read this story.

CHAPTER ONE

LEA

I'm a firm believer of listening to your gut. When I had a foreboding feeling after stepping off the plane at the Philadelphia airport earlier that day, I should have turned around and flown home. Instead, I trudged on and ended up at the biggest draw of the weekend, the Comic-Con like convention, WizCon.

"I have to pee. I'll be right back," I say to my friend Jess. She half-heartedly nods, not even turning towards me.

When Jess is on a mission, it's best not to get in her way. At the current moment she's trying to find the whole reason she signed up for WizCon in the first place, the beautiful Brown Recluse.

Brown Recluse is a Black Widow knock-off but can poison villains with her fingernails. Jess is dressed up as her today, but not going to lie, she looks like one of those kids at school that is purposely trying to not fit in, with her skintight brown tank showing way too much cleavage, dark brown leather jacket, tight brown leggings that shouldn't be worn out of the house without a dress over them, and beat-up Converse shoes. The all-brown outfit compliments her long curly, brunette hair.

Jess's gaze pans the room when she gasps and points.

"O-M-G. There she is! We have to try and sneak a picture." Jess grabs Olive, her non-binary partner, and pulls them down the aisle. Olive is dressed as the non-binary superhero, Commander Hero. Their schtick is wearing swanky business suits, being able to jump really high, and not giving two craps about anyone. I have to say, the business suit that Olive bought with their parents' credit card looks so much like Commander Hero's its uncanny. Olive even has Commander Hero's recognizable dark-green hat on top of their short, black hair.

Olive gives me a shrug and they obediently follow Jess. Jess has been obsessed with Brown Recluse almost as much as she's obsessed with her partner Olive.

I sigh watching them walk off, hand-in-hand. Being the third wheel is the worst, especially when it's your two best friends who are the ones dating. It also doesn't help when one of them had been your kissing buddy and suddenly decided you weren't enough, but instead, concluded your other best friend fit the bill.

I slog towards the exit of the convention hall, lost in my thoughts, when suddenly, out of nowhere a wing is aimed right at my eye. I yelp and jump out of the way right at the last minute. A redheaded girl, fully clad in a white Valkyrie costume with the largest wings I've ever encountered, apologizes.

I really should've canceled this trip, although getting stabbed in the eye would help me not have to witness Jess and Olive's excessive PDA.

The three of us booked this trip six months ago to celebrate our high school graduation and our impending pilgrimage to college but a lot can happen in six months.

The line to the women's restroom is wrapped around the

corner. Guess it isn't only guys that go to these conventions anymore. At least some stereotypes in the world are changing for the better.

"Is there another bathroom?" I ask a muscular bald guy that has *Security* written on his black shirt.

He nods towards the elevator. "Down a level."

The elevator is starting to close, and I slip in, quickly pulling my gold cape in behind me.

I don't have a particular hero that I wanted to dress up as, so I picked out my own costume. Gold cape, white shirt, gold spandex pants, and black flats with my signature bright orange purse. Oh, and don't forget the bright gold *L* across my chest. In all honesty, I kept procrastinating buying a costume until I realized WizCon was only days away, so what I'm wearing now is all I could find on Amazon Prime. I thought I was being cute with the monogrammed *L*. Now it seems ridiculous. When Jess saw me this morning before we boarded the plane, she just shook her head.

"Couldn't even splurge to get a new purse to match?" she had asked me, raising her eyebrows.

I wanted to come back with some kind of witty comment, but my tongue felt thick and heavy, so I took her crap like I always do.

A lone figure lingers in the back corner of the elevator wearing a navy-blue Yankees baseball hat, their face cast downwards.

I push for level two when there is a large bang. The lights flicker and go out. Deathly silence follows but is broken by a curse word behind me. I whip around, trying to make out the figure's face.

"Watch that cape, you almost gave me cape burn," the voice grumbles.

"Sorry. I never knew how annoying wearing a cosplay costume would be," I reply, biting my lip.

When the silence continues, I nervously keep up my word

vomit. "This is my first time coming to one of these things. I should've taken a page out of your book and worn the incognito star look. I would've been more comfortable on the plane flight earlier this morning and gotten less strange looks."

Backup lights flicker on. I can barely see the figure lift his head and look at me directly in the eyes. My heart drops.

"About the incognito star look," he says, his dark eyes full of hesitation.

No way.

No freaking way.

He isn't playing an incognito star.

He is the star of today's show. The last-minute addition that made the entire WizCon event sell out as soon as his name was announced.

A gasp escapes my mouth. I can't physically stop it if I tried.

I'm from the middle of nowhere Ohio. You don't see a movie star on an elevator or anywhere in your vicinity.

Keep calm, Lea, don't scare him off. He's incognito for a reason.

"Oh."

That's what I come up with to say. I mean, what else am I going to utter aloud? Certainly not any of the questions running through my head, like why is he in this elevator alone without a posse of security? Why did he even stoop to this level of a publicity stunt; isn't this type of thing for actors whose careers are on the downward trajectory?

"I should've never signed up for this stupid convention," he mumbles under his breath.

I'm still grasping what to say back. He must've taken my non-responsiveness as an indication to continue complaining.

"Now I'm stuck on here with some megafan and I need to get back to my dressing room in like ten minutes or my agent is going to chew out my ass," he gripes.

That's when I shake out of it. Even though he's a movie star, it doesn't mean he has the right to be a jerk to me. It's not like I stopped the elevator on purpose to get some alone time with him.

I've always heard not to meet famous people in person. Guess they're right.

"I don't want to be trapped in here either," I say sharply. "I have to pee so bad." Probably not what I should be saying to a movie star, but he doesn't seem to have any filters so why should I? What I really want to do is jump up and down to fight off the urge, but I don't want to rock the non-working elevator.

"Not my problem," he says pulling out his phone from his dark skinny jeans.

"It will be if we're stuck on here too long," I say smugly.

"Wait, my phone isn't working." He keeps tapping at the screen.

I fumble in my purse and find my phone. I push the side button, but no shining light appears.

"Mine's dead too."

My eyes lock onto his.

"What's happening?" he asks, panic finally revealing itself on his face, mirroring my own.

I take a deep breath that I feel to my toes.

"Maybe it's some type of power failure?" I suggest.

"What kind of power failure also affects cell phones?" he asks.

I shrug. "One that's powerful enough. I don't know, I'm not some electrician."

He lets out a burst of air. "I don't have time for this. I need to get out of here and figure out what's going on."

"The first thing to do in a crisis is to remain calm." My tone contradicts everything I say.

"That would be the ideal way to react but it's kind of hard because I have so much riding on today."

"At WizCon? But you're like the hit star," I say, my mouth dropping.

"But is that all I'll ever be? Some superhero star associated with comic books?"

I have to bite my tongue to keep from saying what I'm really thinking. *At least you're a star at all; many people would kill to have that job.*

"I only agreed to be the headliner for this event because my agent promised me if I came here, he'd try and look for a non-superhero role for me. I'm only popular with comic book nerds and teenage girls, not the rest of the population and I'd really like that to change."

"That can't be right, you're such a good actor." I can't help myself. He really is talented, even if he is a jerk in real life.

It's also weird talking to him with only dim lighting. I can barely see any of his body language but am able to see the outline of his figure moving to the ground. I join him on the elevator floor. Better to settle in for the long-haul because it looks like we are going to be here for a while.

"Sure, I'm awesome as The Amazing Boy but apparently that's all anyone sees me as. If someone isn't into superhero stuff, they've never heard of me."

"Is that so bad?" I ask.

"I want to be a real actor and win an Oscar. Why am I even telling you this?"

I shrug and realize he probably can't see me, so I say instead, "I don't know. I've heard crisis situations can make people say things they are really thinking. It makes more sense now why you came to WizCon."

"What do you mean?"

I cough. "My friends and I were surprised to see you listed. It seemed, uh, beneath you."

I hear a smack and see his hand covering his face. "Even the megafan agrees I'm doomed."

"Hey now. Megafan? I don't think so. Sure, your movies are fun but I don't have some life-sized poster of you in my room. And even if I did, I'd be removing it as soon as I got home. You're something else."

He makes a sound of irritation. "What do you mean?"

"We're stuck in an elevator with no power, no phones, and barely any lights and you're worried your agent is going to chew you out. It's all about you. What about me? I took this elevator to go to the bathroom and now I'm trapped in here with some stuck-up guy that thinks he's God's greatest gift to earth. I'm getting the crappy end of this deal."

There is silence and a sigh. "Sorry, I'm not used to normal interactions anymore. I forget how to talk to people that aren't famous or obsessed with me. We're all self-absorbed assholes."

At least he admits he sucks.

"It's okay. I'm being pissy too because this trip isn't what I was expecting. And the pressure on my bladder isn't helping."

"Please don't pee on the floor. I don't think I could control my gag reflex and then we'd have even more *fun* bodily fluids to deal with."

That comment then causes me to involuntarily gag. "Gross! Although that's the most normal guy thing you've said since I've met you."

He chuckles. "Yeah. I guess I still have some remnants of my old self."

"Glad you haven't completely sold out. I'm Lea Anderson by the way."

"I'm Jake Johnson, but I guess you already knew that."

I snicker. "Even someone who isn't a megafan would know your name. It's plastered everywhere."

"But not on a poster in your bedroom," Jake quips back.

"Hey, you listened to me," I say.

"I'm not always an ass."

It's quiet for another moment.

"If you aren't here for me, what made you come to this event?"

I chuckle. "You're really egotistical, aren't you? People can come to these things not to see you."

"Sorry, that's not what I meant. Came out the wrong way. I'll try it again. Why are you at WizCon?"

I sigh. "That's a long, complicated answer."

"I'm not going anywhere anytime soon, unless you have some grand plan to get us out of here."

Suddenly the lights flicker for a second and the elevator lurches sideways. I gasp and brace myself against the wall.

"What the heck," Jake says, also grabbing onto the side of the elevator.

"Is it going to fall?" I ask shakily.

"It better not."

The elevator stops moving, and we are back to only having the flickering emergency lights.

"Maybe a good way to pass the time and not think about what's going on would be to tell you my sad story," I say, trying to control my breathing.

"Let's hear it."

CHAPTER TWO

LEA
Six Months Prior

"Pretty, pretty please! The three of us HAVE to go together. You like superhero movies, what's holding you back?" Jess asks, sticking out her lower lip.

She always knows how to make me melt.

"I'm going to have to ask off from work," I say.

Jess rolls her eyes. "It's literally one weekend. The Midnight Diner can spare you."

"I don't know, they're always short-handed. Besides, there's no one confirmed yet I want to see."

"Are you kidding me? Brown Recluse is going to be there. She's my favorite superhero of all-time. You know that!"

"You'll probably barely get a glimpse of her," I respond back.

"But what if I do see her? It would mean everything to me! You're really starting to sound like your parents."

That's a low blow.

Jess keeps rambling. "Plus, many other cool people will be there, and they keep teasing that a huge headliner is going to be announced soon. If it's someone super famous it'll sell out immediately, so we have to get on this now."

"And Olive's already on board?" I ask nonchalantly. I would be fine going with Jess but she's insisting Olive comes too. Which normally would be okay, Olive is another one of my best friends, but things have been heating up with Jess and I'd rather have some alone time with her.

"They also like Brown Recluse and Commander Hero is confirmed in the lineup. Olive's parents have a ton of hotel reward points so our hotel would be free."

I sigh. "You know I love doing things with the three of us, but it would be more fun if it's just you and me."

Jess moves toward me and pulls me close. "We can sleep in the same bed in the hotel room," she whispers in my ear.

I suck in my breath. That would be a dream come true, except minus having my other best friend in the bed next to us.

"You drive a hard bargain, but we'd have to be good if Olive is coming."

"I'm sure we can find a way to be alone, like we always do," Jess says, a glint of mischief in her eyes. She leans in and plants a kiss on me. My misgivings about the trip float away as the kiss gets deeper and more frantic. Just as things are really heating up, Jess pulls herself off me and looks expectantly into my eyes.

"Well?"

I'm still out of breath, wanting more, but manage to say, "Yes. If more of that happens, absolutely yes. I can geek out on all the great historical sites in Philadelphia."

Jess jumps up and down. "I can't wait! This is going to be absolutely epic! I have to tell Olive." She picks up her phone and begins typing away. She looks up and gives me a thumbs up sign. "They're in! Let's do the registration together. Olive's in charge of the hotel room."

The two of us, side-by-side, reserve our spot for this amazing adventure. I'm high off of Jess and the idea of being with her for over twenty-four hours straight. She's giddy with the anticipation of meeting her real-life hero. After we receive our e-tickets, we set down our phones and stare into each other's eyes. I think, at long last, it's going to be the time we say that we love each other. But before I can open my mouth, Jess pounces on me and her lips are on mine. Maybe WizCon will be the time we profess our love. Who knows what can happen?

Three months later, I walk into Jess's room and find her in the same exact position, except with Olive. And she ultimately chooses Olive as her partner. Not me. The one that's been by her side since kindergarten. Her number one fan.

Why didn't I buy the refundable plane ticket?

———

Present Day

"THAT'S ROUGH; you didn't even want to be here," Jake says.

"Jess is a master manipulator except she didn't expect to get caught with Olive."

Jake shifts positions. "So, let me get this straight, your ex is with your other friend and they're both here?"

"You've got it exactly right. I was talked into coming to this thing by promises of kisses. Now all I get to see is my friends kissing all they want. And be stuck in an elevator that may or may not crash at any moment."

"At least now you won't see the kisses?" Jake offers.

I rub my temple. "I've already seen so many that they are imprinted in my mind."

There is a beat of silence until Jake asks, "So, are you a lesbian? Or bi?"

Now's always the fun part, explaining myself. Sometimes I say I'm bisexual, because no one understands pansexual, but Jake is famous, and I hate not being truthful about my identity. He probably knows some people that identify as pan. Maybe he's met my uber crush and famous pan, Miley Cyrus.

"Pansexual. But I've mainly only been with girls. Well, basically one girl, and the worst part is Jess and I weren't actually girlfriends. She never wanted it to be official, probably because she was doing the same thing with Olive."

Jake turns his head towards me and says, "That sucks."

"I feel like I wasted so much time on her. I should've seen the red flags but when you're obsessed with someone, things slip past. What about you? Anyone?"

Jake scoffs. "No way. No time. Here and there I'm with somebody but nothing ever sticks."

"None of those models that you're in pictures with?" Everyone that's a breathing human has seen all the pictures of Jake with gorgeous girls. He's like the younger version of Leonardo DiCaprio.

"No."

"What about any of your adoring fans?"

Jake grunts. "Dating a superfan is such a bad idea. They will never like you for you, or when they find out you're a human being like them, they start to lose interest."

"Sounds like you might be talking from some experience."

I can faintly see Jake shrugging. "Maybe. But everyone in the biz knows it."

Talking with Jake feels normal, as if he isn't some famous movie star that many girls dream about every night. I almost forget about my aching bladder, almost. It probably helps that I can barely see his face, so it's just like I'm talking to any other guy.

I clear my throat. "How would you go on a date anyways; wouldn't you need security?"

His head nods. "It's a pain, probably another reason I never do it. Sometimes they clear out a restaurant, or other times they try and get a dark, back booth. Either way, it's not very fun, especially if there are paparazzi. The incognito look can only take me so far. If I want to keep on the baseball hat, it's not like I can take my date to a fancy restaurant."

Jake gets up and squints at the elevator button panel. He plays with a few buttons while he says, "I wonder if it's a whole city outage?" I take that as his way of ending the subject of his dating life.

As soon as Jake stops talking, another set of lights come on, but they aren't all the lights in the elevator, just one more set. A slight hum begins to sound and the elevator shakes again. I involuntarily gasp. Jake leans against the elevator wall, bracing himself.

"What's going on?" I whisper.

"I think another backup generator kicked in."

The elevator begins a painfully slow descent. The whole time I'm trying to not freak out.

Is it going to crash? Is this going to be my end? I have so many things I haven't done yet. Is Jess going to be my last kiss?

The elevator stops moving and the doors inch apart. It feels like hours until the space is large enough for us to move through.

Jake grabs my hand and pulls me up off the floor. "Run!" Jake says, pushing me ahead of him. He doesn't have to tell me twice. I grab my gold cape so it won't get stuck if the doors slam shut. I twist around to make sure Jake is right behind me. He slips through the doors just as they begin to close. They shutter together with a bang. Pretty sure I will never go back on an elevator for the rest of my life.

Only darkness remains. As my eyes adjust, I notice a few hints of brightness from the emergency lights scattered throughout the hallway. I can just make out the doors up ahead.

"Come on, let's go this way," Jake says. He reaches out and lightly pulls on my hand. "I don't want to lose you."

I clasp his hand and trek behind him. Now I really understand the term *follow blindly*.

After walking down the hallway and managing to not trip over anything, Jake stops and drops my hand.

"Here you go, this is what you've been needing right?" He gestures to a door. I can faintly make out the word: RESTROOM.

"You're my savior right now. You have no idea how happy this makes me. Thank you!"

I'm about to run inside when I turn back to Jake.

"You'll be here when I come out?"

Jake nods. "For sure. We need to stick together right now."

With that reassurance, I proceed with caution.

CHAPTER THREE

JAKE

I don't want to scare Lea too much, but it's clear something is majorly wrong. Time to change into my gear. These civilian clothes won't help if I need to fight some bad guys. That will do me and the world no good whatsoever.

While Lea's in the bathroom, I sprint down the hallway as fast as I can with low lighting. That's all I need, to fall and get hurt before figuring out what's happening.

I reach my dressing room, swipe my badge but nothing happens. I almost smack my head with frustration. Of course it's not going to work if the electricity is off.

I've lost track of how many times the Agent has warned me against what I'm about to do in civilian clothes but it's a dire situation. I'm more in survival mode at this point. Besides, I'm not sure if it'll work anyways. I swivel to make sure no one's watching. Not like I can see much, I really need my Amazing Boy glasses to hone my skills, but it's so quiet that I'd be able to hear the rustle of clothes, patter of footsteps, or sense a heat pattern off a body. I take a deep breath, reach for the door, concentrate as much as I can, and pull.

It starts to slowly budge. I keep dragging the door open until there's enough space for me to fit in and I slip through. I'm just happy it worked this time.

My dressing room is in complete darkness, except for one flickering backup light. I need to get in and out before Lea thinks I've abandoned her. Then I'd really live up to my asshole persona.

I scan the room and use my photographic memory to figure out where my costume is stored. It's never just out in the open. Too easy for someone to steal. Then I remember after the photoshoot this morning my costume was whisked away and put in a large closet until the big event.

I try not to run into anything, especially a large, plush easy chair right near the entrance. I rip open the closet door.

There's my costume in all its glory. Red and gold with a bright red cape. The outfit is all spandex but pretty comfortable. I have no idea where they got the materials, but I must give it to my costume designers, it feels like I'm wearing nothing when I have it on.

I quickly change and leave my civilian clothes on the floor in a heap. I hate leaving them for my team to deal with, but time is of the essence. I need to get back to Lea and figure out what's going on ASAP.

———

LEA

MOST GIRLS WOULD KILL for a chance to stand next to Jake Johnson and would savor every second in his presence. Given the situation, and I'm not most girls, my brain is in high gear thinking of how to handle the current dilemma we're in.

After my trip to the bathroom, I come out to find Jake head to toe in spandex complete with a cape to match my own, except his is red and movie-grade quality. My mouth drops. His costume is even more magnificent in person than on the movie screen.

Mine is the kind of costume that can only be worn once because my gold spandex pants will tear at some point during the day, or the gold coloring will inevitably rub off.

"How did you change so fast? And why?" I ask.

"I couldn't let you be the only one dressed as a super-hero," he says, motioning for me to follow him. "Come on, let's go upstairs to see if we can find out what's going on."

We somehow manage to find the emergency steps and take one at a time back upstairs to the main exhibit hall.

"People will recognize you now that you're in your super-hero costume," I say, my eyes darting around, expecting to see some crazed fan lurking behind a dark corner.

"That's the least of my worries right now. I just want to find out what's happening."

The hallway outside the main exhibit room is empty and oddly silent.

"Is it just me or should there be people roaming around, like us, trying to figure out what's going on?" Jake asks, his head swiveling back and forth.

"And why aren't there any sounds? The exhibit hall can't be that soundproof, right?"

We stare at each other. Jake's eyes are filled with alarm. I'm sure mine aren't much better.

Jake inches towards the large double doors that separate us and the exhibit hall.

"Ready for this?" he asks.

"Let's get it over with."

Jake pushes the right door at the same time as I shove open the left one.

The only sound I hear is the hum of a generator. There is

just enough lighting to see that all the merch exhibit booths, complete with all the POP figurines you could ever ask for, are still intact but that's it. There isn't a single human being in this large space. *How is this possible?*

"This is bad." Jake's standing with his arms crossed.

"Where is everyone? WizCon's sold out," I say, still in shock. *Is this really happening? Where are Jess and Olive? Are they okay?* Even though I don't want to be here with them, I still care about my friends.

"How can thousands of people just disappear in the matter of thirty minutes?" Jake asks.

"What if they evacuated? Is that possible?"

Jake rubs his chin. "I guess that could've happened. But it still doesn't help us."

I eye the room one more time. "I think we need to go outside to see if this blackout is a city-wide thing and maybe we'll run into people from here on the street. They'd be hard to miss."

Jake stares at me. "Have you ever been to Philly before?"

I shake my head. "No. You?"

Jake twists his mouth. "Only for press events and never without security detail."

What Jake's saying isn't adding up. "What were you doing on the elevator without them?"

His eyes dart around the room. "I forgot something in my dressing room."

I cock my head. "Don't you have people to do that for you?"

Jake sighs and folds his arms. "Fine, you caught me. I wanted to experience WizCon just for a second as a normal person. I had a little bit of time before my panel. That's why I wasn't in my costume yet."

"And they let you?" I prod.

Jake coughs. "Well, not exactly. I was only supposed to be gone for five minutes or so. I said I was going to the bathroom and didn't need anyone for that. The elevator ruined my plan. That's why I put my costume on while you were in the bathroom just in case I saw my agent."

My face softens. *It must be terrible to have security around him all the time. No wonder he wants to be normal, even for a minute.* "What did you think of WizCon?"

His hand reaches up to scratch his head. "As soon as I walked in, I knew that it was a bad idea. Someone was bound to recognize me, even with the hat, and I didn't want to start a mob. I hightailed it back to the elevator to go to my dressing room, and then boom, we got stuck."

Jake looks down. "It was stupid of me but sometimes I wish I could be normal. But if I want to work on an Oscar worthy film, that'll never happen."

I give him a sympathetic look. "I have no idea what that's like. Most people don't even realize I exist. Jess has always been the outgoing, more interesting person. I've always lived in her shadow."

"You seem outgoing to me."

I shrug. "Maybe it's only because she's not around. Honestly, she and Olive have never been to Philadelphia before either, so I'm worried about them."

"At least they have each other. I don't think Philly's that terrible of a city. It has bad neighborhoods but what big city doesn't?"

"My grandma is terrified I came here but my parents didn't even think twice."

Most of the time they don't even know I exist. It wasn't like they planned to have me in the first place. I was a *happy* accident, unlike my older sister and brother.

Jake lifts up a black tablecloth at the merch booth closest to him and reveals a purse and a black backpack.

"The only thing that makes sense right now is the evacuation theory. Why else would people leave their stuff here," he mutters, straightening up.

This is too weird. During an evacuation, even though they tell you not to, I'm pretty sure the first thing I'd do is grab my purse.

Jake turns back around and opens the door. "Let's see what the city of Philadelphia is really like."

I take one last look at the desolate room and follow him.

"Are we really doing this? Going outside where there could be a bunch of zombies waiting to eat us?" I ask, hesitation in my voice.

"It was your suggestion," Jake reminds me.

"I know, but I don't always have the best ideas," I say, biting a hangnail. Once I realize what I'm doing I quickly remove my finger from my mouth, hoping Jake didn't notice my gross habit.

"Maybe you're just worried about roaming around such a cool city as *Super L.*" Jake motions to my costume. He's either being polite or missed my finger biting all together. And I guess I have a new nickname?

"If the thousands of people from WizCon are roaming around on the streets right now I really won't look out of place, especially next to you," I say, putting my hands on my hips.

Where did this sass come from? Whenever Jess made fun of something I wore, I hated it, but I never said anything back. And this is someone really famous.

Jake chuckles. "That's true, I saw some ridiculously complicated costumes. I don't even know how they got here wearing them."

"Right? There was one man with tree limbs coming out all over his body."

"Could you imagine the Uber ride?"

"But maybe it's like New York City and Philadelphia drivers are just used to it?"

Jake shrugs. "That's true. It's like the acting world. We're immune to over-the-top people. They're everywhere, all the time."

We begin the descent in the emergency staircase at a snail's pace so not to trip since there isn't much lighting. Jake suddenly stops and I run into his back.

"Ow, you could've warned me," I say, rubbing my nose.

"Sorry, trying to get my bearings. I think this is the ground floor."

He attempts to open the door and makes a noise.

"Wow, this is harder than I expected." He continues to push and finally it budges enough to blind me by the sun.

"Gahh!" I exclaim. I automatically close my eyes. When I slowly reopen them, sunlight streams down on me. We made it outside.

After my eyes readjust and I step through the opening, the first thing I notice are all the people. There are hundreds of them walking around, some in a hurry, but others meandering without a care in the world. Does this mean the blackout isn't citywide?

"The traffic lights are working," Jake says, pointing upward.

I pull out my phone and give a shout of glee. The picture of my tuxedo cat from my phone background stares back at me. "My phone is on again!"

I open the messenger app to see if I have anything from Jess or Olive. Nope, nothing. I type out a message to Jess.

Where ru?? RU OK?

I wait for it to say Delivered but it never happens.

"Jess's phone must still not be working. It doesn't say she's gotten my text."

Jake frowns. "Let me try calling my agent."

He pulls out his phone from his costume and holds it up to his ear.

I have to be honest. It's really odd seeing Jake in his movie costume on a cell phone. I hold in a laugh; it's like seeing a clip from a blooper reel.

After a few seconds he brings his cell phone down and stares at it.

"This is a really big problem," he says.

"Uh … what, the blackout, or the fact you're already getting recognized?" A swarm of girls are making their way over.

"I didn't think I would get spotted already." His eyes scan the crowd starting to form.

"Can we run to the front of the building to see if anyone is still around from WizCon before we find a hideout?" I ask.

"We better do it fast before those girls put my location out on social media."

We jog towards the front of the convention center. I swerve to miss a man sleeping on the sidewalk under the awning of a sandwich shop. *That poor man.* Farther along on the sidewalk there are discarded takeout bags, a needle, and I swear an unwrapped condom. I'm unable to keep myself from gasping. *What kind of place is this?*

Jake turns around. "Just look ahead, not down." *Easier said than done for the girl who's from a tiny town and always curious.*

Outside the front door there's a sea of people wearing all types of costumes from Superman to Pikachu.

I pick up the pace and ask, "Were you just inside?"

A man who could be Thor's stunt double shakes his head. "No, we just got here and are trying to get in, but the doors won't open."

Jake's brow furrows. "That's odd. Why would they lock them?"

"Maybe the blackout automatically causes them to lock?" I respond.

Jake reaches to try. He makes a grunting sound, and the door begins to slightly open. Thor's mouth drops.

"No way. We've been trying to get in for the past ten minutes. How did you do that?"

The man inspects Jake.

"Wait, you're The Amazing Boy, right? Like the real one? I thought you were just a really good look alike but you're actually him!"

"Just like you're the real Thor," Jake says back.

The man raises his eyebrows. "But I can't summon lightning. You actually have superstrength," he says pointing at Jake.

"That's ridiculous," I scoff.

It is weird though that Jake can get the door open and no else can.

"Come on, let's hide inside before any of the other fans find me." Jake pushes me through the partially open door, and it slams shut behind us. I assume the fans can now open the door but when I turn around all I see is the Thor stunt double grunting with all his might and it not moving a single inch.

"Wait, why could you open the door, but they can't? He even looks way more ripped than you, no offense."

Jake turns around, glaring. "I got lucky. Now let's figure out what's going on."

CHAPTER FOUR

We're back where we started. Even our phones revert to the black screen of death.

"Why did you make us come back in here? How's this going to help?" I gripe.

"That empty exhibit hall is really bothering me. Something's not right with it. I should've thought of this sooner."

I scratched my head. "Thought of what?"

"That this isn't just some normal blackout. This could've been a targeted attack."

"Attack? Like a terrorist attack?" I gasp.

"Kind of," Jake says, walking quickly to the escalators.

He takes the escalator steps two at a time. I gingerly step one foot on the first step. It feels weird to be on a non-working escalator. Even though I know it won't happen, I keep worrying that it will begin moving and throw me off balance. I look up and Jake is already at the top.

"Wait for me!" I pick up my pace until I catch up with him.

This time there is no hesitancy when Jake pushes the

exhibit hall doors. Even though I know what to expect, it's still creepy seeing the abandoned room with all the exhibits still in place, when I know just forty minutes before it was filled with people in an array of costumes.

Jake's walking around rubbing his chin. It's as if he's forming a conclusion of what happened, but for me, nothing can ever explain this madness. He pulls out of his costume a pair of midnight black sunglasses and places them on his face, surveying the room even closer.

"Why are you wearing sunglasses indoors?"

When he doesn't turn around, I call out, "Jake, slow down. I'm confused. Why are we back here? Can you walk me through what you're thinking?" I'm now jogging to catch up with him.

"I can't," Jake says, muttering to himself. I can't even imagine how dark things are for him with sunglasses, but miraculously, he doesn't walk into anything. The few occasions I've accidentally worn sunglasses inside never end well and that isn't even during a blackout. Jake wears them in his movies, but it's for getting information from some computer. That can't be happening now so why is he wearing them?

My head begins to throb.

Does he think I'm not smart enough to share what's on his mind? I thought he finally was starting to seem normal until now.

"You keep flip flopping from jerk to semi-normal, back to jerk. Are you always like this?" I ask.

Jake turns back and lowers his sunglasses to look at me. His eyes drip with sadness. "I'm sorry. I'm not allowed to tell you. It's in my NDA."

This throws me for a loop. *What does that have to do with thousands of people missing?*

"NDA?"

Jake sighs, almost in defeat. "A contract stating I can't tell anyone anything about myself."

I blink a few times. "But just a few minutes ago you were

opening up to me. What changed in between going outside and meeting Thor?"

"When I confirmed that this isn't a normal blackout, and we couldn't reach anyone that had been inside the building. Clearly, they weren't evacuated. My agent never shuts off his phone." His voice is deeper with more conviction.

In my stupor, I trip over an extension cord that looks like it had been fueling a dragon before the electricity went out. As I stumble, my first thought is, *People go all out to sell their merch. Such a shame no one's around to buy anything.*

I land on the ground with a thud.

Jake runs over to me and offers me his hand. "Are you okay?"

I ignore him and jump up, brushing off my spandex pants.

"Oh, now I get your attention. I'm fine. Just apparently way clumsier than you and I'm not even the one wearing sunglasses."

Jake raises his eyebrow as he motions to my legs. I look down.

Great. My pale skin is peeking out of a small hole in my gold pants right at the knee. This costume really is a piece of crap. At least there's no sign of blood.

"It's fine. Not like I am planning to wear this costume ever again. I was distracted by the fact you're being weird."

Jake blows some air out of his mouth. "I'm really not used to having a civilian tag along with me."

That comment pushes me over the edge.

I stamp my foot. "Civilian? Actors call fans civilians? You aren't in the military!"

Jake clasps his hand over his mouth. "I meant to say fan."

I take a step closer to him and turn my face up with a defiant look. "I get it. I'm not famous or at all cool. But my friends are missing, and I want to know what the heck is going on. If you know anything at all, can you please share it with me, even if I am a *civilian*?"

He's about to open his mouth but I cut him off and say, "Screw the NDA. How's anyone going to know?"

Jake's eyes dart around the room. "They'll know. They always know."

CHAPTER FIVE

JAKE

Look, I'm not trying to be a jerk or an asshole. I legit can't tell anyone what's going on or who I am, especially not some random girl I just met on an elevator. She could be a plant and working with whoever is creating this mayhem. Or even the megafan she claims she's not. I am still trying to wrap my brain around the fact the convention center became a ghost town in the blink of an eye.

I really do want to be a real actor, but I guess the world doesn't have that in store for me. I need to keep wearing the superhero suit and save the world once again. A new mission has been formed and there's no one else around to help. I guess that's just my purpose in life, and I have to live with it.

"Hey, you. What are you thinking? You zoned out on me again," Lea says, snapping her fingers in my face.

"Just accessing the situation and trying to form a reasonable hypothesis," I say, half-paying attention to her.

Her mouth parts and she runs her hands through her long blonde hair.

"You sound just like The Amazing Boy. Is this some kind

of joke? What have you done with the Jake I met in the elevator?"

Oh no. When emergency situations like this occur it's too hard to play Jake Johnson, especially now that I'm wearing my superhero suit. It's really hard work to act like a stubborn, rich asshole who only cares about himself. The Agent knows who I actually am, but everyone else sees playboy Jake Johnson. The one that dates models and collects fancy cars. I wish the Agent didn't make me have that alter ego, but I have always trusted him because I have no one else.

I've been trained for situations like this when I'm stuck with a civilian during a mission. I'm supposed to keep playing The Amazing Boy, clear her memory, and continue along like nothing's happened, but this time everything is different. The Agent is nowhere to be found to give me a mission report and he's usually the one who takes care of the memories. I need all the help I can get right now, but I don't know how much this girl can actually support me. She's already tripped over a clearly marked extension cord.

That's when we hear it. The kind of boom where your ears continue to ring minutes after it sounds. Even the floor keeps vibrating.

"This must've been the diversion. Come on, people might need saving," I say, grabbing Lea's hand. *And now I really need to go be The Amazing Boy.*

She's in some sort of trance but once I grab her hand, she wakes up from wherever her brain was living.

"What's happening, Jake? Are we in a movie right now?"

If she thinks that, I'm not going to say otherwise, because she's not wrong, she just doesn't realize that it's different from how other movies are made. "This is going to sound crazy, but we need to go to wherever that boom occurred and see if there is anything we can do. I can't explain everything to you but please trust me. I know things seem out of sorts right now and I'm being a completely different person, but I ask you this, if your life was in danger, would you trust The Amazing Boy?" I ask, looking Lea square in the face.

Her baby blue eyes stare right back at me, full of terror.

"Like if The Amazing Boy was real? Absolutely."

"Okay, just keep holding onto that thought and follow me."

CHAPTER SIX

LEA

Ever since Jess royally screwed me over it's hard to trust people, but there is something about the way Jake pleads with me that makes me shut my mouth and run after him, my silver bangles clinking against each other. If there are people hurt of course I'd do whatever I can to help them. I'm not sure what I can do, but Jake seems certain that it's us that has to be there. I mean, it's not like I have anything better to do, and maybe it will distract me from the fact the only person I've ever loved is missing.

We run down the escalator and this time I'm not at all hesitant. I think my eyes are finally adjusting to the darkness. Jake pushes open the door and I squeeze through. He reaches behind me to shut it before the swarm of people in cosplay costumes can get in.

"Sorry everyone, WizCon is canceled," Jake says, pushing through the crowd, removing his sunglasses and stowing them away in his costume. *Wait, so he takes them off when it's actually sunny?* Are they some kind of movie grade glasses that let you see in the dark?

"What? Will we get our money back?" a guy wearing green sweatpants, a green T-shirt, and bright yellow fuzzy horns asks.

Is he trying to be Loki? If so, at least I'm not the only one with a less than perfect costume.

"Don't count on it," Jake says, pulling out his phone. He stares down at it with a puzzled expression. I peek over and see something that says, *MISSION REPORT*.

"Everything okay?" I ask, not wanting him to know I read whatever message he received.

"No," he says, putting his phone to his ear and then angrily shoving it back into his pocket. "Still going to voice-mail. But how did I get this information? He's usually the only one that sends it to me."

Jake really is giving me the bare minimum.

"I was going to ask who you are talking about, but I'm assuming you won't be able to answer because of the NDA," I say sarcastically.

"My agent. Come on, I got us an Uber."

This super rich guy rides Uber? And he knows how to get one?

"Won't the Uber driver recognize you? I'm a little worried that you don't have your security staff." I pan the street to see if any fans are headed our way.

Jake shrugs. "I can handle myself. I'll just give the Uber driver a bad rating if they give me a hard time."

Now that sounds like the Jake I met in the elevator. The driver grumbles hello and asks if we are with Chase, and when Jake nods, the man doesn't even turn back to look at us. Chase must be a fake name Jake gives out, so people don't recognize him.

"So, what's the plan?" I ask, not really expecting a coherent answer.

"Gauge the situation and help as many people as we can," Jake says, still scrolling on his phone.

"But how?"

Jake's silent and I roll my eyes. *How does he think he can help out more than the EMT people that are bound to be there by now?*

The driver weaves in and out of traffic and enters an area with cobblestones and old school architecture.

"This must be the historic section," I say, my eyes glued out the window. Maybe I can get a glimpse of something super cool, like Independence Hall. History is my jam, specifically Presidential history, that's why I'm going to UCLA to study history in the fall. My end goal is to be an archivist somewhere really cool. That's one of the reasons I didn't cancel this trip. I thought maybe I'd see some historical buildings, and anything related to the founding fathers, if I was lucky.

Jake reads off his phone, "It's called 'Old City Philadelphia'. We're almost to our destination."

How does he know where to go? Is it in that weird report message he received?

"Which is where?" I press.

"The Museum of the American Revolution," Jake says, staring outside.

Now that's a museum that would be amazing to work at some day. Think of all the history inside.

"Oh no, it must be right there." He points out his window and I scoot over to look out. A large cloud of smoke is billowing from the side of a brick building and it's clear the smoke isn't going to stop any time soon. In fact, it looks like it's getting worse each second.

"This is good, please let us out here," Jake says to the Uber driver. The driver pulls alongside the one-way street, and I hop out onto the sidewalk. As the Uber is driving away, I spot Jake running straight at the building on fire. He turns around and yells, "Wait for me outside. Don't do anything stupid!"

Me do anything stupid? How about him? What in the world did he think he could do? He isn't actually a hero, just a good-looking actor.

After waiting on the pedestrian signal to give me the go ahead, I sprint across a grassy area to the fire. We must've been one of the first on the scene because there aren't even any fire trucks yet, only people gawking.

Jake's nowhere to be seen. *How did he disappear so fast?* A uniformed guard is near the smoking building, and I jog over to him.

"Have you seen a guy wearing a cape anywhere?" I ask, out of breath.

The uniformed guard scratches his head and says, "Weird to be saying this, but yeah, he went right into the building. I tried to stop him, but he didn't listen to me. I was trying to tell him the museum is closed today so no one should be inside."

That's super weird.

"It's closed on a Saturday? It's a museum. Saturday is their prime time."

The guard shrugs. "I don't know what to tell you."

What is Jake thinking? How can he run right into a burning building? Even if he somehow is shooting a movie, running into a fire seems wrong. He's going to get smoke inhalation or worse.

The shrill siren of a fire truck fills the air and gets louder by the second. *Thank goodness, maybe they can come rescue him.*

The fire truck pulls along the sidewalk, blocking all traffic on the one-way street. Cars blare their horns. Can't they see a building is on fire? *Sorry the fire truck is an inconvenience for them. My friend is in there and he could be hurt.* Well, I guess he's my friend even though we just met. I don't know what else to call him.

A police car is weaving in and out of traffic trying to get to where the fire truck is parked. Once they finally make it, a clean-shaven policeman jumps out and comes over to where I'm standing with the guard.

"What's the situation?" he asks the guard.

"My friend is in there!" I say in a panic, pointing at the museum.

The policeman looks at me and says, "The best thing you can do right now is remain calm; we'll get him out. What about anyone else?" *Because when someone tells you to calm down, that really helps the situation.*

The guard shakes his head. "Nope, not as far as I'm aware. The museum is closed today."

"On a Saturday?" the policeman asks, his eyebrows raising.

"That's what I said. Isn't that weird?"

"Then who are you?" the policeman asks the guard.

"I work as a security guard for the National Park Service and was on my break when I heard the explosion. Normally I'm stationed by the Liberty Bell."

"Why is your friend in there if the place is closed?" The policeman gives me a scrutinizing look.

I shake my head. "He didn't say, he just ran inside." *I'm not lying, I really don't know what Jake is planning to do.*

The policeman sighs. "An untrained person is more of a liability than a hero. I'll go brief the firefighters."

As he's about to leave, a figure takes shape from a side entrance of the museum. As the person gets closer, I can make out a red cape flowing in the wind.

Jake's alive! He isn't coughing or limping. There isn't a single sign of an injury.

"Jake!" I scream, running over to him. "Why would you do that? I thought you were going to die," I say, tears welling up in my eyes. *I hadn't realized how scared I was until I saw that he's okay.*

"I told you not to worry." He turns to the policeman. "Whoever set the explosion broke into one of the exhibits and stole something. There's glass all over the floor. I didn't look to see what it was because I was focused on finding the perpetrators, but I didn't have any luck. I was too late."

I glance over Jake's body, and I can't see a single thing wrong. His costume is intact. Even his hair is picture perfect. Didn't he just come out of a burning building? I know his costume is grade-A movie quality, but nothing can withstand heat and smoke like that, except firemen gear.

"Mister, you could've gotten really hurt. What were you thinking?" The police officer lectures Jake. "Just because you're dressed as a superhero doesn't mean you are one!"

Jake straightens up. "Sorry sir, but this is a mission that The Amazing Boy has been sent on. You should have received a memo from my team about me being in town. Come on Lea, we have to find whoever is responsible for this."

He walks away from the police officer, but I'm frozen in place.

CHAPTER SEVEN

JAKE

I realize talking like a privileged superhero to a police officer isn't the best idea, but I need him to understand that I know what's going on. And how do you respectfully tell an authority figure with a gun that information, especially when wearing a ridiculous costume?

Lea is still stuck in the same spot, so I tug on her arm and pull her behind me. "Come on, we have to find the person who stole whatever was inside."

As we are walking away, I turn my head back and see the police officer glaring at us with his hands on his hips. I veer down a cobblestone street so I can get as far away as possible before he changes his mind and runs after us.

I place my hands on Lea's shoulder. "I know you're probably freaked out and I wish I could tell you more. But you'll have to use your power of deduction to figure things out; I'm sorry."

She gazes up at me with her sky-blue eyes. "I don't understand. It doesn't make any sense. How can your costume be that fire resistant?"

I give her my best quirky smile and nonchalantly shrug. "I have some kickass costume designers."

She furrows her eyebrows. "But why is that needed if you're on a set all day and probably have a stunt double? That seems excessive. And if you're actually shooting a movie now, where are all the cameras and producers?"

That's when I notice the street we're standing in isn't as secluded as I first thought. People wearing brightly colored fanny packs and large brimmed hats are passing us doing a double take. Some have their phones raised, aimed right at me. Times like this make me miss my security detail. It doesn't help that we're in the touristy section of Philadelphia, minutes away from Independence Hall.

Lea shouts at the tourists, "Leave us alone! We're trying to work something out. Do you have any decency? A building was blown up minutes ago."

I notice a hostel sign ahead and motion for Lea to follow me. Little known fact, hostels are great hiding places for superheroes. No one looks twice if you're wearing something ridiculous, and in the United States not many people use them, so you get loads of privacy. Now in Europe, it's a completely different story.

This hostel doesn't disappoint. Only one person sits on the shabby puke green couch in the entranceway, and they are so engrossed in their well-worn copy of *War and Peace* they don't even look up when we enter.

"Can we get a private room for one night?" I ask the guy standing behind the front desk. He looks to be in his early twenties, wearing a faded T-shirt from a random brewery.

"That's fifty dollars," he says in a monotone voice.

I pull out my wallet from one of my many pockets and hand him a credit card. This one has another fake name, Jamie Adams, not even my stage name, Jake Johnson. Yep, that's right. Jake Johnson isn't my real name. It's some name the Agent came up with, thinking it would be more appealing than my birth name. No one knows that name and identity, except for me and the Agent.

I sign for the room and grab the key that's attached to a ridiculously large keychain of the Liberty Bell.

In front of our room Lea pulls on my arm. "What are you doing?" she hisses.

"Trying to hide from everyone so we can figure out our next step. Talking on the street isn't going to work if everyone is going to film us. That'll already be on social media by now."

The door creaks open. *Shit, one bed. I forgot to ask for two.*

Lea notices it at the same time and gives me an *I'm going to kill you* look.

I shrug. "We're not actually here to sleep, only talk."

She rolls her eyes. "Sure, that's what they all say. If I knew you wanted a hotel room, I'd take you to the one I'm staying at. There are at least two beds there."

"No, we need one off the radar and under a fake name. You never know who might try and find us."

She flops on the bed. "What name did you use? The same one from Uber? And who would try and find us?"

"No, another fake one." I purposely avoid her second question. I don't even know where to begin.

Lea blinks for a second. "Wait, is Jake Johnson even your real name? Now that I think about it, it kind of sounds made up. Like it's too perfect."

I shake my head. "No and before you ask, I'm not telling you my real name. It could compromise your safety."

Lea sticks out her lower lip. "I'm stuck in this one-bed hostel room with you and you won't even share your real name with me?"

"That's right. It's for your own good."

I sit down on the bed, but far from Lea. I don't want her to think I'm going to try anything. I'm not that kind of guy. Jake Johnson might be, but that's not really me.

I scroll through my phone to find the mission report. It details the exact villain we're looking for. Long dark scraggly hair, full beard, and weathered, tan face. A black eye patch covers his left eye and he has a full tattoo sleeve. *Are we hunting a pirate?* To complete the cliché, his villain name is One-Eyed Barnacle. He better not have a parrot for a sidekick. *How is this my life? And how do I go about explaining this to Lea?*

"Whatcha' looking at?" she asks, getting closer to me.

I try covering up my phone with my hand.

"Uh … nothing?"

She jumps off the bed and sticks her hands on her hips.

"Stop being a jerk! If I'm going to help you, I need to know what's going on."

Maybe if I give her the clues, she'll figure it out herself? It might be nice having someone else know my deepest secret.

I make an exaggerated yawn and my phone *accidentally* flies out of my hand and lands near Lea. After picking it up, she studies my phone carefully. "Mission Report. One-Eyed Barnacle. Likes breaking and entering. First stop, the Museum of the American Revolution." She glances back up at me, her eyes wide.

"What is this?" she asks.

I shake my head. "I honestly can't tell you. What does it look like to you? Talk it out, like the contestants do on *Who Wants to be a Millionaire.*"

She gives me a questioning look. "You've seen that show? Isn't that for old people?"

"What can I say, I get bored on flights and it's something easy to watch."

She looks back down at my phone. "This seems like some kind of clue card. Or something that James Bond would get from M."

She gazes off into space. "Maybe this is some kind of weird way of method acting. To get yourself into character. Or to make it seem like the filming is more authentic if you don't know who you are acting against."

I twist my lips. "I cannot confirm or deny."

She must really think I'm shooting a movie right now. I mean, she wouldn't be wrong, I'm always being filmed, but it's more complicated than that.

I shouldn't have expected her to get it so soon. It's not like civilians think the superheroes they see on the screen can actually be real.

"So, this mission report. Do you have to find this person and fight him for the film? He looks like he belongs on a pirate ship."

I raise my eyebrows. "Essentially. It's a new way of acting." *That's not a lie. It really is a different way to act.*

"But where are the cameras? How is this all getting filmed? And did the Museum of the American Revolution really get blown up or was that part of the script?"

I shrug. "That's above my paygrade. I just do what I'm told."

Lea scratches her head. "That doesn't worry you? And how do you figure out where to find these bad guys?"

This is the tricky part.

"My agent usually gives me tips along the way, like this mission report, or I'd call him when I get stuck, which is more often than I'd like. That's the stuff they will edit out of the movies. But this time he isn't around. I don't even know how I got this report."

I get up from the bed and start pacing on the well-worn brown carpet. There's a dark spot on it near the window. Hopefully not dried blood.

Lea's eyes are following me as I pace, like a cat tracking its owner. "But how does this help me find my friends? Filming some superhero movie?"

"I think it's all connected. That this is all part of the movie but somehow, I have been kept in the dark about it."

"How can thousands of people disappearing be a part of a scripted movie? There's no way all of that could've happened while we were in the elevator. What possible explanation could there be?" Her voice sounds wary.

Maybe she'll figure it out eventually, but we are losing precious time while she's thinking things through.

Lea studies me. "Okay, so this is a superhero movie but also like James Bond. He, like you, still needs help figuring things out, which isn't a bad thing."

"I guess so, but I'm not as cool, and I don't sleep with all the women that help me, just so we can make that clear. That's not why I brought you to this hostel. If I wanted to do that, it would be somewhere way nicer."

Lea gives a small smile. "Even if it was, I can't sleep with someone I just met. I'm demisexual."

I'm trying to wrack my brain to remember what that means. I hadn't realized until now how much I need to get up to speed with my LGBTQ+ terms.

Lea must sense my confusion because she says, "It means you're only sexually attracted to someone when you form a connection with them. One-night stands don't work for me. Trust me, I've tried."

I raise my eyebrow. "Oh? So other people besides your friend?"

Lea plops back down on the bed. "After Jess picked Olive, I went through a dark time when I wanted to erase the pain and be with anyone. Turns out that doesn't even work for me."

I sit back on the bed next to her. "Hooking up with someone without feelings isn't all it's cracked up to be. It's weird and awkward. And then you never see them again. I'd take someone I care about any day."

"Until they make your heart shatter into a million pieces," Lea says, looking away, but not before I see her eyes start to water.

CHAPTER EIGHT

LEA

I need to prove my usefulness so Jake, or whatever his real name is, doesn't drop me at the first opportunity, especially since I'm not actually supposed to be in this movie he's making. He does seem a little lost without his agent giving him tips so I can help him try and figure out where this Barnacle guy, who looks like very bad news, is hiding. This means I need to stop thinking about Jess, like yesterday.

I'm still very confused about the logistics of how all this works. Does Jake not have a script? I really thought all the superhero movies I've seen are scripted down to every single sentence. But here he is, winging it, trying to figure out where to find the villain. The whole premise is odd. It still feels like there's something Jake isn't telling me, but I can't pinpoint it.

I hand Jake back his phone and dig mine out of my purse. No new text messages from anyone, which isn't too weird since Olive and Jess are the only two people that text me. It's not a shock I haven't heard from my parents. As long as I return home at some point tomorrow, they probably won't even check in.

When I told them I wanted to go on this trip my mom barely looked up from her computer to acknowledge my presence. She nodded and said to have fun. My dad discussed it a little more with me, as in, *If we don't have to pay for any of it, it's fine by me.* But they are okay with shelling out loads of money when my older brother's baseball team went to states a couple of years ago. They got hotel rooms for the entire family, even my grandparents, and bought us an expensive three course meal, so we could watch him excel. And let's just say we didn't stay at your typical run of the mill hotel; it had valet parking, a bellhop, and even a spa.

I can't let my parents' disinterest in my life distract me now. I have a chance to do something cool and different and I need to prove to Jake it's worth lugging me around.

"What about checking out Independence Hall? It's full of history and the perfect spot to feature in a film," I suggest.

Not going to lie, I really want to visit the site. The place where our founding fathers stood. It's probably the number two spot to visit for history buffs in Philadelphia, number one of course being the Liberty Bell. I might as well take advantage of the situation.

Jake types on his phone and says, "It's right down the road. The mission report doesn't give any other hints of where One-Eyed Barnacle is going, and I can't think of any other places off the top of my head so we might as well have a look."

I try and hide my smile. I've secured a place on his team, for now.

While I'm on my phone, I do another quick Google search, this time to see if there's any information about the Museum of the American Revolution and what was stolen. I quickly skim the top article and shake my head.

"It's bothering me that we don't know what was stolen, but I just checked, and the news only says that something valuable was taken at the Museum of the American Revolution, with very few details. It's a *developing* story."

Jake's looking out the window and turns back to me. "In the meantime, we can try and stop this pirate from stealing anything else."

———

ON OUR WAY to Independence Hall, I try to engage Jake in some small talk but he's not having it.

"So where are you originally from?"

"Nowhere you'd know."

That's usually when the person expands with more information, but Jake says nothing else.

"You never know, I could be a geography nut and know random towns."

Jake turns to look at me, with one eyebrow raised. "Are you?"

I twist my mouth and say, "No. Just into history a ton. But it doesn't mean I haven't heard of places."

Jake continues onwards and, this is growing to be a pattern, me jogging to catch up with him.

"What are we going to do if he's at Independence Hall?"

"You can stay out of the way. I don't want a civilian, I mean, non-actor, getting injured. I'm a trained professional so I know how to handle situations like this."

Ouch, that hurts my ego.

"Then what's the purpose of me even following you around?" I ask bitterly.

Jake stops and looks at me. "Sorry if I sounded like a jerk. When I'm on a mission it's all I can think about. I'm not used to having someone else along. You weren't part of the plan."

I chew on my lip. "Do you want me to leave?"

He shakes his head. "No, that's not what I'm trying to do. I just don't want you getting hurt."

I scrunch my eyebrows. "How would I get hurt on a movie set?"

Jake looks at me for a second. I can tell his brain is hard at work from his penetrating stare. It's almost like he's trying to sort out some kind of story to tell me. "I don't use stunt doubles. I do everything myself and it can get intense real fast."

"I don't want to slow you down. Let's keep going and I'll stay out of your way."

Jake points down the street, and after we turn, we come upon a large grassy area with a brick building with tons of white windows and a tower at the top with a spire and a clock.

"We made it!" I exclaim. Before now I had only seen pictures of Independence Hall; seeing it up close is so much cooler. I can't believe I'm at the place where both the Declaration of Independence and the U.S. Constitution were signed.

As we get closer, I can just make out a line of people near the building.

Jake stops. "Great. More tourists."

I stand next to him, arms crossed. "Of course there's tourists. It's one of the most famous historic buildings in Philadelphia. What did you think?"

"I was hoping it would be closed like the Museum of the American Revolution. I can't go near the area with all those tourists. I'm immediately going to get recognized."

"Or we use it to your advantage to get ahead of the line. Can't we ask for a private tour?"

Jake stares at me. "Who are you going to ask? The security guard? He'll probably laugh at us. My agent has to negotiate private tours well in advance if I need one."

I shrug. "You never know until you try. Better than getting mobbed by all of those people."

"Fine, let's go, but you have to do all the talking."

This is a change of pace. Normally it was Jess that always had to be the center of attention and the one to charm everyone. Let's see what I learned from her.

The line is longer than I anticipated but as we approach, I hear a couple of screeches and girls around my age pointing their phones at us. Well, correction, at Jake. No one would give a second look at me, especially with how disheveled I must look. And don't forget about the growing hole in the knee of my gold pants.

"Can you hurry up and do something before someone pulls out a body part for me to sign?" Jake grumbles.

"Alright, alright."

I pass by the other tourists in line and keep saying excuse me, excuse me. There are some protests, but most people don't even notice me, they are too busy turning towards the commotion. I get to the front of the line at the security checkpoint and spew out, "So that person right there is the famous actor Jake Johnson, also known as The Amazing Boy. If you don't let both of us through right now, all these people are going to erupt into chaos trying to get a picture or his autograph. So can you do us a solid and just let us through and give us a very quick private tour?"

The security guard blinks at me a few times and then focuses on Jake. A couple girls are already out of line; one is posing for a selfie. Jake really is a good actor because his smile for the picture almost looks genuine.

The security guard glances at his watch and says gruffly, "Fine. I don't need to deal with this right now. There are already more tourists than usual because the Museum of the American Revolution is closed. I don't need to handle a mob either. They don't pay me enough."

"Thank you so much, sir. Jake, come on!" I motion for Jake to join me.

He scrambles away from his adoring fans and starts to walk through the line. He doesn't have to push through too hard; it's like the sea of Jordan splitting in two as he walks past them, their phones up close to his face.

"Shouldn't you have a security detail if you're that big of a star?" the security guard asks, giving Jake a stern look.

"I usually do but they're on break so I'm here with my publicist, Lea," Jake says, nudging me.

"Uh yes. Normally I would've called ahead for a tour, but this is an unscheduled stop and we had been hoping you'd accommodate us," I say in my best grown up tone.

"Your publicist wears a superhero costume?"

Jake smirks. "What can I say, she's my superhero."

Groan. But if this gets us in the building, I'll be whoever I need to be.

The security guard makes a pfft sound and gestures for us to go through the metal detector. I give Jake a worried look. *Will any of his gadgets set it off?*

He doesn't meet my eyes and walks on through. No blaring sounds emerge. I'm partially in when it beeps like crazy, and I jump a foot in the air. *Are you kidding me? I'm the one that sets it off?*

"What do you have on you?" the security guard demands.

"Nothing!"

The security guard roots around my purse and then looks at my wrist.

"I bet it's all your bracelets. Take them off and go through again."

I slip off my silver bangles, hand them to the guard, and gingerly step in the metal detector. I should have remembered that. I had the same thing happen at the airport, but I didn't think a tourist attraction would have such a sensitive security sensor.

No beep. "Okay you're clear to go. The tour guide is at the back of the building. I can't get you a private tour because there are already a couple individuals waiting back there, but I can stop anyone else from joining."

That will have to do. Hopefully, none of the individuals are The Amazing Boy megafans.

"Okay, sir. Thank you for your help," I say, pushing my bracelets back on my wrist.

The small group we find around back should not give us any problems. There is a gray-haired lady wearing a huge sun hat and sunglasses and an almost bald man wearing a visor and those clip-on sunglasses that attach right to your prescription glasses. Given the sunny skies and not having any hair, he probably should have opted for a baseball cap. The other couple are probably in their thirties, with a stroller and a screaming toddler. He throws a stuffed lamb on the ground, only causing him to yell even louder.

Perfect, this will keep everyone distracted while we search around.

The tour guide wears a gray button up shirt with a gold badge right above the left pocket and a National Park Service patch attached to their shirt sleeve. Her khaki ranger hat and green pants with a black belt completes the look. She listens to her walkie talkie for a second, gives us a quick glance, and then says, "Okay folks, we're having a smaller group today so let's get started." *Even the tour guide isn't fazed by our costumes.*

She begins her spiel about Independence Hall, and I try to listen as much as possible. This is my jam and why I want to become an archivist but it's hard to pay attention because of the screaming child and Jake constantly monitoring every movement. I want to be able to help him out, so I half pay attention and keep an eye out for anything suspicious.

We follow the tour guide into the building, and I have to keep my giddiness in check. I am standing exactly where our forefathers signed the Declaration of Independence! Well, not the exact spot but super close to it. There's a room set up how it possibly looked back in the seventeen hundreds. It's not the original furniture of course, but it still seems pretty realistic to my untrained eye. But nothing else catches my attention, no shadows lurking around or anything amiss.

I catch Jake's eye and he shakes his head. Guess he feels the same way. As the guide talks even more about life when the Declaration of Independence was signed, Jake pulls me off to the side and says, "This is all wrong. One-Eyed Barnacle couldn't have been here. This space is too confined and guarded. And there doesn't seem to be anything of value, since the tour guide just said it's all replicas."

As cool as this room is, I agree with Jake. Unless this villain wants a quill that was probably made in China, there aren't many options.

"We need to get out of here so we don't waste any more time," Jake says, tapping his foot.

I know what usually works for me when I need to get out of a situation in a hurry. As the tour guide pauses to take a breath I say, "Excuse me, I really need to use the bathroom. Can my uh … client, Jake, and I be excused?"

I almost called him my boyfriend which would have been super embarrassing, especially for Jake. He'd never be seen with someone like me; I'm not his typical flavor, even if he says all the models are only for show. I'm more the girl next door, not the girl that actually gets the popular person. I couldn't even keep Jess.

The tour guide gives me a long stare before responding. "Yes, you can leave, just go down the hallway and out the door, but fair warning, you will have to go back through security if you want to return. And we can't do another semi-private tour for your client."

Jake's already heading down the hallway so I say, "We got what we needed but thanks for the tour."

I squint outside as the sunlight reaches my eyes. The door drops us right outside near a road, no longer even in the grassy knoll behind the hall.

"Now what?" I ask.

Jake runs his hands through his dark brown hair.

"Now we try and find another lead."

I chew on my lip. I feel terrible that I took us down the wrong path. I need to right this, so I don't get left behind. I spot an open bench under a tree and head there. As soon as I sit down, I open the Chrome app on my phone and type, *Villains in Philadelphia.* When in doubt, use Google.

The first option that pops up is a tattoo parlor with the name villain in the title. The second hit is a comic bookstore. *Okay time for a different tactic, unless pirate man is deciding to add a new tat to his collection.*

"What are you up to?" Jake asks, sitting next to me.

"Searching where a villain would hide in Philadelphia."

I delete the previous search and type, *Famous villains in Philadelphia hideout.* I scan the hits and most of them are about Philadelphia sports players, but one catches my eye. The title is: *20 Real-World Places That Could Be the Secret Lair of the Next Marvel Villain.*

BINGO. This has to have something Philadelphia related if it popped up in my search. I show my findings to Jake.

Jake scoffs. "Marvel, come on. They aren't even cool superheroes."

I roll my eyes. "You have to admit, their movies are pretty good."

"That's because they can actually reshoot scenes, unlike my method. When you're in the thick of fighting a villain my way, you can't ask them to stop and try the fight scene again because the angle was wrong, or that you didn't get a one-liner in. My shots are more real."

"But yet you want to get out of it and become a real actor," I retort, scanning the article for anything Philadelphia related.

Number eighteen reads *The Imposing Architecture of Phil-adelphia City Hall Is Sure to Attract (Evil) Attention.*

I shove my phone in Jake's face and point to the screen. "What about here? It's in the middle of the city and has lots of rooms for hiding places. Even if he's not there, it's close to a lot of other places in the city."

Jake rubs his chin. "That could be a valid hiding place or even his next target. It's worth a try. Good work!"

I glower. *He told me I did a good job! Maybe he'll keep me around.*

CHAPTER NINE

JAKE

Even though Marvel superheroes are lame, whoever wrote that article about Philadelphia's City Hall is spot on. It really would be the perfect place for a villain to hide. I've been around the world but still get impressed by cool buildings like this one. The architecture looks Gothic, but Lea corrects me and says, "According to this article, it's Second Empire style and also the largest municipal building in the world, with seven hundred rooms."

I whistle. "Seven hundred rooms? We better get in there fast to see what we can find; it's going to take us forever."

Before moving any closer, I look up at the building towering down at me. Lea also shares with me that William Penn, the city's founder, is at the top of the most prominent spire. We saw it during our Uber ride down Market Street, like a beacon calling to us.

This stupid Barnacle guy better be hiding here because I really don't feel like playing the superhero anymore. It would be nice to be a normal tourist and actually see the rest of Philadelphia. And Lea likes history, so I'm sure she'd be game to go check out the

Liberty Bell and other tourist sights like Ben Franklin's grave, especially since we didn't get to spend much time at Independence Hall. I felt bad pulling her away from something she clearly enjoys, but we don't have time to mess around.

"Where do we start?" Lea asks, her eyes wide gazing at the building.

"The entrance?" I suggest. "Although I have no clue where that is."

My eyes dart around, willing the people milling about not to congregate around us. I pull out my glasses that look like sunglasses, but really aren't. There are bodies in the rooms at City Hall, but not too many. We are lucky it's a Saturday or I bet all the rooms would be filled.

"Are you going to fill me in what those glasses do?" Lea asks, raising her right eyebrow. "Or are they just part of your costume to make you look cool?"

Hiding my powers from her is getting to be so much harder. Why did I have to sign that stupid NDA?

"Uh … yeah, I have to complete the look in case I run into One-Eyed Barnacle, and they start filming us."

Lea squints at me. "There's still something you're not telling me but I'm not going to keep bothering you if you don't want to tell me."

I hate being my asshole persona and hiding who I really am. Lea seems like a cool person, and it sucks to treat her this way, but I know it's for the best. The less she knows, the better.

Without saying anything else, she marches over to someone with a black T-shirt, black pants, and an earpiece.

"Do you know how we get inside?" Lea asks. He looks down at her.

"Ma'am, it's a Saturday. City Hall is closed on the weekends to the public."

Lea bites her lip. "But we really need to get inside, we've come so far to see this building. I'm from Ohio and am only here for this weekend and I'm told that City Hall is one of the coolest places to visit."

"All due respect ma'am, but City Hall is much nicer on the outside than inside. Inside is like any other municipal building, nothing out of the ordinary."

"But I'm trying my best to check off all my boxes for the weekend," Lea says, her lips quivering.

Is this an act? If she can cry on command, I'd need to get some lessons from her. That's one acting technique I've yet to master.

The guard's resolute look begins to break. No one can ever stand to see a teenage girl cry. It's even weirder seeing one about to lose it wearing a cape.

The guard sighs and motions for us to follow him. "Come on, I'll see what I can do. I think there are some employees in there working overtime, just don't bother them."

My mouth gapes open. If it would've been me, I'd bust open some door that is already worse for the wear, try to evade any security cameras, and make the Agent pay for any damages after the fact. We usually make so much money on these films that any material damages along the way are fine. As long as I don't hurt anyone or break any really big laws. Breaking and entering is usually okay if a villain is involved. In the long run, most of the time the police side with us, as long as we get the villain.

But Lea's tactic is genius. Hiding in plain sight. The guards can't come after us if we're invited inside.

We follow our new guard friend to a side door. He pulls out a set of keys, puts one in the keyhole, and the door pops open. He stands at the entrance and calls to a curly, gray-haired lady sitting behind a desk, "Hey Ethel, these kids want to see City Hall for some reason. Is it okay if they do a quick lap?"

Ethel removes her wire-rimmed glasses and narrows her eyes. "It's a weekend."

The guard shrugs. "They're tourists that are only here for the day."

Lea pipes up, "It's been my dream to see the inside and I'm going to give a report on it when school starts again."

Ethel sighs. "Fine. I'll get you signed in. You're lucky I came in today to get through some work."

"Thank you so much," Lea says, her face brightening. She gives the guard a large smile and he returns it. I even find myself grinning. Her happiness is infectious.

After showing ID, Ethel types a few things into her computer and the printer spits out two name tags. As she hands them over to us she says, "You can walk around the building for thirty minutes, that's it. Come back here and I'll sign you out." She narrows her eyes. "And you better not have any weapons to go along with these costumes. This is the side door so there are no metal detectors, and I don't want to do a pat down," Ethel says sternly.

"No ma'am. These costumes are just costumes. No weapons at all," I say lying through my teeth. I can feel my dagger pressing against my calf. Even if she'd pat me down, there is no way she'd find it. The costume designer thought of it all, even a side pocket inside my pants for a dagger, along with some kind of cloaking device that will throw off a metal detector.

Lea gives me the side-eye. Glad to know she already can tell when I'm lying.

"Fine, fine. Just do your lap and get back here. By then I hope to be finished all this work."

Lea and I hurry away before Ethel says anything else. After we're out of earshot Lea whispers to me, "No weapons? Where are the ones I've seen in the movies?"

"Hidden safely away. They're only for dire circumstances and not detectable," I whisper back.

We continue walking down the hall and I toss my name tag in a garbage can. Lea slips hers in her orange purse.

The security guard isn't kidding. The inside of City Hall looks like its straight out of an 1980s crime show, very old school and gritty. Maybe that's how they came up with the Philadelphia Flyers mascot's name Gritty? It's as if the lights are only partially shining. I take a breath and cough. Why does it smell like a mix of wet dog and an old bookstore?

"So, what's the plan?" Lea interrupts my thoughts.

"We need to quickly find if any of these rooms could have One-Eyed Barnacle."

Lea twists her mouth. "How will we open the doors though?"

"Leave that to me," I say cryptically.

CHAPTER TEN

LEA

I've come to find in my short life that older buildings with a gorgeous exterior usually disappoint you once inside. Philadelphia City Hall is no different. With its flickering lights, musty smell, and colorless walls, the place needs more than a facelift. When the *Queer Eye* gang came to Philadelphia the other year, the interior of City Hall should have been their focus.

Now Jake is talking about breaking down doors. Maybe that can be the first step of the restoration process, but it's not very discreet.

"You just said you're not going to pull out your weapons unless necessary," I protest.

He places those ridiculous sunglasses on his face again as we're walking around.

"Who said anything about pulling out a weapon? Don't worry, I won't hurt anything. Besides, from the look of this place, I'd be surprised if the doors even lock."

He stops for a second at each office door, stares straight

into it with his glasses still firmly on his face and then keeps moving, as if he knows no one is inside.

"Aren't you going to try some of the doors? How do you know no one's there?" I ask. I want him to tell me what he's doing.

"I didn't hear any movement," he says abruptly.

Those glasses clearly help him tell if someone's in there or not. Maybe they are X-ray vision glasses. Would that mean he can see through me? My face instantly grows warm thinking of that.

I look down at my watch. "We've already been gone five minutes. Do you think Ethel is going to stand by her thirty-minute rule?"

Jake turns his head towards me. It's disconcerting not being able to see his eyes, but not going to lie, those glasses make Jake really look like The Amazing Boy in all his glory. My heart races for half a second. How is it possible I'm running around the city of Philadelphia with this super famous guy and the object of so many people's desires?

"Did you see all that paperwork on her desk? She's going to completely forget she saw us once she gets back to that."

I stop. "Wait, so we aren't even going back to her?"

"That's how this works, Lea. We get in, try to get the bad guy, and get out before the authorities show up."

I raise my eyebrow. "Don't they know you're only shooting a movie?"

Jake gets closer to a door and says, "Yes, but they aren't always on board. Sometimes they think I'm some vigilante trying to get notoriety. I guess that's sort of accurate, but I do know what I'm doing, for the most part."

"Without your agent?" *Oops.* That just slips out. I didn't mean to sound doubtful.

"Well, someone's helping me if they're sending me this mission report. And I've got you," Jake says, turning to me, giving me a sheepish smile, a piece of his brown hair falling in his face. *Okay, I can see why everyone swoons over him. He's pretty darn good looking.*

"I wouldn't put all your eggs in one basket on me. I've never done anything like this before," I say, biting the side of my finger.

Jess was always the one thinking of schemes and pulling me into some kind of madness, like the time we glitter bombed Olive's locker after their winning goal led their lacrosse team into the playoffs. Olive was so mad and kept finding glitter in their things for months that I don't think Jess ever told Olive it was us. Not Jess's best idea of the year.

"Doesn't seem like that to me. You're the one who charmed that guard to let us in and … wait, someone's in that room," Jake says, his voice dropping a level to a whisper, pointing to the door up ahead.

I give him a wild look. "How do you know?"

He runs to open it before I have time to protest. It doesn't budge. That's when he does something I'll never forget. He takes a deep breath, crouches down, and pushes it in.

"What're you doing?" a female voice calls out. "My door was locked!" The door at this point is open.

How did Jake just open a locked door?

The pieces are starting to fall into place. In the movies the character The Amazing Boy has superstrength, is fire resistant, and can feel body heat. It's starting to seem like Jake can do all the same things. I don't have too much time to think about it because a girl with blonde hair in a tight top bun shoots up from behind a tiny desk. She's wearing a navy-blue pencil skirt and a loose short sleeve beige blouse. I gauge that she's nineteen or twenty. She looks too young to work here, but maybe she's an intern for the summer.

"Sorry ma'am, looking for any corruption," Jake announces.

Does he make up lines like that on the spot or is he given a bundle to memorize for scenarios such as this? And why is he being all weird? Are we being filmed right now? I don't see any cameras around.

"Aren't you that superhero from the movies?" the girl says, her eyes wide.

Jake smiles. "I am The Amazing Boy, here to see how I can help. Have you seen anyone that looks like this?" He pulls out his phone, and I see a flash of the pirate guy before he hands it to her.

"No, he would be hard to miss. He looks like a less sexy Johnny Depp," she comments. "What's he done?" she asks, her eyes back gazing at Jake.

"Stole something from the Museum of the American Revolution and we're trying to return it," Jake says, looking around the room.

He said *we're* trying to return it. I'm a part of his team!

That's when the girl notices me. "Who are you?" she asks, looking me up and down.

"Uhhhhh," I stammer.

Jake slings his arm around me. "She's here to help me out. She's Super L," he says, giving me a smile.

Why did I get a big L on my chest? I guess this nickname is here to stay. Super L sounds like another *The L Word* spin-off.

"Where are the camera crews?" the girl asks, peering behind us. "I didn't know they were filming a superhero movie in City Hall today."

See, she's as confused as I am.

"We're just practicing right now while they're setting up. So, you haven't seen anything weird in City Hall except for us?" Jake asks.

"Nope," she says, grinning, thinking she is playing along with the movie script.

I'm starting to think differently. Is this actually for a movie or is this real-life?

"If you're still in town later tonight, let me know. I'm

finished around five and I could show you some tourist sites," the blonde says, giving Jake a coy look.

Jake coughs. "Sorry ma'am, no rest for the weary. I've got a city to save but I'm flattered. If you do see anything suspicious though, call this number." Jake hands her a red and yellow business card with only digits on it. She effortlessly grabs it with her perfectly manicured pink nails.

"Absolutely," she says, winking. "What if I need someone to check to make sure my bed doesn't have any scary intruders in it?"

I'm holding back my urge to roll my eyes. Are girls really like this? And I guess the bigger question is, does it work?

Pink splotches appear on Jake's cheeks.

"In that case, I'd recommend calling the police. We've got to search the rest of the building now." Jake spins around and legit sprints out of the room. I wave at the girl and say, "Better luck next time."

The door slams behind me and I see Jake already halfway down the hallway.

"Hey, wait up! She's not following you, you don't have to run," I say, panting.

Jake changes his walk to be slightly slower but only a tad.

"Girls like that can be a lot," Jake says, running his hand through his hair. "I never know how to respond."

"Her pickup line was a good enough reason to blow her off."

"And she'd be bad for my Amazing Boy brand. He's wholesome and sweet. I guess if I was in my Jake Johnson costume, I would've had to say yes, but at least I'm wearing this," Jake mutters, pulling his sunglasses off his face.

"Your Jake Johnson costume?" I repeat. "Jake, what is going on?"

Jake blinks a couple of times, and he mumbles something under his breath.

I hold up my hand. "Save the lies. I can't believe I'm

saying this but I'm pretty sure you're a real superhero. I don't know how that's possible but it's all I can think of that makes sense."

Jake's face betrays nothing. *He really is a good actor.* "I'm not sure what you are talking about," he says, turning away from me.

I stamp my foot. "Stop it. I know something's going on and you have your NDA, but if I'm going to help you, I need to know the whole story. The real you."

Jake winces at the last part and he takes a deep breath. "I can't tell you, but I will say you must have graduated high school with good grades."

My heart pounds a mile a minute against my chest. *Superheroes are real?! Does that mean Brown Recluse is real too? Or any of the Marvel superheroes? Is there really a Hulk?*

My eyes must be bugging out because Jake grabs my arm.

"It's okay, I know it's a lot to take in. Let's start with the easy stuff to explain. What you saw me wearing in the elevator is the *Jake Johnson* outfit that my agent makes me put on. And I have a certain persona that I need to upkeep, sexy asshole playboy. One that messes around with lots of models and is a complete tool. I guess that helps separate The Amazing Boy from *the person,* so people don't realize I actually have powers."

"Your attitude in the elevator was all an act?" I ask.

Jake's mouth is tight. "Partially. Don't get me wrong, I was irritated that the elevator stopped, but I channeled all that into how Jake would react. I couldn't go full blown into The Amazing Boy because you were around."

I shake my head. "Then who are you really if you're not Jake Johnson or The Amazing Boy?"

Jake grimaces. "I can't tell you that. But it's nice that I can now be myself around you."

I give him a small smile, "I'm glad to hear that. I'm not a fan of jerk Jake."

Jake's eyes brighten. "Really?"

"Who would be?"

Jake shrugs. "I thought most girls prefer bad guys, so it was pretty easy to fall into that stereotype, but I still don't like it. And I'm not lying when I said I really don't have time to date. Most of the girls I'm photographed with are just there to show my *brand*."

We near the end of what has to be one of the longest hallways known to mankind and turn right. Jake stands up straighter and whips his glasses back on.

"Be on alert. Someone's coming towards us." And sure enough, a short figure appears around a corner. The person stops and rubs their chin. "The Amazing Boy! We weren't expecting you today. I thought you'd be a bit too tied up to find us. Why didn't that work," he mutters.

Even though this guy is almost out of my eyesight, I can tell this is not One-Eyed Barnacle. He's not very hairy and both eyes are intact so unless One-Eyed sprung for a haircut and suddenly came upon a new eyeball like Thor did in Infinity Wars, this is not our guy.

Jake puts his hand out to stop me from moving forward.

"Don't move, I don't know anything about this person," he whispers. He stands as tall as possible and saunters down the hallway.

Do I follow him or hide behind a door? I'd really prefer the hiding behind the door option, but I can't let Jake be by himself, not after he's trying to figure out what's going on to help my friends.

"Are you One-Eyed Barnacle's lacky? The person he sends to do his dirty work?" Jake calls down the hallway. There's a slight echo.

A cold, merciless laugh comes from this man's mouth.

"You should be glad it's only me and not *him*. That girl of yours would already be gone."

My stomach turns over. "Gone?" I squeak. *Oops, I hadn't meant to say that aloud.*

"Cool your horses, girl. He likes to take valuable items, not hurt them, and from where I'm standing, you're the most valuable item to our friend The Amazing Boy here. I'd watch yourself," he says, erupting in another heartless laugh. The closer Jake gets to this guy, the more I can see he's really short. Probably around my height of five feet, five inches.

"I'd love to stay and tell you more, but this location has been tainted by the likes of you. Don't keep looking for us or the girl goes." Before either of us can blink, the man is gone from the hallway. Jake picks up his pace and runs the rest of the length of the hallway and looks both ways.

"How did he escape that fast?" Jake asks, with a mystified expression on his face. "I don't even sense him."

Never good when the superhero is confused.

"I'm not the one to ask. I'm still wrapping my brain around that I'm being used as collateral to hurt you," I say, trying not to whimper.

Jake hunches over. "This is why I'm not allowed to get close to anyone."

I suck in a breath and say, "I'm fine, go look for him. I'll be right behind you."

Jake nods and takes off to his right.

I jog to keep up with Jake. I exercise on occasion but after hanging out with Jake, I can tell I need to pick up my pace during my morning runs.

Jake's scanning the rooms, still wearing the glasses. He stops and turns back towards me.

"I can't find him anywhere."

I lightly touch Jake's arm. "Don't be too hard on yourself. He sprinted away before either of us realized what was going on."

Jake shakes his head. "But now we have no idea the next place on their list."

I pull out my phone. "More googling?"

Jake blows out his breath. "We got lucky this time and I screwed it up."

"If we can get lucky once, I bet it can happen again," I say.

Jake scratches his head. "We might need a different tactic. The internet can't know all the ins and outs of Philly."

"Need some help?" a voice calls out.

I turn around to see the blonde waving to us outside of her office, as if she's waiting for the right time to interject.

Jake looks at me and shrugs. "Can't hurt. She might know more hiding spots."

I try not to show that I'm hurt that he doesn't like my googling idea. "Sure, makes sense." I nod while inwardly thinking, *she just wants to sleep with you. We shouldn't be wasting time on dead ends.*

CHAPTER ELEVEN

JAKE

Do I really want to see that thirsty model-like blonde girl again? I mean she isn't bad to look at, but probably high maintenance and that doesn't work well for me. It's hard to take time to send flowers when I'm saving people's lives. And spoiling someone doesn't fit with my bad boy brand anyways.

The goal for involving this girl is to get some Philly insider info and move on to the next location before Ethel looks up from her paperwork. Besides, this girl has my calling card, which has a tracking chip in it so the Agent will know how to find her when we need to erase her memory.

We're all staring at each other in this girl's office. I clear my throat and say, "We could use some local knowledge if you have any. Our villain has decided to hide elsewhere in the city. If you were a villain, where would you hide in Philadelphia?"

She scratches her head with her pink fingernails. "The Philadelphia Museum of Art is pretty cool and iconic. Or the

Academy of Music if this villain is like the Phantom of the Opera."

I shake my head. "I don't see this guy being that cultured. Anything grittier, like City Hall?"

She thinks for a second and says, "Oh, I know! The Eastern State Penitentiary! Al Capone, that famous mafia guy, was even imprisoned there."

Now that sounds right. It's worth seeing this girl again just for that knowledge, even though I can tell Lea wants to be anywhere else. We could've done her googling idea but talking to locals sometimes works the best.

"Thank you very much ma'am for your service. We'll go check that out. Do you know how to get there from City Hall?" I say, using the polite language I'm told to use when dealing with a civilian.

"It's not too far of a walk from here. Too bad you can't fly, The Amazing Boy," she says winking.

Yeah, you and me both wish that. Why can't I have cool abilities, instead of only being able to sense heat sources through buildings, withstanding extreme heat, and having super-strength. I'm pretty lame when you think about it.

"We'll add it to the list of skills we want added for the next movie," Lea says with a straight face.

"You can do that?" the girl asks, her eyes widening.

Lea shrugs. "The Amazing Boy is the one that brings in the cash, why shouldn't he have input?"

If only they knew. I can tell my team what hat I want to wear as Jake but that's about it. My one item of control. Except now. Things feel different than before. The Agent being out of touch has been scary but at the same time it's nice to have the freedom to figure things out without everyone telling me what to do. And there hasn't been any punishment for letting Lea tag along. *At least not yet.*

But I know, even if the Agent isn't around, the cameras are. They always are. That's why I gave Lea the warning earlier. She deserves to know she's being recorded, even if she doesn't realize the whole extent. I don't know exactly how it works, but it always happens like this. I get a mission, do what it says and at the end, the Agent and I have a pre-screening to watch the footage. The footage is always edited before I see it, so I really don't know how much is filmed but I err on the side of caution and assume it's everything. Well hopefully not the bathroom. Better not to think that the guy who helps me make millions hears me taking a dump. Even superheroes poop.

I look down at my watch and see too much time has lapsed for my liking. Time to find a way to end this conversation.

"Thank you for your help, ma'am." I reach out to shake the blonde's hand. She grasps it and lingers holding my hand for more than is socially acceptable.

"You're welcome. This is fun. It's like a scavenger hunt with one of my favorite actors. I'm Meg by the way," she says, finally letting go of my hand. At least her hand isn't a sweaty mess. I'll give her that.

"I'm Jake, and this is Lea."

Lea tips her head towards Meg and Meg returns the nod.

"Need some company? I've lived in Philly all my life, so I know all the inside places if Eastern State isn't where your guy is hiding."

I see Lea roll her eyes. Honestly, I agree with her. One civilian for me to have to worry about is enough. Nothing against Lea or civilians in general, but usually I spend more of my time worrying about them than focusing on the problem at hand. I especially don't need a fangirl that really is aiming to get in my pants.

"Thank you, ma'am, but Lea and I have things covered right now but I do appreciate your offer of assistance," I reply.

Meg's face falls. "Oh, well okay. A friend of mine works

there, I'll give her a heads up you're coming. Maybe she can let you in for free."

I give her a genuine smile. *Maybe she's not that bad.*

"That'd be much appreciated, thank you for your service," I say walking towards the door.

"Enjoy the rest of your day working on a Saturday," Lea says waving.

As soon as we are out of hearing range, I let out a long breath.

"Everything okay?" Lea asks, giving me a side eye.

"Interactions like that are just draining. I have to watch every single thing I say."

Lea follows me and says, "I can't even imagine what that's like, everyone loving you. It's the opposite for me. I hate it when people don't love me."

Maybe that's why she didn't like Meg. She didn't give Lea the time of day.

I shrug. "She didn't love me. She loved the idea of me or who she thinks I am. In reality, she probably wouldn't like me. I'm pretty boring and wouldn't pay her enough attention."

Lea shakes her head. "You're a real superhero. Literally the opposite of boring but I can see how all that attention would get draining. You're just trying to live your life."

"While saving the world. Speaking of, let's try this side door that's far away from Ethel and get over to that penitentiary. We need to snag One-Eyed Barnacle before he finds a new hiding spot or steals something else."

WHEN I OPEN the Uber app, it flashes that there is a surge and besides being expensive, which doesn't bother me, it's going to be a thirty-minute wait for a ride. We don't have time to stand around. I bring up walking directions to the

Eastern State Penitentiary. It's about a mile and a half walk, so thirty minutes for the average person, but I can do it in about twenty. I explain to Lea the situation.

She eyes me warily. "I already have trouble keeping up with you. Can you at least not go too fast?"

"I'll try my best but it's hard to do when a city needs saving."

Lea stops in her tracks. "What do you mean the city needs saving?"

I'm in too deep not to tell her what's going on. She's the one that figured out my secret. The Agent will just have to erase her memory when this is all over anyways; what's the harm in telling her? We'll just have to edit these sections out of the movie.

"One of my powers is to feel body heat; the glasses I wear help me focus that power and make out more of the shapes. Before I got these glasses, I could read the body heat, but was not able to figure out how many people it came from, or where. I just knew people were in buildings. With this tech, I have a better sense of where and how many."

"Woah. I knew your character in the movies could do something like that, but I didn't understand how. Why were you wearing them at the convention center?"

This is where it gets tricky. "The first time we were in the big hall, I didn't sense any body heat at all, so I didn't even bother putting on my glasses. But as soon as we went outside and everything seemed fine with the rest of the world, I knew something was off inside."

Lea is still not moving. "What happened when we went back in?" she whispers.

I want to lie and not tell her, because it's really unsettling, but that won't do her any favors. I motion for Lea to keep walking. Maybe it'll be easier to break the news when I don't have to look at her.

"When I put the glasses on, body heat radiated through

the exhibit hall. Like hundreds and hundreds of bodies. I have this hunch that all the people are still there, just through some kind of cloaking method that evaded my normal powers."

Lea gasps. "Everyone's still there, just frozen?" she says slowly.

My eyes soften. "I'm not sure. It's like some kind of spell that didn't affect me, or you for that matter. Maybe because we were stuck in the elevator."

Lea's face darkens. "And this One-Eyed Barnacle can help us reverse whatever is going on at the convention center and get Jess and Olive unfrozen?"

"That's the hope. It's the spot where all the superheroes were stationed for the day, so I feel like he wanted us out of his way while he went through with some evil plan to steal something from the Museum of the American Revolution."

The pedestrian stop sign changes to walk and we jog across a busy intersection. "That's why Dave said that he was confused why you were around."

I nod. "Exactly. I think I was supposed to also be affected by that spell so I couldn't foil their evil plan. I have to find this One-Eyed Barnacle guy to get back what he stole and stop anything else from happening."

"And this is all unscripted? None of this was supposed to happen?" Lea says.

"Yeah. Today I was just supposed to make an appearance at WizCon, not chase some bad guy, again. It would be nice to have a break for a change."

Google Maps tells me we are only five minutes from our destination.

I was right, time flies when you have something life changing to discuss.

"Are all of the other superheroes in movies actually superheroes too?" Lea asks. "Like Thor can't be real, right? How can there be an actual God of Thunder?

"Some are, and some are just actors. Don't worry, Marvel and DC superheroes are all fake. That's why some of their superheroes and villains are ridiculous. Like Thanos? A big purple dude that collects gemstones? Come on. Pretty lame."

Lea looks physically relieved. "Phew. I was really starting to worry that everything I ever knew was wrong. At least it's only some people that are real superheroes."

I pick up the pace. Time to get this show on the road so we can be done as soon as possible. "My goal is to be a real actor doing real movies. That's what I originally started doing but once I fell into the superhero genre, it just won't seem to go away. Especially if stuff like this keeps happening."

That's when a huge stone building comes into my view.

CHAPTER TWELVE

LEA

I point to the sign sitting in front of the towering stone structure. *Eastern State Penitentiary is closed for a private event.*

"Isn't that suspicious? The Museum of the American Revolution and City Hall were both closed and now the Eastern State Penitentiary is also shut down for the day?"

Jake rubs his chin. "Very. It also means there is a good chance One-Eyed Barnacle is inside. Guess we have to find a sneaky way in."

I inspect the former jail. "It can't be that hard, it's pretty torn down as it is. There's got to be a weak spot somewhere, especially with your powers."

Jake winces. "You aren't able to see this in the movies, but my superstrength is hit or miss."

"What do you mean? Does it work like half the time? Or only when you're in dire need?" I ask.

Jake isn't looking at me. "It works most of the time, just sometimes there's a fluke and it won't. We edit footage in the movie to make it work all of the time. They can't have The Amazing Boy showing any sign of weakness."

"Oh …" I'm not sure what else to say without sounding disappointed.

"Sorry I'm not who you think I am," Jake mumbles.

I touch his arm. "No, it's not that. I'm just trying to process how this whole superhero thing works. When I figured out you were a real superhero, I just assumed all the powers were real, which was my bad. Of course, things are going to be different."

"They're real, just exaggerated in the movies," Jake says defensively. "And don't always work when I need them to."

I'm curious about his powers, and how he even knew he had them, but now doesn't seem like the right time to ask.

"We can figure out some other way to get in then. You breaking down a wall would cause too much disruption and damage anyways. What if we say we're part of the special event?" I ask.

Jake looks down at his costume. "Depends on the special event. If it's a black-tie wedding, we're a little underdressed."

Good point. "Unless it's superhero themed. How do you wear this all day? I'm so hot." I fan my face with my right hand.

Jake laughs. "My suit is made from similar materials that Under Armor uses, so it really doesn't bother me too much. That and I'm used to it by now."

"The Amazing Boy," a voice calls.

Oh no, not some fan coming to bother us. That's all we need right now.

We both turn towards the voice and I'm not able to hold in my groan. *Meg found us.*

"Are you freaking kidding me?" I say under my breath.

Jake's face is contorted. He's doing his best not to look annoyed. It must be taking all his acting abilities to do so.

"Meg," Jake says. *He's dropped the polite act and saying ma'am. He must be pretty annoyed.*

She saunters over to us and puts her arm around Jake. When she does so, I notice that her fingernails are no longer pink. *How did she change the color so fast?*

"Right after you left, I texted my friend who works here and she told me it's closed for the day. I thought I'd come over and help you out," Meg says, pulling her blonde hair out of her bun. It comes down to almost her waist and it only increases her hotness factor.

"That's so nice of you," I say sweetly.

Meg shrugs. "It's the least I can do. It's not every day I get to help a movie star," she coos, turning towards Jake, her arm still around his shoulders.

It's very convenient that Meg knows someone that works here. But she is employed by the city, and I bet they have the best connections.

"Come on, she's waiting for us at the entrance," Meg says, walking in front of us.

Jake and I exchange looks. His eyes are wary. "I don't have a better way of getting in. I guess we try this and see what happens," he whispers to me.

Meg's already talking to her contact, a girl with long dark brown hair in dreads and dark skin. She's dressed almost identical to Meg, a black pencil skirt, bright pink blouse, black heels, and a fashionable pink bag. Is every girl in Philadelphia secretly a model?

The new person's face erupts in a large grin as we approach, and her hand shoots out. "It's so nice to meet you, The Amazing Boy, or I guess I should say Jake. And it's good to meet you, uh ..." She falters as she looks at me questioningly.

"Super L," Jake says, while shaking her outstretched hand.

I want to groan. *I guess that name really is sticking.* "Calling me Lea is fine." I also shake her hand.

Meg's friend cocks her head at me. "Are you going to be introduced in this new movie that's being filmed because I don't remember you from any of the other ones?"

"Yep, my first appearance." *If I don't get edited out for being an awful companion.*

She gives me a scrutinizing look. "You must be super new; even the gossip sites haven't mentioned you yet."

Jake rescues me and says, "Last minute addition. We thought we'd change it up a bit and appeal to our female fans. Too many male superheroes."

I wholeheartedly agree with that. There needs to be more women superheroes that are queer, quirky, and not stereotypically hot. Someone more normal. *I guess like me?*

"I love that! I'm Gina by the way and I'm excited you're here at the Eastern State Penitentiary. Were we supposed to know you'd be here filming? I'm sorry if something got dropped," Gina says, her brow creasing.

"It's a very last-minute pit stop. We won't be here long. We just want to look around for future movie locations. It's just the two of us," Jake explains.

"Okay, great. I wish I could take you around and give you the full tour, but I need to prepare for tonight's event. Meg here should be able to help you out. She's been here enough," Gina says, giving us another one-hundred-watt smile.

I'm already getting a better feeling about Gina than Meg. She isn't fawning all over Jake and she seems super genuine.

"Thanks for letting us in, I know you probably had to pull some strings," I say, returning her smile.

Gina shrugs. "Honestly, it's not that big of a deal. Plus, this is pretty cool; there aren't many movie stars that show up at our prison."

Meg gives Gina a quick hug and after Gina pulls away, Meg turns to Jake and says, "Let's take a look around."

"What do you know about this place?" I ask Meg curiously. It's so spooky, way darker and scarier than City Hall. I guess one would hope so since it had literally been used as a prison.

"It's used for ghost tours at Halloween," Meg says shortly. I wait for her to elaborate but she doesn't.

Ghost tours make sense though. I'm already getting creeped out walking down the damp, dark hallway. The white paint on the wall is almost completely gone; it probably even needed a paint job fifty years ago. I can almost feel the ghosts' penetrating presence. I'm sure a lot of inmates died in these cells. I shiver and look over at Jake. He doesn't seem bothered in the slightest. This is probably like an everyday occurrence for him.

"Okay, we need to be quiet, in case One-Eyed Barnacle is lurking around," Jake says, pulling out his glasses.

I nod and Meg looks intrigued.

"You look so real right now. This is amazing. You can turn on your acting skills at a moment's notice," she says, clapping her hands.

She really doesn't understand anything going on. I thought maybe she got that Jake was actually hunting a villain, but I guess not. It did take me a while to figure it out. I need to find a way to distract her while Jake keeps looking for One-Eyed Barnacle.

"Is there a gift shop? I love gift shops."

Meg looks straight ahead. "Probably but it's not going to be open right now. But I can take you to see an important cell. Trust me, it's better than any gift shop."

How does she not know if there is a gift shop or not? I always have to stop at one before leaving a museum. I can take a little bit of history home with me.

I follow her, hoping Jake gets the hint, but he's still trailing after us, using his glasses to gaze into the cells we pass.

How are we going to get rid of Meg? We really don't need this clueless fan trailing us. I'll never get Jess and Olive unfrozen at this rate. *I guess this is how Jake felt about me in the elevator before finding out I'm not a megafan.*

We reach a cell at the end of the hallway and my eyes widen. There is a desk with a light that's turned on, a chair with a green cushion on the seat, a bed with a fluffy pillow, and a nightstand with fake flowers on top of it. A fedora hangs on a coat rack, along with a black trench coat.

"Woah. Why's this one so fancy?" I ask.

"Al Capone's cell," she says, staring into the room.

"This is supposed to be what his cell looked like? I've stayed in hotels that are crappier than this."

"Like the place we're set up in now?" Jake states, scanning the room.

"I wasn't going to mention that, but, yeah, that hostel room has way less character than this prison cell."

Meg gives us an inquisitive look. "Why would two movie stars be staying in a crappy hotel?"

"Part of the plot for the movie," I say quickly.

Meg's right eyebrow lifts but she doesn't say anything. She pulls out a bunch of keys and fumbles for a little bit, which gives me the perfect view of her black fingernails. Something about them still bothers me. It takes me a long time to take off polish and reapply, probably why I stopped painting my nails. Doesn't seem worth the trouble to me. How did she change colors that fast? And why would she want to? She doesn't seem like the black nail polish kind of girl.

She tries multiple antique keys until one unlocks the cell and she slips inside. Jake and I both linger outside the cell. She beckons for us to join her. "You can come inside and look around. Gina told me it's fine."

I guess it's okay if Gina said so. Almost in a trance, I walk through the doors and step through time, at least that's what it feels like.

"Didn't Al Capone kill like a ton of people? Why would he get such a nice cell?" I ask.

"The prison owners were scared of Al Capone's wrath, that's why it's so nice," Meg explains, making a beeline to the coat rack. She feels the fabric of the trench coat and sighs. My stomach turns. *What is she doing? You don't touch things in a museum.* Her oily hands are going to ruin it.

Jake lingers outside the door, his eyes darting around. "Come on, Lea. We should keep looking around."

Meg plucks the fedora off the coat rack and places it on her head. It does not fit her style at all, just like the nail polish. The pit in my stomach starts to grow.

"How does this make me look?" she asks, her eyes daring me to say anything.

"Uh, different? You shouldn't wear that. You might damage it," I say, biting my lip.

She's petting the hat on her head like a prized animal. "Don't you worry, I'll be careful. Why don't you both pose for a picture and then you can take one of me in my new getup. You can use the photos to show your producers what a great place this is for a shooting!" Meg says.

"No, we don't have time for that," Jake says sternly, looking down at his watch.

Meg's eyes turn to slits. "So, you're going to make me do this the hard way."

Meg steps out of the cell, fedora and all, and leaps into Jake, pushing him into the cell, right where I'm standing. I collapse on the bed, with Jake on top of me, his glasses tumbling to the floor. I hear the cell door slam shut and the distinct sound of a clicking lock.

"No!" Jake yells, scrambling off me, lunging at the door. He grabs a hold of the cell door and rattles it, like a toddler trying to defeat a baby gate. It doesn't budge. I get up off the bed and join him. I shake the bars too, just to be sure. It's probably the sturdiest thing in this building.

Meg has a demonic look on her face. "You escaped our plan at the convention center so we had to improvise. Let's see you get out of this, The Amazing Boy."

CHAPTER THIRTEEN

JAKE

Normally being locked in a room with a cute girl wouldn't be the worst thing in the world but when you are trying to find a villainous pirate to save the cute girl's ex-girlfriend, it's not an ideal situation.

"Have fun you two. Looks like you are in for a long night, together. At least the accommodations are comfortable," Meg says, smirking. Her eyes are as cold as ice. Suddenly she doesn't seem so hot.

"Why are you doing this? And who are you?" I ask.

"After you ran into Dave at City Hall, One-Eyed Barnacle gave me instructions to get you out of the way."

Lea's mouth drops. "You're working with One-Eyed Barnacle, and that other man at City Hall?" She's standing next to me, her hands grasping the cell door.

She gives an exasperated sigh. "That's Dave. He always ruins everything. I told him not to get caught. If it wasn't for him, you would've had no idea we were even there."

What a terrible sidekick name, Dave. Not even anything similar to One-Eyed Barnacle. Did they call him Dave the Doofus?

Meg keeps rattling on. "I heard you talking to the city worker, this Meg person and it was perfect. And she had already called her friend to let her know you were on the way to Eastern State Penitentiary, and what a coincidence, this place is on the list for me to hit up. I became her but thank God you know the truth now. I'm so sick of her clothes. How can anyone wear a skirt so tight?"

Meg transforms right before our eyes. One moment she has long blonde hair and blue eyes in her skirt and nice shirt, and the next second she's wearing black jean pants, leather boots, and a black T-shirt. Her long black hair is pin straight, and she has on so much makeup under her gray eyes.

I'm not the least bit surprised. Most villains and their side-kicks have powers. It's a known attribute in my world, just like I have superpowers. I worriedly look over at Lea to see how she's handling this new development.

To her credit, she hasn't fainted yet, but her face is whiter than normal, which isn't saying too much because she's already a pretty pale person.

"What just happened? You're not the city employee, Meg? I'm so confused right now," Lea says, her eyes growing wide.

"Get it together, sidekick," Meg says sneering. "You clearly aren't up to the caliber of The Amazing Boy and you're just bringing him down, like now. You're the reason the both of you are locked in a cell. But lucky for me, you guys are a package deal."

Lea wipes her eyes, looking away. This isn't all on Lea. I should have spoken up about my doubts and not let her in the cell. Enough is enough.

"You can make fun of me all you want, Meg, if that's your real name, but leave Lea alone. She wasn't supposed to be involved in this mess." I give Meg a look of death.

Meg laughs. "You can call me Hallie, but that's also not my real name just like Jake Johnson isn't yours. You and I are similar like that. No one will ever know the real us."

I flinch. *How does she know that?*

Hallie stares at Lea. "And don't you worry your pretty little head. That Meg girl is still back at her civil servant job, serving a society who cares for nothing but themselves. She has no idea I'm pretending to be her."

I figured that is the case, but it's nice to hear that Meg isn't tied to a chair somewhere. I don't need another person to save, especially one that keeps hitting on me.

"If you do manage to get out, don't come looking for us. Next time we won't be so nice," Hallie says, walking away. Her swagger is even different now that she's revealed herself. It's filled with confidence and purpose. She turns around for one more quick look.

"Oh, and if you didn't figure it out already, this place won't have an outside event tonight. We're the ones that rented it out for the entire day." She winks at us. "I'm going to tell Gina that you had to leave to scout out another location which means no one will come and rescue you. Good luck!" She gives a cackling laugh and disappears around a corner.

Lea's still staring after Hallie with a terrified expression on her face. I put my hand on her arm reassuringly.

"It'll be okay. I always manage to get out of situations like this, I promise."

Lea turns to me, her blue eyes still wide.

"I've never met anyone so evil. She doesn't seem to care about us at all," Lea whispers.

I pat her arm. "I know it's hard when you first meet someone like that, but not everyone in the world is good."

"How did she change forms?" Lea asks, rubbing her temple.

I'm not sure how to respond to her question. Maybe the most truthful but yet basic answer will work.

"She appears to have superpowers just like me. But hers are more mimicking, so she can impersonate other people."

Lea shakes her head. "This is crazy. How can all these individuals have special powers, and no one has the slightest idea."

"We have people that work very hard to keep everything a secret," I say.

She doesn't know the half of it and she never will since her mind will be wiped as soon as the Agent makes an appearance.

"This Hallie person left us here without a way to get out," Lea says flatly.

"But she did leave us with resources," I say, pulling out my phone.

Lea's eyes brighten. "I guess she did!"

I look down and realize I spoke too soon. *No signal.* Probably from being stuck in this dungeon-like fortress.

"Never mind ..."

"Guess you don't have any reception either," Lea says, sitting on the side of the bed staring down at her phone.

I sink into the desk chair and prop my legs on the end of the bed. Lea eyes the cell door and then looks back at me.

"How are you feeling about trying out that superstrength?"

I start tapping my heel against the bed frame. All this talk about my superstrength is giving me performance anxiety.

"Best case scenario it'll work, but I'm not feeling great about it right now," I say, breaking our stare.

"So, it's not like the Hulk and you need to get angry for it to work?" Lea asks.

I shake my head. "No, nothing like that. I've had it work when I'm in very distressing situations but then sometimes it doesn't, and my agent has to send back up for me," I say, staring at my sneakers.

"Oh," Lea says softly.

She's probably thinking that I'm super lame, rather than a

superhero. I always tell everyone that I'm working with upfront that it doesn't always work. I don't want to be held accountable if someone needs it to work and it doesn't. The Agent gets it and he always promises to have my back, except for this one time I really need him.

"What about picking locks?" Lea asks.

"I didn't need to learn that. People could just come get me out if I was ever stuck."

Lea falls back on the bed, her head hitting the pillow. As she closes her eyes, she says, "I'm not falling asleep, I'm still thinking, I promise."

"I wouldn't fault you if you took a nap. It's been a really long day," I say.

"But Jess is counting on me," Lea mumbles. She opens one eye and peeks at me.

"You don't have to sit on that creaky old chair. It's probably super lumpy. I won't bite," she says.

I scratch my head. "Are you sure? I didn't want to assume it was okay to be in that super small bed next to you."

Lea shuts her eyes again. "It's totally fine. I trust you. You're nothing like what the gossip columns say. *Jake Johnson's at it again. Two dates with two models in one night.*"

I go over to the side of the bed and lay down, making sure there is as much space as possible between us. The bed, even though it isn't the comfiest one I've ever laid on, is feeling pretty good right now.

"Oh yeah, I remember that one. Those pictures with the models were from a photoshoot. My agent paid the gossip site to run them to upkeep my bad boy persona."

Lea turns onto her right side facing me, both her eyes open. "You're joking."

I turn my head towards her. "Nope. The night in question, I was in my condo working on a *Star Wars* LEGO. Everyone needs a hobby to relax from work. LEGO just so happens to be mine." A weight lifts off my shoulders. I've never told anyone about my LEGO habit. Not even the Agent, but I'm sure he knows. *He knows everything.*

Lea covers her mouth with her hand to smother a laugh. "I wouldn't have taken you for a LEGO and *Star Wars* enthusiast, but I love it. My hobby is learning as much as I can about history, especially presidential history. It's a goal of mine to see anything related to the Presidents of the United States. That's why I was geeking out so much over Independence Hall." Lea looks down. "Jess thought it was super nerdy, so I didn't talk to her about it very much."

This Jess person sounds awful. Why would she say all these terrible things to Lea?

"Hey, if it makes you happy, then who cares what anyone else thinks."

I need to take my own advice too. Who cares if LEGO doesn't go with my bad boy persona. Honestly, I think my bad boy persona is what needs to go.

Lea slowly nods. "I'm starting to realize this. I'm also still stuck on what's happening right at this moment. That I'm in bed at some creepy prison next to one of the most famous movie stars in the world."

"I don't know how famous I am, but we do keep getting stuck together in some weird situations."

"This time we're sharing a bed that a gangster might have used," Lea adds.

I chuckle. "I doubt this is Al Capone's real bed."

"I sure hope not. It probably would be so gross by now, with lots of bed bugs," Lea says wrinkling her nose.

We're silent for a minute. "For the record, I never thought I'd be in this situation either. Or even that I'd be The Amazing Boy."

Lea inspects my face and after a moment says, "I've been dying to ask this. How did you become The Amazing Boy?"

I place my hands behind my head. "Do you really want to know? It's not all it's cracked up to be."

Lea motions to the door. "Does it look like I have anywhere else to go? And this time I don't have to pee."

CHAPTER FOURTEEN

JAKE

"My mom tried to be an actress, but nothing worked out for her, so she wanted to live vicariously through me."

"And your dad?" Lea asks.

I shake my head. "Never met him. I still have no idea who he is. My mom never told me. She said it's better if I don't know. He left when I was young. According to her, he'd try and take away all my 'hard-earned money.'"

"As a kid, I was doing commercials left and right. She'd take me out of classes for all kinds of acting calls and gigs. Eventually she ended up homeschooling me. And not very well. I still don't know anything about the United States government."

Lea shrugs. "Even being the huge history nerd I am, there's more to life than learning the branches of government. And it's never too late to learn."

"I guess, but I feel like I missed out on a lot besides my

studies. I never got to experience friendship. Or really being a kid. It was always learning lines and preparing for the next audition."

I'm keenly aware the both of us are still laying together on a mobster's bed. Lea's staring at me intently, clearly invested in my life story. When was the last time I was in bed with a girl and all we were doing was talking? Probably never. Most of the other girls I took to a hotel room immediately jumped me. None of them knew my true name and what I'm really like. Lea still doesn't know my name, but this is the closest I've come to telling anyone.

"That had to be hard. I really didn't like school that much, but it's where I started to really love history and realized I wanted to be an archivist. And met Jess," Lea says, shifting her eyes from mine.

It's not fair to Lea that she's this broken up about someone who hurt her so bad. Lea's going to hell and back for this girl, and I'd bet anything that Jess, once she's unfrozen, will never appreciate it.

Lea picks at her fingernail. "How'd you figure out you have superpowers?"

"When everything started to go down, I was already getting homeschooled. I was sixteen and on the set of a cop show no one's ever heard of. We were in the middle of shooting a scene where a building catches fire with a bunch of hostages inside, and the cops are supposed to burst in and save them at the last minute."

Lea's playing with a strand of her hair, eyes still focused on me.

"I was in my trailer waiting to be called for my scene when I heard a bunch of screaming. I burst outside and first saw the smoke billowing up into the sky. Fire was leaping out of every part of the building. Windows, doors, the roof, you name it."

"How did they not have a backup plan if something like

that happened?" Lea asks, her brows furrowed.

"It was a low-budget TV show; I'm surprised they even used real fire. Clearly, they shouldn't have. I tried to find out if people were still inside, but no one was paying any attention to me. Finally, I just focused on the building and sensed that there were three people inside. Don't ask me how I knew, I just did. I felt their heartbeats and counted. I couldn't tell exactly where they were, but I knew they were there."

"I have a feeling I can guess what happened next, especially since I experienced it firsthand today," Lea says. Her focus still hasn't wavered from my story as she is playing with one of her many silver bracelets on her arm.

"I didn't think twice and ran inside. I can still hear my mom screaming my name."

"How did you know you weren't going to get burned?" Lea asks.

"For as long as I remember I've never been scared of fire. When I was around seven, one of my mom's candles fell over. The flame landed right on my hand, but I didn't feel it and there wasn't a mark. I never told her and didn't think much of it, except that experience helped me not be afraid of fire."

Lea's eyes were wide. Maybe my superpowers are cooler than I think.

"In the burning building, the flames were leaping all over me, but I didn't feel a thing. It was as if I was covered in water and the flames couldn't touch me. I had trouble finding the people inside though from all the smoke, but finally they came into view. Two of them were tied together, a man and a woman, both on the floor passed out and another man was lying on the floor next to them. It was one of those impossible choices. I picked the two people and hoisted them on my back and maneuvered my way out the back of the building. I took them outside and went back to get the third person."

"I can't believe you went back in after that," Lea says, her mouth wide.

"I had to save that last person. He was much easier since he wasn't tied to anyone else, but at that point the building couldn't have been structurally sound anymore and I was dodging falling debris left and right, but I managed to get him outside. Because I put the people on the side of the building, no one even noticed them out there, so I called my agent and then my mom to ask for their help."

"How did your phone still work?" Lea asks.

I shrug. "Beats me. It's always like that. Even though my costume is flame resistant it really doesn't need to be. Whenever something is on me, it's immune from the flames, my phone included."

Lea shakes her head. "That's so wild. I'm sure your mom was freaking out."

I nod. "She thought I was a goner. My agent and my mom came running around the side of the building and when they saw me, they stared at me like I had horns. I still remember my mom's look of terror. It was as if she didn't recognize me. My agent though, I could almost see the dollar signs popping out of his eyes, like that stupid emoji. He ran over to me and said, *You can't tell anyone about this. The media will blow this apart. Let me take care of it.*"

Lea moves her head closer to me. "How'd he take care of it?"

I suck in a deep breath. "He untied the people and called the medics over. He explained that the three individuals must have gotten themselves out and everyone bought it because I didn't look like I'd been involved at all. My mom wanted to take me to the hospital, but the agent kept saying, *They are going to ask what happened to him and what can we say?*"

"At least your mom wanted to make sure you were okay," Lea says, giving me a sympathetic glance.

That was then. Now is now. She doesn't even know who I am anymore.

"After the burning building incident, my agent tested a

few other scenarios. It became very clear I'm fire resistant, can sometimes use superstrength, and that I'm able to sense people through buildings. My agent is the one that came up with the idea of The Amazing Boy and sold the idea to studios, a real-life superhero. Marvel was still all the rage, so they loved the idea. Someone that was kind of like our own hometown Peter Parker."

"When I first started out, we were going to be honest and say that the movies were based on real events and have me be my superhero self all the time, but during a test session, we found people were extremely confused and upset by the concept. They didn't understand how superheroes could exist in real life and became agitated, not even wanting to see all the movie footage we had planned to show them."

Lea grimaces. "Understandable. My mind is still completely blown, but I'm trying to act chill. Not sure if I'm doing a good job."

I take her in. I had been wondering. It seems to me like she is cool with the whole thing except for the few nervous twitches, like playing with her bracelets, or picking at her nails.

She catches my eye. "It's something that you don't really want to believe, because it means so much more exists than you ever thought was possible, including creepy villains."

"That's exactly it. If I'm a superhero, what else in the world is a lie? So we changed tactics, not to freak anyone out. I became The Amazing Boy when I'm fighting villains, which is what's used in the movie footage, and Jake Johnson all the other times, complete with a whole new personality."

Lea shakes her head. "That's the part I don't get. Why can't you be yourself, instead of some made up douchebag?"

"My agent said I needed to be a completely different person. No one should know who I really was from my past, and I had to leave my old life behind, including my mother. Villains, since they are actually real, could use her as collateral. That's why I don't ever use my other name. I don't want anything to ever get tied back to her."

Lea's eyes soften. "Do you get to talk to her at least?"

I look away from Lea, trying to keep my voice under control. "She doesn't remember who I am. My team erased all her memories of me for her protection."

Lea gasps and grabs my hand, "Jake! Or whatever your name is … that's so awful. I can't even imagine. How could they do that?"

I can't help it; tears start to form in my eyes, and I try to move my head away so Lea doesn't see. I know I'm not successful when she says, "It's okay. It really is. How can you not be sad?"

"I know it's for her safety, but I had no clue it would hurt this much. It's almost as if she's dead. I have no family and friends, just fans who don't know anything about me," I say, my voice breaking.

"You have me now." Lea pulls me to her and gives me a hard side hug. I bury my face into her hair. If only I could have someone like Lea in my life. I don't have the heart to break it to her that there is no doubt in my mind when the Agent comes back, Lea's memories of me will also be erased, unless I can somehow convince him she can be a sidekick introduced in this film. But I doubt he will agree to it. It's always just the two of us.

The hug breaks and I lay my head on the pillow again next to her.

"Thanks for listening to me. I've never told anyone that story before," I say. I'm squeezing my hand in a fist.

"Never? You really need some outlet, like a therapist."

I shake my head. "There's no way I'd be allowed to have one of those. They could out me. No one is supposed to know."

Lea studies my face. "That must be lonely."

"A bit, but I'm used to it by now."

It looks like she's about to say more when I hear, "What are you two doing? You can't be in there!"

I scramble off the bed and run to the cell door and Lea's right beside me. The girl that works here gapes at us, her hands on her hips.

"Gina, we're stuck!" Lea exclaims.

"What do you mean you're stuck?" She fumbles with the lock and swears under her breath.

"How'd this happen?"

"Meg locked us in," I say, realizing this girl is not going to believe her friend stuck us in this situation.

Gina scrunches her eyebrows. "Wait, why would she do that?"

"She literally turned into someone else before our eyes," Lea says and immediately clasps her hand over her mouth. "I'm sorry," she mouths at me.

What is Lea doing? That's just great. Another memory to erase.

Gina gives us both a confused look. "Um, what?"

"Long, complicated story, ma'am, that I doubt you will believe. Are you able to get us out of here? We have some other tasks we need to complete," I state, straightening up.

"Don't call me ma'am. You make me feel a million years old," Gina snaps, rooting in a bright pink bag. She keeps rummaging and her face turns cloudy.

"Are your keys missing?" I ask innocently.

Gina meets my eyes and they're filled with panic. "I'm dead. I'm going to get fired. Where did they go?"

Lea speaks up. "Meg probably stole them when she hugged you. And I'm sure it has something to do with her superpowers." As soon as she utters those words, Lea's face turns whiter than normal.

Gina raises her eyebrows. "Superpowers?"

"I didn't mean that," Lea stutters.

Gina comes closer to the cell and crosses her arms. "Your face says otherwise. What is going on?"

CHAPTER FIFTEEN

LEA

Gina isn't wrong. Jess always told me I'd lose in an instant at strip poker. Which might be how I was the one who had to remove most of my clothing when Jess wanted to play one time. I thought I was going to get lucky that night, by winning the poker game of course, but instead I'd made myself look like a fool yet again.

Now here I am divulging that superpowers exist, something Jake has worked so hard to keep a secret. He is going to get in so much trouble. I give him a look of panic. His face is strained, as if he can't decide whether he's mad at me or not.

"I guess it doesn't hurt to try this now that Gina knows about superpowers. Stand back," he orders us.

I give him a questioning look. "What are you going to do?"

"Our last resort option. We don't have time to keep standing around." He plants his feet firmly, takes hold of the cell door with both hands, and tries pushing it open. He keeps grunting but no luck. I'm afraid he's going to bust a gut, so I place my hand on his shoulder.

"Stop! I don't want you hurting yourself. I didn't know it would be that painful. It looks so easy in the movies," I say frowning.

"Nothing's ever like the movies."

Gina stands there staring at us. "What about the lock?" she asks.

"He says he can't pick locks," I respond, staring down at the rusted key lock.

"If you're trying to do what I think you are, can't you crumble it with your hand to make it open? The thing has to be brittle being so old."

Jake maneuvers his arm outside the cell door and gets ahold of the lock. He grunts as he pushes against it. I can tell he's using all of his strength to make it move. His face turns red as he squeezes it.

"I don't know. It's too …" Jake starts to say and then I hear breaking metal.

"You did it!" I say, clapping my hands together.

Jake lets the pieces of the lock fall out of his hand and pulls his arm back inside the cell. "The fact that it was so rusted did help, but I guess my skills finally showed up when I needed them."

I look over at Gina and her mouth is agape. "What just happened?" she asks, her eyes wide, staring down at the pieces of the lock on the ground. "I was just playing along when I suggested crumbling the lock. I didn't think you could actually do it."

"No need for that key anymore," Jake says, brushing off his hands. "But you're going to need a new lock."

"And I'm still going to need the rest of my keys," Gina says sharply.

"Then let's get going, we need to catch a bad guy. Or bad guy and girl. Or bad people," I say.

Jake shakes his head. "If you're going to stick around, we need to get you some better one-liners."

"Was I right that you have a bunch of lines that you have to memorize and pull them out of your pocket when you need them?"

Jake opens the cell door and motions for me to go through. I happily comply.

"Of course. I need to be prepared so I'm not fumbling my words while also fighting a bad guy. Otherwise, my agent gets annoyed when he has to keep dubbing my lines."

Jake shuts the cell door. Gina's still silent. We both stop talking and look at her.

"Are you waiting for me to say something? Because I sure as heck don't know the right questions to ask. I know you said something about superpowers, and then I just saw this display. It seems Jake's actually a superhero but that can't be a thing, right?" Gina asks, crossing her arms.

"I said the same thing earlier today. I even saw him run out of a burning building without so much as a scratch," I say.

Gina's wringing her hands together. "I don't know what to make of this."

"I know it's a lot to take in, but I'm sorry, we don't have much time. If we're going to find Hallie to get your keys, we need to hurry," Jake says.

He's dropped his polite demeanor again. Maybe it's because Gina figured out the truth or yelled at him for calling her ma'am. I don't blame her. I'm only eighteen-years-old so I would feel weird being called ma'am, and this girl only looks a little older than me.

"Wait, who's Hallie?" Gina asks.

"The girl here earlier wasn't Meg, just someone that looked like her. Your friend Meg is still at City Hall with no idea that you thought you saw her," Jake explains.

Gina blinks her dark brown eyes a couple of times. "Are you sure you guys weren't doing drugs in Al Capone's cell?"

I shake my head. "I've never done drugs in my life."

"Okay, I'll play along, especially if you think I'll be able to get my keys back."

"Oh, and a hat," I add in.

Gina's right eyebrow shoots up. "What hat?"

"The Hallie person walked out of here with the hat from Al Capone's cell," I say.

Gina's mouth drops. "Are you kidding me? That's super valuable. It's one of Al Capone's iconic fedoras. Where do you think she went? We need to get it back as soon as we can," Gina says frantically.

Jake sighs. "That's always the hard part. I wish I knew Philly better to figure out where else she, Dave, and One-Eyed Barnacle would hide."

"One Eyed-Barnacle? This just keeps getting better and better."

"You can say that again," I reply.

"Do you need help finding them?" Gina offers. "The sooner I get the fedora and keys back, the better."

"Do you have any ideas where a villain would go in Philly?" Jake jumps in.

Gina's face lights up. "I might! I'm actually from Philly."

"Really? How long have you worked at the Eastern State Penitentiary?" I ask.

Gina flushes. "I'm actually interning here right now. I go to Temple University but this is my summer internship."

"Having you around will be even better than googling!" I exclaim.

Jake knits his eyebrows together. I guess I should have asked him first before I invited another person along on our adventure. I didn't even think but why wouldn't he want extra help? Then I remember how he said his agent and team are very secretive and how he can't even see his own mother anymore.

I give Jake my best *I'm sorry* look and after a moment, he shrugs. "It will be good to have an insider's perspective."

Gina's face drops. "I can't leave though. We have an outside rental that I need to help with."

Jake and I exchange a look.

"We found out it was Hallie, aka Meg's lookalike, and One-Eyed Barnacle that rented out the place to have it empty. I guess you'll be having an event that no one's going to show up to," I say gently.

"Are you kidding me? We've spent the past couple of weeks getting ready for it! They bought one of the most exclusive packages too, complete with a cocktail hour right by Al Capone's cell." Gina's gripping her hands into fists. "I need to let my boss know ASAP." She pulls out her phone from her bag and starts typing away.

Jake's eyebrow raises. "Maybe it was a backup plan to get the fedora?"

I mull this over in my head. That's not a bad idea.

"Are you thinking they are stealing things all over the city?" I ask.

Jake starts pacing, kicking up some dirt from the ground. "It would make sense. There has to be some kind of end game. Right now, we know they stole something at the Museum of the American Revolution and here. And who knows, they could have also taken something at City Hall and we just didn't see it."

Jake stops right in front of Gina.

"What are some places that have valuable items in Philly?"

"The Philadelphia Museum of Art is very iconic and ..."

"Meg already suggested that too and Jake thinks it's too mainstream," I offer.

Jake begins his pacing again. "That was when I thought they were trying to find a hideout, not steal more stuff. That could be a good option."

Gina scratches her chin. "Well, Philly also has less mainstream places too. What about a gross, cultural spot that's off the beaten path? It's called the Mütter Museum and is full of weird things."

Jake suddenly stops. "Wait, I think I've heard of that," Jake says. He leans against Al Capone's cell.

"It's a collection of weird medical items. My girlfriend's interning there so she can let us in, and it's kind of on the way to the Philadelphia Museum of Art so we could hit up both."

Jake scratches his head. "Is there anything worth stealing there?"

Gina nods. "For sure, especially if they're into strange things. And taking a gangster's fedora is pretty odd to me."

I narrow my eyes. "I just had a thought. How do we know you're actually Gina and not Hallie? You could be trying to lead us in the wrong direction."

Jake straightens up and looks on guard. "Very true. I'm pretty sure Hallie's a shapeshifter so she could be Gina right now."

Gina holds up her hands. "Why would I let you out of the cell?"

"You didn't let us out. I did," Jake says inspecting Gina.

"Right, well I tried to, but my keys were gone."

I blow a piece of loose hair out of my face.

This is all so confusing. I want to believe Gina, I really do, but Hallie broke my trust. People breaking my trust seems like a pattern, starting with the root of the problem, Jess. How do I believe anyone? Is Jake really Jake? *Wait, that gives me an idea.*

"Jake, have you dealt with shapeshifters before?"

He looks up at the deteriorating ceiling as he's thinking. "Once or twice. Why?"

"Are there any patterns or something we can use to determine if Gina is herself?"

Gina puts her hands on her hips. "I can hear every word you're saying about me."

"I'm sorry, I just don't want to get fooled again," I say.

"One way to tell is in the eyes. If it's a shapeshifter, something is normally off. They are dull and lifeless. Or sometimes even an odd color."

We both turn to Gina and peer into her dark brown eyes.

"Now I'm feeling really self-conscious," Gina says, blinking more than usual.

Gina's eyes have a healthy glow to them. I don't see anything sinister or dull although they do look pissed off.

I glance at Jake, and he gives a slight head nod.

"Sorry, we've been fooled once, and I didn't want it to happen again," I explain.

A memory comes rushing back to me.

"When Hallie was Meg, I noticed her fingernails were black and earlier that day Meg's were bright pink. Is that a way to tell too?" I ask.

Jake nods. "Sometimes shapeshifters don't get all the details right, so they can forget something small like that."

"Now we know how to look for Hallie in the future, the black fingernails."

Gina holds up her bright blue manicured nails. "Are you guys good now?"

Jake clears his throat. "You're all clear. Sorry for the interrogation but we're learning to not trust anyone on this mission."

Gina's face lightens a little. "It's fine, just unsettling. We better get going if we want to go to the Mütter Museum and the Philadelphia Museum of Art. It's a bit of a hike from here and I really need to get those keys back. I'll text my girlfriend to expect us."

Jake and I exchange a look. *Do we want another person to get involved?*

"What if we go to the Philadelphia Museum of Art first and then the Mütter Museum? I'm thinking there are way more valuable things to swipe at an art museum," Jake says.

Gina shrugs. "Okay, fine. I'll just let my girlfriend know we might stop by at some point."

As Gina is texting, I casually move closer to Jake, who is cleaning off his weird heat sensor glasses on his suit. I'm glad he remembered to pick them up off the cell floor before we left.

"I guess Gina's a part of our growing group of misfit superheroes?" Jake says, eyeing her up.

"Who are you calling a misfit?" I quip back.

Jake shoots me a smile. "I was talking more about myself. At least my superstrength worked crumbling the lock."

A smile is a good sign. Guess he's not too irritated at me for accidentally telling Gina that superpowers exist.

"She's already being helpful," I offer.

"I know, but I still don't trust her. And the more people that know, the more my NDA has gone out the window," Jake says, putting his glasses in his pants pocket. *I wish my costume had pockets. All I have is my orange purse that Jess hates.*

"You technically didn't tell me or her. She figured it out herself. But this will be the last person, I promise," I say.

Gina looks up from her phone and says, "My girlfriend is super stoked to meet a superhero!"

Jake blinks.

Oops.

"Okay, well Gina's girlfriend will be the last person, I swear," I say, giving him my best puppy dog eyes.

Gina looks between me and Jake. "What, was I not supposed to tell anyone who you are? How could you expect me to keep something like that a secret from my girlfriend? We tell each other everything."

"See, that's what I've been trying to tell him. I don't get how it's been kept a secret for this long," I state.

Jake sighs and says, "Now that my NDA is completely shot, I'll tell you how. My agent wipes the minds of anyone that finds out. That's why I'm worried. I don't want you to not remember me." He looks at me, his eyes filled with sadness.

My mouth drops a little. "Wipes their minds? How is that possible?"

Jake shrugs. "He has his ways."

Gina grabs her head. "Wow. That is some shady shit. I don't know who your agent is but he better not mess with my mind."

"Uh, yeah. Your agent sounds pretty terrible."

Jake avoids my eyes. "He got me to where I am today, so I owe him everything."

"But what kind of life is that?" I protest. "You can't talk to your family, you aren't allowed to have friends, and it sounds like he pimps you out to women for your *bad boy* brand. That's all pretty messed up if you ask me."

"But I didn't ask you. Come on. Let's go to this art museum so we can get your ex back," Jake growls.

CHAPTER SIXTEEN

JAKE

L ea knows the right words to really piss me off. Of course I want my mom to remember me. I'd also like to have a few friends and I don't want to be paraded around with women I could care less about. But I'm in this deep, how can I ever get out? Plus, I'm super famous, well at least with teen girls. Isn't that the dream?

I need to solve this mission and then talk to the Agent. Maybe this can be my final superhero movie and I can be the real actor I want so I can build an actual life for myself instead of being scared that a villain will take out everyone I care about.

We're walking to the art museum when a phone rings. It's one of the stock ringtones that are pre-programmed into an iPhone, so I know it's not mine. The Agent had one of his crew members program different ring tones for different people in my phone so I can tell who's calling, but the tones are all from the soundtrack to one of The Amazing Boy movies.

"Hey hon, what's up," Gina asks, answering her phone. "Woah, slow down. What do you mean the security alarm just went off?"

I already have my phone out and am googling the way to the Mütter Museum. I run across the street hoping Gina and Lea are following. Luckily, it's not too far down the road.

It has to be One-Eyed Barnacle or one of his lackeys. There are very few coincidences when villains are involved.

I hear Gina behind me saying reassuring things on the phone like, *It'll be okay. We're on our way now. Hang tight.*

After about five minutes, we approach a stone building and a small girl wearing a gray business suit with long straight black hair runs out, waving her hands.

"You weren't kidding when you said you were close by! The security alarm is so annoying today. We've had issues with it in the past so I'm not too worried, but today feels different. It just won't stop!"

"Are the police here?" I ask, whipping my head around. I don't need any more run-ins with them.

The girl shakes her head. "No, my boss told them not to come. We're just waiting for someone from our security company to show up and shut it off. But I thought it was kind of weird, after what happened to Gina today."

She turns towards me. "I'm Ashley Ling. My girl here didn't even introduce us."

I'm not going to stick my foot in my mouth again like I did with Lea and ask how Gina and Ashley identify. They can tell us if they want. Plus, we need to focus all our energy on finding One-Eyed Barnacle.

Gina covers her mouth with her hands. "Sorry, hon! I'm just so all over the place with my keys and the fedora missing."

"That's okay, I get that." Ashley looks at me and says, "I

know who you are but who's this?" Ashley uses her thumb to point towards Lea.

Before I can respond, Lea jumps in and says, "I'm Lea, well I guess I'm now Super L according to Jake."

"Are you a new cast member? Where's the rest of the crew?" Ashley asks.

Wait, does she not actually think this is real? Maybe Gina didn't explain things right. If that's the case, we can keep her thinking this is just a movie.

Lea smiles. "Not quite. I'm helping figure out what's going on and trying to unfreeze my ex-girlfriend," Lea explains like it's no big deal that she has an ex that's frozen.

If I was alone right now, I'd do the biggest over exaggerated face palm. Did she not hear Ashley just say she thought Lea was a new cast member? This is when I wish Lea and I could speak exclusively to each other through our minds.

"Say what? Frozen? You didn't tell me that!" Gina says, her eyes about to pop out of her head.

Ashley claps her hands together. "This is so exciting! It's just like the movies!"

Lea gives her a smile. "Jake's been nice enough to let me tag along to try and figure out what the heck's going on. I'm only in town for the WizCon event and that's where everything went down."

"Sorry to break up the party, but we really need to get this moving along and see if we can find One-Eyed Barnacle before he leaves again," I say fidgeting.

I already messed up finding him twice before, I will not let him get away a third time.

Ashley's face lights up. "One-Eyed Barnacle? You're freaking kidding me? That's the best name ever for a movie villain!"

"What is he, a pirate?" Gina asks, hands on her hip.

"If you see a Johnny Depp as Jack Sparrow lookalike,

that's the guy," I say, walking towards the entrance of the museum, hoping they will follow.

"I haven't seen any of those movies," Ashley says. "Why would a security alarm go off because of this guy? And wouldn't he have cameras surrounding him?"

"No, the camera work is done all inconspicuously, almost as if it were real," I say. I guess she does still think a movie is being filmed. "The security alarm would go off if he stole something, for the movie of course." I exaggerate the *for the movie part*, shooting Gina and Lea a look. No need to let someone else in on our secret if she still thinks this really is just a movie stunt.

Ashley frowns. "Maybe that's why my boss isn't concerned about the alarm. Maybe he got a heads-up about this and didn't share it with me."

"Don't worry about it. Movie people have their ways. So, can we just walk in here without any tickets?" I ask, hoping to hurry them along.

"Yeah, follow me in. I've got you covered," Ashley says, opening the double doors. Unlike the rest of the places we visited today, this one is not closed, and has lots of tourists with backpacks wandering around the entranceway, looking annoyed. I don't blame them; the security alarm *is* really loud. A small child is hanging onto his mom's pant leg crying and she is on her knees talking softly at him, rubbing his back.

A sign that reads *Tickets* is off to the left and Ashley calls over to someone manning the ticket counter and says, "These three are with me. I'm showing them around on a personal tour to find a shooting spot for the new Amazing Boy movie."

What I wouldn't give for my New York Yankees hat and Jake Johnson alter ego right now. A million eyes turn toward me, and I hear a few shrieks. Flashes from camera phones are going off and I growl, "What are you thinking? People are already on edge from that alarm. Do you want a stampede?"

Ashley smiles sheepishly. "Sorry, but I thought it'd be

some good PR for the museum and make people less pissed off. Think of everyone that's gramming us right now tagging you and the museum!"

"Yeah, that's really great, and it's going to make it even harder to find One-Eyed Barnacle now that you announced his arch-nemesis has arrived," I say, growing even more angry.

I need to figure out how to drop everyone. Maybe not Lea, but Gina and Ashley need to go. If Lea's going to stay around, we will have to set some ground rules or at least one rule: *Don't tell anyone that I'm really a superhero.* Is that so hard?

Lea's biting a fingernail looking at me anxiously. At least she gets that she royally messed up. I look around and see a family restroom sign. Without thinking, I grab Lea's arm, open the door to the restroom, and push her in. I slam the door shut.

"I'm sure one of your adoring fans got all that on video," Lea says, running her fingers through her disheveled blonde hair.

"I wouldn't have to have this conversation with you if you hadn't originally told Gina that Hallie has superpowers," I snap.

Lea's face crumples. "I'm sorry. It just slipped out of my mouth. I'm used to being lied to, not the one covering something up. It's not who I am," she whispers.

I take a deep breath. I need to curb my Jake Johnson anger. Lea's outburst at the Eastern State Penitentiary wasn't on purpose. And I, of all people, understand how hard it is to hide yourself. I've just become immune to it, and I forget how hard it was for me at the beginning too. Another reason that I have no friends. It's easier to keep a secret when you have no one to tell.

"After everything that happened with Hallie, we really need to be careful who we trust."

Lea's eyes are downcast. "It sucks. Gina and Ashley seem so cool."

A knock sounds against the door. "Someone's in here!" I yell.

A muffled voice that sounds like Gina says, "I know. We saw you and Lea run in. Ashley's working to get the hallway clear so you can come out undetected."

"Now she does that? What happened to getting good PR?" I ask, exasperated.

The door opens a smidge. "I talked to her, and she didn't realize you wanted secrecy. I know she's a little over the top, but her heart eventually gets in the right place. I'll let you know when it's safe to come out."

"Thank you, Gina." As the door shuts, I look over at Lea and she offers me a small smile.

"Can we at least try and work with them, at least until we find Gina's stuff?" she says.

I blow out a puff of air. It will be helpful to have two people that know the Philly scene.

"Fine. But if either of them messes up again, it'll just be the two of us."

Lea nods. "That's fair. At least you aren't threatening to kick me out."

"I can't, you're Super L," I say.

Lea straightens out her cape and says, "I guess I am, but I still don't have a superpower."

"It's not something you'll see right away. The longer you work with me I bet your superpower will shine through."

"What if I don't have one at all. You had no idea you had powers until you rescued those people," Lea whispers.

I place my hand on her arm. I can barely remember why I was so angry. Lea has this way about her that calms me down. "It's okay if you don't have one like me. People can have superpowers in different ways."

Her face starts to turn a pinkish hue. "Thanks for giving me a chance."

I give her a sheepish smile. "I think I should be thanking you for understanding that this is complicated for me. I'm used to working alone and doing things my way."

She nods. "Absolutely. How could it not? You've been through so much, but I do want to help, in any way possible."

How can someone be this sweet? And nice. For the first time ever, I feel comfortable sharing stuff about myself with someone.

We lock eyes and I notice a dimple on Lea's face. She's also staring intently back at me, and I feel the air around us change. My stomach flip flops. *Wait, what's happening?* Does Lea sense it too? Or is it just me?

Another knock sounds. My hand is still on her arm, and I quickly pull it away.

"Coast's clear," Gina says through the door.

Whatever was there a second ago is smashed by Gina's news.

"Come on, let's find One-Eyed Barnacle before the news breaks that we're here for him," I say, opening the door.

CHAPTER SEVENTEEN

LEA

I never had a *moment* with a guy before, but I swear that's just what happened between me and Jake. Especially with that look he was giving me. I could have sworn he was checking me out, but that can't be the case, right? He's super famous, and well, I'm me.

I've had crushes on guys I've been friends with throughout the years, but nothing ever materialized. The guy always thought of me as a friend and then Jess became my main priority, until she picked someone else.

That leads me to my next question; now that I'm finally getting a peek into Jake's real world, do I want to know even more about him? Am I even ready to like someone else? And the big question that always surrounds me is, after I get to know him, will I be attracted to him?

I don't have much time to think about these extremely complicated questions because before I know it, Jake has disappeared out the bathroom door.

"I'm coming," I shout over the stupid security alarm.

As I'm walking through the door, Gina raises her eyebrow. "If you two wanted to get a room, Ashley could have found somewhere more romantic."

"Can't get much more romantic than Al Capone's cell though, right?" I say back.

Gina's laugh is large and melodious. "That's for sure. I honestly thought you were in there to get it on."

My blush grows deeper. "No! We just met today. Plus, Jake's not the player he's portrayed in the media. Besides, I don't think I like him like that." *Right?*

Gina gives me a knowing look. "Not that I like guys or anything, but if I did, I bet it would be hard not to think about someone like Jake."

"Yeah well, I think I'm still hung up on my ex that I need to unfreeze."

Gina gives me a side glance. "True, but usually your ex is an ex for a reason."

Isn't that the truth. Maybe it really is time to move on. Jess certainly has.

"Come on, the tourists aren't going to stay away forever." Jake motions for us to follow him.

"Does he even know where he's going?" I ask Gina.

Gina shrugs. "I'm assuming someone like him just kicks down doors and asks questions later."

"You're not wrong about that." *When his superpowers work.*

We pass through an open doorway and what first greets me is the smell of chemicals.

"Gah! What's that god awful smell," I say, trying not to gag.

Gina laughs. "That happened to me the first time I got here too. It's formaldehyde. Most of the weird things in the museum are soaked in it and kept in jars. It keeps them from decaying."

Decaying? "What kind of place is this?" I'm afraid to hear a response.

Jake's leaning over a wooden railing, taking in the room below us. "You weren't kidding when you said this place is all kinds of weird."

"Tell me about it. On my first date with Ashley, she told me it was her dream to intern at the museum that keeps organs in jars."

My hand automatically goes up to my mouth. "And you went on a second date with her?"

"What can I say, she intrigued me. And I've never turned back." Gina looks star struck. *I would have killed to have Jess be that captivated by me.*

Jake's leaning against the railing, looking deep in thought. I poke him and say, "What's going on up there?"

"We need to find an area where One-Eyed Barnacle would hide if he's still here or think about what he might steal. The problem is there are just so many people downstairs in the exhibit area. I guess Ashley couldn't clear that part."

Gina shrugs. "She can only do so much. It's kind of hard to make any kind of announcement with the annoying security alarm."

"Why didn't the visitors leave when the security alarm went off?" I ask. I rub my temples. I'm starting to get a headache with the constant blaring.

"Might be one of those situations where if no one is panicking, they keep going about their business. I don't blame them, if I paid for my ticket, I wouldn't want to leave." Gina turns on her heels and says, "I'm going to go see if Ashley needs anything. In the meantime, I'd recommend keeping a low profile."

"Have you seen what we're wearing? We're basically sitting ducks," Jake grumbles.

"That and the fact that everyone and their brother knows who The Amazing Boy is. Oh, looks like we've already been spotted," I say, motioning to the group gathering at the bottom of the antique wooden steps to the right of us.

"You're an actor. Can't you fake them out?" Gina asks.

"I can try. At least WizCon is supposed to be taking place right now so that's a good excuse for Philly people to be dressed in costume."

Gina snaps her fingers. "Oh smart, blame it on that. Try not to get into too much trouble while I'm gone."

I'm still overwhelmed by the smell but also intrigued by the oddities that lie ahead. Can't ever say that in my eighteen years of being alive I've seen organs in jars before.

"Want to look around? Maybe weird things will be the distraction we need until we can figure out if they were actually here," I say.

Jake's eyebrows shoot up. "As intriguing as that sounds, I'm worried that those fans down there might eat me alive," Jake says, pointing down the steps.

The group below us keeps growing, mainly filled with girls my age. Some of them are screaming up the steps at Jake. Why can't this museum be vacant like the other places we visited today?

"I'm also really worried that even if One-Eyed Barnacle and Hallie had been here, they aren't anymore. It's been too long since the security alarm went off," Jake says, his eyes darting around.

"You never know until we look. Let's get this over with," I say and take a step down the antique steps. They lead right into the sea of fans, but I keep taking one step at a time. I turn back and Jake's following me.

"The Amazing Boy, we love you," one girl with messy purple hair calls.

"Can I have my picture with you?" a curly blonde girl yells, waving her pink sparkly iPhone case in front of her face.

"Are you a new character in the movies?" a guy asks, staring straight at me.

I hear Jake say behind me, "Don't answer. Just keep moving."

It's weird not to talk to someone shouting in your face, but I figure Jake has better experience with this than I do. I reach the final step and before my feet touch the ground, someone is tugging on my sleeve.

"Can I get a picture with the both of you?" a brunette girl with choppy bangs asks.

I try to pull away, but her manicured hand with black nails is clasped tight. A deep, unsettling feeling sits in my stomach. *She can't be Hallie, right?*

Then I remember Jake's advice. I stare directly into this girl's eyes and involuntary gasp. What looks back at me are gray, glassy, and devoid of feeling. Jake's immediately by my side, trying to remove Hallie's clenched hand on my arm. She's grabbing so tight I'm starting to lose circulation.

"Nice to see both of you again. I didn't think you'd escape that quickly," Hallie, in this new form, sneers.

I keep pulling my arm to get away, but no luck. "We need the museum keys and Al Capone's fedora back," I say, whispering as much as I can. I don't want to attract even more attention than we already have.

Hallie cackles. "I don't think so. That fedora is mine. Finders keepers and all. Speaking of, One-Eyed Barnacle sends his regards and he's sorry he couldn't meet you."

"How do you always find us before we can track him down?" I say exasperated.

Hallie uses her other hand to throw some kind of iridescent purple ball on the ground. It explodes and shimmery smoke fills the room. Jake and I start coughing at the same moment. Warning bells are going off in my brain, and this time, it isn't from the security alarm. *What is going on? Did she just throw a glitter bomb at us?*

All the background noise of fans yelling abruptly ends. When the smoke begins to clear, I can see that the fans standing by us are completely frozen. All I can hear is the security alarm screeching. I feel cold all over and my hands start to shake. My eyes immediately grow and move to Jake's face.

"What did you do to them, Hallie?" Jake demands. He meets my glance and gives me a slight nod. At least he's feeling okay. *Do these kinds of things happen to him all the time?*

Hallie grins, showing all her teeth. "Nothing different than what we crafted up at the convention center, except this time there's no need to hide our work. We were just being extra cautious there since there were so many superheroes around."

I involuntarily gasp. "Does that mean you can unfreeze everyone?"

Hallie rolls her eyes. "Of course I can, but what fun would that be? Besides, we don't want all the other superheroes getting free and coming to help The Amazing Boy, now do we? These people here, I'll free them as soon as I leave, but no, the people at the convention center will just have to wait until this is all over."

"All over? What does that mean?" Jake inquires.

Hallie chortles. "You'll just have to wait and see. Tell your friend sorry about the keys and fedora, but I still need them."

"Still need them? Are you going back to the Eastern State Penitentiary?" My voice wobbles. I don't want to seem like a scaredy cat, but it's hard to not show how I'm feeling. I'm not trained like Jake, nor do I have any powers to defend myself and Hallie's grasp is still strong on my arm. *That's going to leave a mark.* My pale skin bruises so easily.

"No, we got what we needed there, but even if we were, I wouldn't tell you," Hallie says.

I'm tucking away all of Hallie's statements to analyze with Jake after she leaves.

I take a deep breath to steady my voice and get a huge whiff of chemicals. My nose wrinkles. *How does Ashley work here all the time or is that smell from the smoke ball that Hallie just threw?* That's when I notice Jake's holding his mouth and I hear the distinct sound of a gag.

"I'm going to …" and before he finishes his sentence, he moves his face closer to Hallie and vomit spews out of his mouth. I can feel a slimy substance dripping from the arm that Hallie has a hold of. I look over at Hallie and she takes her free hand to wipe Jake's vomit from her face. Thank goodness she doesn't have a power where her eyes can shoot out lasers, because if she did, Jake would be a goner.

"I'm sorry, I really didn't mean to do that. I told Lea when we first met, I have trouble controlling my gag reflex," he says, his cheeks bright red. I nudge him with my free arm, but he doesn't look at me.

Now I'm really limiting the amount I'm breathing. Between the smell of this place and now vomit, it's going to take a lot for me not to spew my guts out too. I'm glad I haven't eaten in a while, there wouldn't be much to come up.

Hallie drops my arm and I move it back and forth, trying to get some feeling back into it. She flings her head like a dog after it gets wet, and vomit flies every which way. I duck and close my eyes to try and not be on the receiving end of it. When I open them back up, Hallie's transformed back to her normal self, complete with her all black-outfit and black hair.

She's smirking when she says, "I'm done here. At least I can change my form to get out of these soiled clothes, unlike both of you."

"Doesn't it get tiring doing One-Eyed Barnacle's bidding? And having to clean up the mess?" Jake asks. He's back to standing up straight; his cheeks have more of a pink hue than the previous red.

Hallie's eyes flick to the puddle of puke on the ground near her. "This mess looks more like your doing than mine.

Clean-up in aisle three, the one with hearts in jars!" She chuckles at her own joke.

Jake grits his teeth. "Why is Dave not around anymore?" I quickly ask. I want to add something to show I can be of help and also let Jake compose himself. He's taking deep breaths in and out.

Hallie's forehead creases and she sneers, "He's on an easier task. If he's given anything remotely difficult, he royally screws up, just like at City Hall and the Museum of the American Revolution. I always have to do the hard work because I actually get it done right."

"You can change your appearance; shouldn't you get a higher rank than him?" I probe.

"I'll get what I've earned soon enough. I'm not working this much for shits and giggles. I've said too much already so I must bid you adieu, again. Hopefully, I won't see you anymore, but I highly doubt that. Until next time!" Hallie says, waving. She runs up the steps, two at a time.

"Wait! What about the people here? And can you also pretty please unfreeze the people at the convention center?" I call after her.

Hallie stops and turns around. She's staring intently at the frozen figures. She reaches into her pocket and throws another purple ball on the floor. This time I shut my eyes, knowing what's going to happen next. When I reopen them, the smoke is already clearing, and Hallie's gone. The people beside us are starting to move. There's a shriek and I hear, "Ew, don't step on that!"

JAKE and I try to break free, but we are still surrounded by a mass of people trying to get a selfie with Jake. I've never had the urge to be famous, but if I did, this experience would make it vanish in an instant.

Being in a crowd of rowdy fans in a museum full of dead things reeking of chemicals and vomit is not the ideal way to spend a day in a new city. Nor is it a good way to continue connecting with the guy I might or might not have a tiny crush on. One small blessing is these people could care less about me; Jake's fully got their attention.

My whole body is feeling warm, with all the bodies pressed up against us, and the mix of smells reaching my nose makes my stomach turn over. My heart's beating rapidly; I just need to sit down, maybe that will make me feel better. That's when an idea pops into my head.

"I don't feel so well," I say very loudly.

No one's paying attention to me. Jake's busy trying to get everyone off him. One girl has her forearm out with a pink sharpie demanding he sign it. Maybe I should have let Hallie keep them frozen. We need Jake's security detail ASAP. I'm not the one that's the paid actor but I'm going to have to do something.

"I feel so warm, I think I'm going to ..." I say, trailing off. I close my eyes and just let myself sink to the floor.

"Is she okay?" I hear a voice ask. I keep my eyes clamped shut.

"Okay everyone! Show's over, we have a medical emergency, please clear this floor immediately," a voice echoes throughout the area. There are groans and the sound of footsteps moving away from me.

I squint through my eyes to see if everyone's gone. I can just make out Jake kneeling over me. He rubs my arm ever so slightly.

"Lea, can you hear me? Are you alright?" he asks. His face is creased with worry.

My heartbeat is returning back to its normal pace, and I don't feel like I'm out in the sun anymore. I nod and whisper, "I wasn't feeling too great, but I also thought this might make people leave us alone."

Jake's eyes widen for a second and then he lets out a deep laugh. "You're really good at this." He says quieter, "Maybe you really can be my sidekick. It's nice having someone else around during the thick of things. Thanks for helping me out back there when I wasn't feeling too great."

I move my hand to his and squeeze it. "Of course. We just need to stop and get something to wipe my arm off with before we leave here."

Jake's eyes widen. He pulls a tissue out of one of his pockets and pats my arm. "I'm so sorry. That's really gross. Unfortunately, you got to experience first-hand a part where my agent would cut some footage."

"Are you okay or are you faking it?" Ashley leans over me, her long black hair hitting me in the face.

I blow a puff of air. "I'm fine now that all those fans are gone."

"That was some quick thinking on your part. Provided me the perfect excuse to clear the room." Ashley nods approvingly.

She gives me her hand to help me up and I accept it. Once I'm back on my feet I really take in the space around me.

"Woah, you weren't kidding when you told Gina you work at a place with body parts in jars. How can this be legal?" I ask. I am transfixed by a display of hearts and now I have to hold in the urge to gag. I fan myself with my hand to help slow down any more reactions from returning.

"You told her I said that?" Ashley says, swatting Gina, who's standing beside Ashley with her arms crossed.

"I had to, it's too good of a story," Gina exclaims. "Ashley loves this place. It's starting to grow on me."

"This place isn't for everyone," Ashley says.

I close my eyes. There's no way I can ever be a doctor, even looking at these sorts of things makes me want to go back and lie on the floor. I root around in my purse. I need something to ground me. I open my eyes when I find what

I'm looking for. My signature body spray, vanilla lavender. I press the top a couple of times and mist flies out. I move it all around me.

"You can say that again." I'm about to spray it again when Ashley's hand clasps the top of the bottle.

"I don't think it's a great idea to have more chemicals mix in this area. Now it's smelling like a field of flowers covered in puke and pesticides. Let's just move to a different spot. Do either of you like history?" Ashley asks, looking back and forth at Jake and me.

I can't stop my hand from shooting up in the air. That's how much I have a passion for history, my hand has a mind of its own, even when my brain is overwhelmed.

"Yes! I'm going to UCLA for history in the fall. My dream is to work at a museum someday and be an archivist," I share.

Gina's eyebrows raise and Ashley says, "Woah, UCLA? That's legit. Then you'll love what I'm going to show you," Ashley says, motioning for us to follow her. I'm squirming in anticipation, while also hoping it's not too gross.

We approach a glass case and Ashley says, with her back turned to the display, "We have a box that contains slides with portions of Albert Einstein's brain! How cool is that?" She leans in close to us and whispers, "He died in Princeton Hospital and the person that performed the autopsy took Albert Einstein's brain. And now we have parts of it here."

I squint my eyes thinking maybe I'm missing something, but nope, the case is still bare. I exchange a glance with Jake.

Jake makes a motion to the empty glass case. "Ashley, hate to break it to you but there's nothing in there."

Ashley turns around and gasps. "How's that possible? The case isn't even broken!"

"This must have been what Hallie stole!" I exclaim. "Is the security alarm hooked up to this case?"

Ashley takes deep breaths.

"It is but I swear I checked it! What is going on?"

"Hallie might have somehow tripped the alarm before she stole it," Jake says, turning to me.

And we helped provide the best distraction ever, bringing a real-life actor to the scene.

I take a closer look and see some scratches on the display case's lock. Jake might not be able to pick locks, but I'll bet my purse that Hallie can, or she somehow used one of her smoke balls to take her prize.

"Hon, come on, don't worry, Lea and The Amazing Boy are helping find my stuff, and I'm sure they'll help us get Albert Einstein's brain back too," Gina says, rubbing Ashley's back.

"I don't understand. What kind of movie are you making that involves people actually stealing really valuable items? And how did they take it?" Ashley runs her hands through her hair. "I'm going to get in so much trouble. I can't lose this internship. My parents will be so disappointed. They came here from China to give me my best life and now I'm squandering it!" Ashley says, her eyes filling up.

I feel so bad for her. She's here at her internship, helping as best as she can, and some awful person steals something under her nose. She also doesn't know that Hallie seems to have access to some kind of spells, so there's nothing she could have done differently.

I shoot Jake a look that I hope he interprets as please tell her the real story and that it's really not her fault. Hallie has a track record of getting the best of all of us.

He sighs. "Sure. What's one more person?"

CHAPTER EIGHTEEN

JAKE

I give Ashley the downlow on One-Eyed Barnacle, Hallie, and even Dave. If the Agent wasn't frozen right now, he'd kill me. But maybe I can convince the movie production editors to delete this section out before he sees everything that happened while he was frozen. That would be the best-case scenario.

I really hate breaking my NDA but at this point I don't know what else to do. Besides, the Agent can just wipe their memories once he's back in action. Well, hopefully not Lea's. I'd like her to keep solving things with me. For a civilian, she's been more helpful than I'd ever thought, as long as she still wants to be around me after that vomit incident. I cringe just thinking about it.

After my whole spiel, Ashley sits down on the ground.

"Hon, what are you doing?" Gina asks, peering down at her.

"I'm afraid I might faint, and it's not from the vomit,

flower, and chemical mashup. This is all too much. How can people have superpowers in real life and villains exist?" She's hunched over, hugging her knees into her chest. Gina gets down next to her and rubs her back in a circular motion.

Lea nods. "I get that. It's pretty crazy. Honestly, I just found out about it today too."

Ashley's eyes widen. "Really? I thought maybe that was your cover story and you've been working on this movie all along."

Lea's face turns tomato red. "Oh, that's so nice, but no. I'm in town for the WizCon convention and got stuck this morning in an elevator with Jake."

"Which seems like ages ago," I say.

"Now that I think about it, it's been so long since I ate something. Maybe that's why I feel off," Lea says, leaning against the empty glass case. Her face is paler than normal.

"You should come join me on the floor," Ashley says, patting the space next to her. She's full on laying down on the ground. At least my puke isn't anywhere near this area.

"Hon, I'm sure the lovely aroma doesn't help," Gina offers.

"Smells don't bother me," Ashley says, her eyes closed.

Gina wrinkles her nose. "That's because you're around a gross chemical odor all the time. Luckily the stink doesn't follow you home. There's no way I could stand that."

Ashley gives Gina a light kick from the ground and Gina pulls Ashley into a hug.

Lea and I stand there awkwardly watching them hug it out on the floor of the weirdest museum I've ever visited. I shift my gaze from their PDA.

Instead, I see a case with brains in jars and farther down the museum, there's a lot of skeleton heads and it feels like they are staring at me. Just heads, not the rest of the body. I've seen some weird stuff before, but nothing like this museum. I look away. It almost feels like the skeleton heads are all turned towards me, judging me for my missteps and not figuring things out sooner.

I need to get out of here, not only to find One-Eyed Barnacle, but so I don't have weird dreams the next time I sleep, although, who knows when that'll be. At least there's still that room in Old City in case we can actually find time to rest. But then there's that whole one bed thing. I can just sleep on the ground although I also have a fancy hotel suite I can crash at, but that's under my Jake Johnson name, and anyone, villains and paparazzi, might be staking that out as we speak.

Can I never get any peace and quiet? I'd love to be able to start a new LEGO set but I'm never in one place long enough. I've been eyeing up the Millennium Falcon one, but with its seven thousand plus pieces, it would take me years to complete.

"Jake, did you hear what I said?" Lea tugs on my arm.

I shake my head. "No, sorry. I got distracted by all the things in this room. Ashley, how do you not have nightmares?"

Ashley and Gina are both upright at this point. How long have I been out of it?

Ashley shrugs. "I guess I'm used to it by now. But I am going to need some strong medicine to get the sound of the security alarm out of my brain."

"You know how they seem to be gathering items at each spot? Maybe the items they are stealing are all connected? Hallie left the Eastern State Penitentiary with the keys and Al Capone's fedora, and Albert Einstein's brain is missing from this museum," Lea says excitedly, her arms waving all over the place. "Maybe we try and find places with other items that could be related?"

I scratch my head. "You could be on to something. But why those items? They don't seem to have much in common."

"You said a case was broken into at the Museum of the

American Revolution. We still don't know what they took there," Lea says. "We tried googling it earlier, but the news articles only talked about the blast, not what was stolen."

Ashley gasps. "Wait, I saw an email about that earlier from a museum listserv I'm on. It said that some musket from revolutionary times was taken, and the thief somehow used a cannon to blow a hole in the wall."

"A cannon! One that old can still work?" Lea gasps.

I don't want to scare Lea and our new friends, but Hallie seems to have some powerful items up her sleeve if she can freeze a room with some kind of smoke ball. Who knows what else she can do, including making a revolutionary cannon work.

"This doesn't help Ashley and I recover our stolen items. We need to get them back pronto before our asses are handed to us," Gina says sharply. "We are not going to lose our internships because we're helping you."

"For sure, we don't want that to happen. The big question is what are they going to steal next because that's where we need to go," Lea says, scratching her head.

The four of us stand quietly, ruminating on that question, when I hear Lea's stomach grumble.

"I know what we are doing now, grabbing food. It's not going to help anyone if you faint from hunger, so let's find something to eat while we plan our next move," I say, motioning to the steps.

Lea starts to protest when Gina says, "Even though I need to get that stuff back, I agree with the superstar. I haven't eaten since six this morning and it's like past two now!"

"I actually just had my lunch and can't leave yet. I need to somehow figure out a way to hide that Einstein's brain is gone," Ashley says, biting her lip.

"What about putting a sign in the case that says, *Sorry for the inconvenience, Albert Einstein's brain has been removed for research purposes and will return soon?*" Gina suggests.

"That's genius," Ashley says, leaning over to kiss her cheek. "You'll be a museum curator soon enough! I'll just have to make sure that no one who actually works here sees it."

"We will do all in our power to bring back the brain," I say more confidently than I feel, when I am really thinking, *How am I going to do this without the Agent?*

I must be convincing because Ashley gives me a huge smile. I am not feeling as secure in our aptitude. We've had a lot of lucky guesses, but our luck is bound to run out at some point.

CHAPTER NINETEEN

LEA

At the exit of the Mütter Museum, Ashley wraps herself around Gina. "Be careful! Don't do anything stupid," Ashley says.

As they are intertwined, I avert my eyes, feeling a pang of jealousy. That's what I had wanted Jess and I to be like. Always there for each other and not caring who sees it. We had a ton of inside jokes and behind closed doors we'd kiss, but as soon as we were around anyone else, it would return to being strictly friends. Always hiding how we felt about each other. I should have known what we had wasn't special.

They broke apart and Ashley waves to us.

"Go get those bad guys! And if you need anything, just have Gina text me. I can see if I can get out early."

Outside, even though there's the hum of traffic and horns beeping, at least we are free of that awful blaring security alarm. I take a deep breath and my lungs fill with clean air. Well, they are probably filled with city smog mixed with a whiff of car exhaust, but I'll take that any day instead of the chemical vomit blend. Counting my blessings, one smell at a time.

"Gina, any quick spots to grab some food?" Jake asks, pulling out his phone.

"You do realize you're in The Amazing Boy costume. Anywhere we go is going to quickly get mobbed with fans dying to see you," I remind him. We do NOT need a recurrence of what happened on the steps of the museum.

Jake frowns. "Right. My agent usually would have a trailer set up somewhere with catered food for us to pick up. And any other time I'm out, I'm usually incognito."

Gina moves her dreadlocks behind her ears. "I can grab food for us and meet you at Rittenhouse Square. It's a cute park about ten minutes away and no one should pay you any attention."

"How's that possible? We're both wearing superhero costumes," I ask.

"All kinds of people hang out there. Trust me, once you see it, you'll understand. What do you want to eat?" Gina asks.

"Anything fast," Jake says, still looking down at his phone.

I still can't get over seeing The Amazing Boy google directions. Superhero movies will forever be ruined for me. Thanks a lot, One-Eyed Barnacle.

"Same, I'm not picky. I'm so hungry I can eat almost anything," I reply.

Gina nods her head in approval. "You're my kind of people. I'll meet you in the park soon."

Jake points left and motions for me to follow him. As usual, I have to jog to keep up.

"I'm going to try and avoid any larger streets to not attract a crowd. I don't want another Mütter Museum incident. I can't ask you to fake faint twice in one day for me."

I laugh. "I don't mind. Helps me increase my acting skills if I'm going to keep hanging around you."

Jake's back stiffens right after I speak. *What did I say wrong?* I thought we were making some headway.

"Are you sure you want to keep being around me? This can be dangerous."

After a few more turns, we land in front of a park with loads of green trees, shrubs, and even ornate fountains; the kind with a statue in the middle and water coming out of its mouth. I didn't realize big cities had pretty little parks like this.

There are benches lined up along the sidewalk and tons of people walking small little dogs but Gina's right, no one pays any attention to us, probably because we aren't the only costumed characters. Iron Man and Captain America are sharing a bench chowing down on sandwiches and a little further down, Batman is walking a poodle. Were they here dressed up for WizCon, or do people regularly dress up as superheroes in Philadelphia?

"I've always imagined Batman owning a slightly bigger dog," I joke.

Jake's silent. I know my jokes are usually pretty stupid, but I'm not used to getting zero response.

"I'm going to ask those people dressed as Marvel characters if they were at WizCon," Jake says, walking over to their bench.

At least we are in the same line of thinking, even if Jake's not actually telling me what else is going on in his brain.

Captain America's about to take a bite of his lunch when he looks up and sees us. He sets his half-eaten sandwich on an upside-down Captain America shield. I nod in approval. What a great idea, using that as an oversized plate. Now that I'm closer to them, both of their costumes aren't too shabby, nothing like Jake's but also not as crappy as mine. The weird thing though is this Captain America has brown hair and the Iron Man is blond. Shouldn't they have switched costumes?

"Sorry to interrupt your lunch, but we were wondering if you were able to get into the WizCon Convention today? We tried, but the doors were locked," Jake says.

Captain America and Iron Man share a glance and they both shake their heads. Captain America speaks up first. "No, man. We were out of luck. I guess they oversold the event or something. We're going to file a complaint and try to get our money back. We decided to make the best of it and explore Philadelphia on these cool scooters. You can join us if you want." He points to two scooters on the grass behind the bench.

Jake pulls me close to him. "Thanks for the invite, guys, but I'm here on a date with my girl, and we're about to eat some lunch. You enjoy yourselves though."

My face burns.

Iron Man nods. "Totally get that. Yo, your costume is seriously good. Where did you buy it? I need to invest in one like yours."

Jake releases me and brushes off his sleeve. "I'll never reveal my sources. Thanks for your help."

Once we are out of their earshot I ask, "Where are we going to sit? We can't be too close to them because they'll figure out you were lying when Gina comes along."

A shirtless guy in tiny bright green shorts rollerblades past us, yelling into his phone. Two women in business suits are talking to each other, eating salads on a bench nearby.

"Hello. Earth to Jake," I say, waving my hand in front of his face.

"Oh, sorry. Let's try the one next to Batman and his poodle. It'll look like we're all together."

We sit and Jake's playing around on his phone. Why is he suddenly ignoring me? Jess did the same thing near the end when she was sleeping with Olive. But Jake was fine less than thirty minutes ago. What happened between then and now?

"What's with you? Are you reverting to your douchebag personality?" I ask, crossing my arms.

Jake's neck snaps up and he shoots me a panicked expression.

"What're you talking about? No, I'm trying to figure out One-Eyed Barnacle's next move."

It seems more than that.

"I can help you. You're like completely freezing me out again and it sucks," I say.

If only I had the courage to say something like that to Jess. Instead, I let her walk all over me and my heart. But since that happened, I regret every day that I never stood up for myself. And now, even though it's not her I'm talking to, at least I have the option of telling Jake that I'm hurt. Besides, with the way he's acting, it's highly likely I'll never see him again after this adventure, so I really have nothing to lose by telling him how I feel.

Jake's mouth opens a little. "I'm sorry. Getting close to people is something I'm not good at or used to." He sits quietly for a second as he squeezes a hand into a fist. "Actually, I'm terrified of getting close to people because I know it can't work out. The last time I had someone important in my life, I got massively hurt."

"What do you mean? What happened?"

He leans his elbow on the park bench armrest to prop up his head. "Do you really want to know?"

"When you put it like that, how could anyone say no? Now I want to know even more."

Jake sighs. "You know how I told you my mom doesn't remember me and how my Agent wipes the minds of anyone that gets close to me?"

That's not what I was expecting him to ask me. "Yeah, but

I still don't understand how he gets away with that. And doesn't the person see themselves in the movie?"

Jake shakes his head. "No, my agent makes it so the person doesn't even go see the movie or if they do, they won't recognize themselves. And that's why I have an NDA, which you can see is going swimmingly."

I'm trying to wrap my brain around what Jake shared. "So, that's why you have no friends or any serious girlfriends."

"Exactly. I almost got into a relationship with a girl about a year ago, and before I could even ask her out, my agent made her forget everything about me." Jake hangs his head. "I'm worried that when my agent gets unfrozen, he'll do the same thing to you."

I instinctually grab my head. *I don't want anyone near my memories.*

"First off, doesn't someone have to agree to having their memories erased? It sounds so sketchy, and I don't agree to that at all."

Jake's forehead creases. "You would think. But it might come down to semantics. Once your memories are erased you won't know you didn't agree to having them erased because you wouldn't even notice anything missing."

My mind is spinning. *How can any of this be possible?*

"Your agent seems so shady. How can I get him to not erase my memories?" I ask.

Jake scratches his head and takes a moment to answer.

"Being officially in this movie and signing an NDA. You can formally become Super L."

I gaze off at an empty park bench across from us. "That would mean my family and friends would have to forget who I am, right?"

Jake's face falls. "It does and I know no one would voluntarily want to do that."

I rub my chin. "I don't know. My two best friends are

sleeping with each other and my family thinks I'm a disappointment. It might not be too hard if they forget me," I say, warming up to the idea.

Jake's mouth drops open. "*You* a disappointment? How is that even possible? You're one of the smartest people I've ever worked with."

"That's really nice of you, but to be fair, you usually work alone. And you haven't had the pleasure of meeting my older brother and sister. They are both brainiacs and star athletes. I can't do any sport without falling over so I'm the lesser child."

Jake's mouth turns downward. "That's awful your family is like that."

"They didn't even care that I came here and probably wouldn't notice if I didn't come home until my job called them and told them I missed work."

"I'm sure that's not true," Jake says, giving me a sympathetic look.

I pick at one of my silver bangles. "No, I'm not kidding. I'm the baby of the family, the *happy accident*. They are always forgetting about me. The one time on vacation at a lake it was time to go home and all of them packed up the car and headed out. I woke up about an hour later and found the vacation rental completely empty. They were already halfway home at that point. Them actually forgetting I exist wouldn't be much different than how it is now."

Jake lightly touches my arm. "I'm sorry, that must be hard."

I shrug. "It's all I've ever known. I'd be on board with being your sidekick, if I'm allowed, and that it's okay not to have any superpowers. Besides, I'm enjoying spending time with you so it'd suck if one day I woke up and couldn't remember you and this adventure."

Jake's gaze softens as he looks over at me. "Do you really mean that? Even with all this crazy stuff going on?"

I nod. "I've never had this much happen to me in my life. And even though bad guys are after us, in a weird way, it's kind of fun. It gives me something to look forward to."

Jake nods. "I know what you mean. You get this adrenaline high." He looks me in the eye. "I also really don't want you to forget about this. Being a superhero is a lonely world and until now, I've forgotten how fun it is hanging out with someone that's not my agent and doesn't mind when I vomit on them."

He catches me off guard and I laugh. "Is that how you pick up all your models?"

He raises an eyebrow. "No, only the girls I actually like."

I blink a couple of times, trying not to show my mind going into overdrive. *Wait, is he actually saying he likes me? There's no way, right? And do I want him to like me? Do I feel the same way? I think I do, but I just met him, so it's really hard to tell. He's fun to hang out with and really sweet but could a romantic spark ever be there?*

"It's nice having someone wanting to be around me, the real me, not famous actor Jake Johnson," he says, still staring into my eyes.

I have a feeling I'm blushing. I'm so not used to someone giving me this undivided attention.

"Sorry to break up this beautiful moment, but here's your food." Gina jumps in front of us, holding up a brown paper bag leaking with grease. I yelp and drop Jake's gaze.

Gina looks sheepishly at me. "Sorry, but I didn't know how else to get your attention. You were pretty engrossed in each other."

Jake clears his throat. "How did you find us so fast?"

Gina points to the Batman bench. "All I had to do was find the benches of weirdos. Although I have to say it's smart trying to blend in with the other cosplayers."

Jake gives his charming smile. "Thanks. I have a good idea here and there."

I nod towards the brown paper bag she's holding dripping liquid. "We need to eat whatever you got us before it becomes a pile of grease."

"Oh no," Gina says, putting a napkin under the bag. She motions for me to scoot over, and I move closer to Jake. Like really close. I can feel his leg pressing up against mine.

"I had to get you both cheesesteaks. These aren't from a famous place, but I wasn't going to run all the way over to *Geno's*."

"How much do we owe you?" Jake asks.

"With drinks, I'd say you owe me sixteen dollars each. You can just venmo me. Do superheroes venmo?"

Woah. Sixteen dollars for a sandwich and a drink? Guess I'm used to small town prices.

Jake's shoulders move up and down as he laughs. "Yes, I venmo."

Gina pulls out her phone and shares her Venmo QR code. "Hey, since I only learned superheroes exist, I know nothing about how that works."

After we pay her, Gina hands over two footlong foil wrapped subs and a couple of bottled waters. Jake downs the water in a couple of swigs and moves onto his sub. I peel back the foil wrapping and the smell that greets my nose immediately causes my stomach to grumble. Melted cheese and diced meat encased in a crisp roll sits before me. I pick up half of it and put the other half back in the wrapping. I look over at Jake and he has a cute little grin on his face.

"Gina, this is exactly what I need right now, great choice," he says as he takes a large bite. Some cheese gets caught on the side of his mouth and he licks it off with his tongue. I quickly look away, feeling like I spotted him during an intimate moment with him and his food. I also take a mouthful and a small moan accidentally slips out of my mouth.

"Oh my gosh, this is *so* good! I've had cheesesteaks before, but nothing like this."

Gina laughs. "Glad you like it. Now hurry up and eat so we can get my stuff back!"

She's already a quarter of the way through her cheesesteak. "How did you eat it that fast?" I ask, trying to gulp down as much food as I can. I can already feel, even after a couple of bites, my stomach getting full.

"Practice. Lots and lots of practice."

We're eating so intently we don't talk much.

"This really hits the spot. Good call, Gina," Jake says, licking his lips. He wipes his face off with a napkin. I haven't touched the second half of my cheesesteak.

"I seriously can't eat this entire thing. I feel like a rock is in my stomach, but I don't want to throw it out." I groan, folding up the uneaten half back into the foil.

I motion with my head to a man sitting on a bench by himself with what appears to be all of his belongings. "Do you think it's okay to give to him? Like he wouldn't mind a half-eaten cheesesteak?"

Gina's eyes soften. "That's sweet of you. Sometimes it's hard for me to remember to offer them something because there are so many homeless people here. It's really sad. I'm sure he'd take it."

I walk over to the man half asleep on the bench. He opens his left eye as I approach. "Do you want the other half of my cheesesteak?" I ask timidly. "I promise I didn't take a bite at all."

His other eye snaps open and a grin appears. "You're my superhero! I'll take that, thanks Miss L for thinking of me."

I hand him the foil clad sub.

"God bless you, dear," he says, quickly unwrapping the contents and taking an enormous bite. My heart warms. I'm glad someone can make use of it.

I walk back to the bench. "Ready to go?" I ask.

Jake's staring at me. "That was really nice."

I shrug. "Wish I could do more."

"Still more than most people would do," Jake says. He gets off the bench, tosses his wrapping in the garbage can, and rubs his hands against his pants. "The big question is where do we go next?"

I scan the park. Captain America and Iron Man are on a grassy area near the street, pretending to punch each other.

"But he killed my mom!" Iron Man shrieks.

Gina jumps up off the bench, her eyes wary. I put my hand on her shoulder. "It's okay, I think they're acting out a scene from the Marvel movie *Civil War*."

Gina's eyebrow raises. "I clearly haven't seen enough superhero movies because I thought Captain America and Iron Man were friends. I was about to tell Jake to get in there and break that up."

Jake shakes his head. "Even if that was real, I rarely get involved in interpersonal fights with normal humans. Villains stealing stuff and hurting innocent people, yes, but not something that doesn't have to do with me. Sometimes people need to figure out their own problems themselves."

"Speaking of villains, Gina, any more ideas where someone interested in stealing valuable stuff would go after the Mütter Museum?"

She scratches her head. "I can't think of anywhere more important than the Philadelphia Museum of Art, so we should head back ..."

Gina is cut off by a scream across the street. "Stop that man! He's a thief," a woman shrieks.

A man darts in between cars and disappears behind a building. He's holding a strange shaped object under his arm. He also vaguely looks like the guy we saw at City Hall.

"I think we've got our answer. Come on, let's go," Jake says. He sprints across the street to where the burglar vanished. I try to follow, but he's too fast.

"Slow down, my feet are killing me!" Gina yells behind me.

I stop right by Captain America and Iron Man's display and see their discarded scooters. I pick one up and hand it to Gina.

"Here, let's take these. Jake and I met these guys, I'm sure they won't mind, too much."

Gina drops it on the ground. "No way. I'm not stealing something."

I'm already on my scooter. "We have to get your stuff back. This isn't stealing, it's borrowing."

"Hey! What are you doing?" Captain America's arms are crossed.

"I'm so sorry, but a civilian needs saving! We will bring these back to you soon, I promise!" I click the *on* button and I'm off, with the wind whipping in my face, my blonde hair and my cape flowing behind me. *Maybe I really can be a superhero.*

CHAPTER TWENTY

JAKE

I'm not going to lose the lead this time. I can do this, even on my own. I don't know where Lea and Gina went but I'm not going to worry about that now. All that matters is getting this guy and making him talk. We need answers.

I have the advantage. This guy, who I'm pretty sure is the same stooge from City Hall, is short and his legs don't carry him like mine do.

We're dashing down the sidewalk of a highly pedestrian trafficked area that smells like spoiled garbage. I keep having to jump out of people's way and apologizing while avoiding large pieces of trash, like a couch alongside the street that almost takes me out. *The city really needs to get a handle on all this trash.*

As I'm racing past everyone, I see a couple cell phones raised, probably filming the whole thing for the masses. At least it can help Lea find where I'm at.

The man turns and gives me a distressed look when he sees how little space is between us.

"No, you can't catch me, he will kill me!" He shrieks and tries to run down a small side street but cuts the corner right into a pedestrian. One-Eyed Barnacle's goon drops to the ground like a bag of rocks, along with whatever is under his arm.

I position my shoe on top of his chest.

"You aren't going anywhere now," I say valiantly. I turn my head to look at the large man this guy accidentally ran into. He doesn't even seem off balance.

"Are you okay, sir?" I ask.

The pedestrian nods and looks at me closely. "Aren't you that superhero person from the movies?" he asks.

"I am. We're filming and this is a part of a scene. Sorry you were impacted."

The guy shrugs. "Hey, as long as I'll be in a movie, I don't care!"

"This isn't a movie. Please help me, he's going to kidnap me and do unspeakable things to me," the goon under my shoe exclaims.

The pedestrian peers down at the stooge and back at me. "You sure you're filming? I don't see cameras anywhere."

I have to think fast. "The cameras are very hidden because it's supposed to be as if we aren't filming." I pull out my phone and show him a few pictures from a couple of days ago when I was on a movie set. "See, it's really me."

The pedestrian nods. "You guys are really good. Almost had me fooled. Good luck with the rest of the shoot."

He walks away as the stooge continues to complain and whimper. I bend down and pull him up, holding his hands behind his back. I slap on a pair of handcuffs from one of my many pockets.

"Time to return whatever you stole." I pick up the weird shaped item the stooge left on the ground. When I see what it is, I almost drop it. The item is bronze, with a sculpted head, nose, eyes, and ears, mounted on a slab of marble.

Luckily the eyes are closed, but it's still extremely disturbing.

"What the hell is this?" I ask, forgetting to use one of my canned one-liners.

"Schubert's death mask," he grumbles.

I frown. "What does that even mean?"

"Famous people used to get a cast of their face before they died. This one is Franz Schubert, a classical music composer. Thank God it didn't break when I fell, the boss would kill me if anything happened to it."

"You're kidding me." I turn the *death mask* over in my hands. This was on some ancient composer before he died? *Gross.*

"Why does One-Eyed Barnacle want this, and the other objects you and Hallie are collecting for him?" I ask.

"None of your business," Dave spits back at me.

I sigh and close my eyes. Time to be The Amazing Boy. My eyes snap open as I straighten up and say, "We can either do this the easy way or the hard way. Easy way you tell me what you know. Hard way is I'll get you to tell me what you know. Either way, you lose out." I make sure my voice is as menacing as I can make it.

He sits back on the ground. "No. Neither. The boss will come rescue me before you do anything."

"I highly doubt that. Guess it'll be the hard way."

I pull out a pill container from another one of my fancy pockets. This suit is pretty amazing, if I do say so myself. It lives up to my namesake. If Lea is allowed to stick around, she'll have to get her own Super L suit, one without a hole in the knee.

I kneel on the ground and work to pry open his mouth while trying to make sure he doesn't bite my fingers off. It's like trying to get a cat to take a pill. The hazards of the job but at least I've been told I have good worker comp benefits if anything ever does happen.

He struggles until suddenly he stops moving and stays still. It must have finally disintegrated. I look around hoping no one saw me accost this man. A couple of people have stopped to stare.

"It's okay, we're filming!" I say brightly. I crouch in front of the goon, trying to block him from the public. I stare into his unblinking eyes.

"Why are you, Hallie, and One-Eyed Barnacle collecting random objects around the city?"

"To become powerful," Dave says in a monotone voice.

"Why those objects?" I ask.

"They are predicted to give powers to whoever owns them. And if he has them all, he'll be the most powerful supervillain ever."

I roll my eyes. *How basic.* Very similar to the Marvel Infinity stones but these objects won't neatly fit into a gauntlet. I go through the list of objects in my head. A musket, possibly something from City Hall, Al Capone's fedora and the keys from Eastern State Penitentiary, part of Albert Einstein's brain, and this death mask from somewhere nearby.

"Where's the next stop?" I ask.

"The big museum," he says still in a monotone voice.

"For what?"

"One-Eyed wants that one for himself so he didn't tell us. Hallie and I got the rest," he says, barely blinking.

I need Gina to interpret this information for me. I'm pretty sure the big museum would mean the Philadelphia Museum of Art, but we don't have time for mistakes. I also can't help but want to see Lea again too. I pull up the messenger app on my phone and stop. *I don't have Lea's number.*

I open Instagram and see if I can find her on there. It doesn't help that I can't remember her last name, so I do something I never do, publish my own Instagram post. I have a PR team who usually does this sort of thing, because using social media is worse than the dentist, but times are dire.

I snap a picture of the street sign closest to us, Moravian, use some fancy filter, and post it with the caption, *Super L, we miss you. @ Sixteenth and Moravian.* That'll get the press going and maybe help cement Lea's future as my sidekick. Either that or I've just royally pissed off the Agent.

CHAPTER TWENTY-ONE

LEA

Gina and I fly down the sidewalk on our *borrowed* scooters.

"I still can't see Jake anywhere," I yell. The sidewalk is so filled with pedestrians that it's hard to spot anything. At that moment a man, his face looking down at his phone, is in my path. I quickly steer to the right, just missing him.

His surprised face pops up. "Watch where you are going!" he hisses, shaking his fist at me.

"Sorry!"

"Why did I follow you on this stupid thing, I'm afraid I'm going to fall off," Gina screams behind me. "And we don't have on helmets!"

"Someone please help me! He was taken from me!" A high-pitched voice screams.

I veer off towards the noise and come upon a woman in her fifties, with wire-rimmed glasses, short curly hair, wearing a long, flowered skirt and a light pink blouse. She's waving her hands all over the place and tears are flowing down her face.

I turn off my scooter and take a deep breath. *What would Jake do?*

"Ma'am, what's happened? Who was taken?"

She squints at me, wringing her hands. "Schubert was taken! I don't know why anyone would do that." A sob erupts from her mouth.

Schubert? Isn't that the name of a composer? My tenth-grade music teacher was obsessed with classical music and taught us all the names of composers and I'm pretty sure Schubert was one of them. Maybe one of his music scores was stolen or something signed by him?

"We're here to help you get him back. Can you show us where he was stolen?" I ask, setting the scooter against a lamp post. Gina props her scooter on the side of the building, pursing her lips. *I really hope these don't actually get stolen while we're in here.*

The woman nods, motioning up to a set of wrought iron doors with elaborate patterns etched into them. The doorknobs are even a golden sheen. There's a plaque next to the door that says *The Curtis Institute of Music Milton L. Rock Resource Center*. After going up a few granite steps, we come upon an empty circulation desk and a set of carpeted steps. The entire room is blindingly white. To my right is another set of doors that are open, displaying hundreds upon hundreds of materials. They look too big to be books, maybe music?

"It's up here," she says, pointing to the steps.

I look behind me at Gina and shrug. *Guess we better keep seeing this through.*

The woman takes the steps slower than I'd like but she's the one leading the way, so I have to deal. On the last step she turns around and says, "Be careful, there's glass everywhere."

She's not wrong. Shiny shards of glass on the carpet reflect off the light.

"My heels and I will stay on the steps, thank you very much," Gina announces.

I tip toe in my black flats to the wall and lean up against it.

"Here's the case where Schubert was displayed. It's not even widely known that his death mask is shown here so I don't know how they found out," the woman explains.

The glass case is indeed very empty. Only a small plaque that's inscribed with the words *Death Mask/Franz Schubert* remains. Under that in small lettering it says *Mounted by Franz Schubert's descendants and dedicated by them in deep gratitude.*

I gasp. I have heard of death masks!

"You have a death mask of a famous classical music composer," I shout. If I wasn't trying to avoid glass at the moment I'd jump up and down. *This is an archivists' dream.*

The woman pushes up her glasses and sniffs. "We *had* Schubert's death mask. And don't sound so surprised. This is the Curtis Institute of Music. We're a very well-renowned music school, of course we have Schubert's death mask and it's not the only death mask we own. We even have a hand cast from the composer Franz Liszt."

"Oh, so you're like Juilliard," I say.

The woman grits her teeth. "We're nothing like Juilliard. We're even more selective and our students don't have to pay a cent to come here."

"I wish I played an instrument! I could use a free education," Gina says. "I've been living in Philly my whole life and didn't know this school existed."

The lady glares at Gina. "We're highly regarded in the classical music community."

Gina puts her hands on her hips. "Yeah, enough for someone to swipe something from you."

To diffuse the situation I say, "Ma'am, we're going to try and get that death mask back for you. What does it look like?"

The woman scoffs. "How in the world would you two help? I've wasted enough time talking to you. For all I know you both could be working with the person that stole the item, looking for the next object to swipe. I need to call the police."

I wince. Granted, I am dressed in a ridiculous costume, but I hate not being taken seriously. *How does Jake do this all the time and be successful?*

The woman whips her phone out of a pocket in her skirt. *Crap.* We need to get out of here before the police show up and ask us any questions. "Good luck with them. In the meantime, we'll work on getting it back for you, no need to thank us."

Gina's already halfway down the steps and we slip out of the library's colossal doors onto the street. As soon as the doors slam shut Gina says, "She was a bundle of joy."

"Talk about stuck up. We better find Jake and see if he caught that man. Any ideas?"

Gina scratches her head. "I'm sure he attracts a crowd wherever he goes. Let's trace our steps back to where we lost track of him and go from there. We can also return our scooters. You should count yourself lucky no one took them while we were in there."

I lead the way back to the park and sure enough, Captain America and Iron Man are still there, this time sitting on the ground playing a card game. As I approach, Captain America jumps up.

"You actually came back!"

I disembark from the scooter and push it over to him. "I always keep my word. Sorry about that, we had to check out the disturbance happening. Superhero business. You understand."

He nods approvingly. "You're even better at this cosplay stuff than we are. Mad props. But where did The Amazing Boy go?"

"Your guess is as good as mine," I say, twisting my mouth. As Gina's handing her scooter to Iron Man, a couple of giggling girls pass us. "He's only a few blocks away! I wonder who Super L is?" I overhear one say.

Gina and I glance at each other. "That has to be a sign," I exclaim.

"Nice to meet you, but duty calls," I say, running to catch the girls. They're wearing ripped jean shorts and similar flowery tank tops. "Are you talking about Jake Johnson?" I ask.

They stop and blatantly stare at my chest. I'm really hoping it's because of the big *L* that's plastered there. "O-M-G! He posted a really cryptic post on his Instagram, and I think it's about you!" The blonde one shoves her phone in my face. I take a quick look and there's Jake's Instagram.

The post is clearly one he put up himself. The picture shows a green street sign and a caption that makes my heart skip a beat. Jake Johnson referenced me on his Instagram. The Instagram account that has over sixty million followers. How is this my life?

I return the phone and thank them. "Where's Sixteenth and Moravian?" I ask.

One of the girls points diagonally. Not helpful.

"I know where that's at. Let's go before everyone else finds him," Gina says, pulling my arm.

The girls behind us are whispering really loudly. "That has to be Super L! I wonder if she's in any other movies and what her insta handle is? He didn't even tag her."

Yes, I am Super L and I'm proud of it. Who knows what I'll do next? I just need to get through this day and unfreeze my friends. But when this is all said and done, it's essential I do an overhaul on my Instagram grid before I will ever consider turning it public. No one needs to see my bangs from ninth grade.

CHAPTER TWENTY-TWO

JAKE

I must have been out of my mind posting that picture. Or underestimated how quickly people that weren't Lea would find me. Now more than ever I wish I was wearing my Jake Johnson clothes so I can fly under the radar. My red and gold costume makes me an instant target, especially when you're standing next to someone in handcuffs.

"Look, there he is! The Amazing Boy, who's Super L? Can we get a picture with you?" A group of tweens are quickly approaching.

I grab onto Dave's arms so he won't try and run while I'm distracted.

"Sorry, I'm on official business right now. I'm trying to return something stolen back to its rightful owners."

They're taking out their phones and snapping pictures. At this point I really don't care.

"Is Super L your girlfriend? I hope not!" one girl says.

I wish I could have a girlfriend or even a friend but how would that even work? I'm always in random spots filming and fighting villains. Oh and don't forget the fact the Agent would just wipe their mind.

If Lea signs on with me, I could see her almost all of the time and there is no way her mind would get wiped but I can't get my hopes up. She says she wouldn't miss her family and friends, but she doesn't realize what it would be like. I'd never wish this on anyone. And the Agent never hesitated to wipe someone's mind before, why would this be any different?

I faintly hear my name and I turn towards the voice.

"Jake!" Lea's running towards me, her gold cape flying behind her with Gina on her heels. She reaches me out of breath. "I thought we'd lost you and I didn't know what to do since I don't have your phone number and I thought I'd never see you again," she says all at once.

I smile. "Look at you, you found me through my vague post."

Lea gives me a sheepish grin. "I can't take credit for that. Some of your megafans were talking about your Instagram and we put two and two together."

"Either way, you found me and the stooge."

"Hey! Who you calling the stooge? I have a name!" The truth-telling pill must've worn off already. He's back to his grumpy self.

I still have my hands around his arms, straddling the death mask under my armpit.

"Lea, can you grab this mask thing from me? I don't want it to fall and break. It already had one tumble today and survived, I'm not going to risk another."

Lea reaches and takes the object from me. She looks down at it and her face lights up. "I know this thing should be creepy to me, but I can't get over how awesome it is. I'm literally touching history right now."

I smile despite the circumstance. It's cool she knows what makes her happy. I wish I had the chance to figure that out, instead of being forced to take this job. Who knows what I could be doing instead. Maybe learning how to design a bridge or a roller coaster?

Lea delicately places the item under her arm. "We talked to the lady who runs the place where it was stolen. I should go return it to her, she was really upset."

Gina speaks up and says, "I'll take it back to her while you guys figure out what to do with the stooge."

"Stop calling me that," he says, "My name is Dave!" His face is getting red.

"It's a terrible villain name so I'll keep calling you the stooge or goon," I reply.

Lea hands Gina the death mask and Gina shudders. "I'm going to return this as quickly as possible before I have night-mares about this creepy face."

"Wait, before you go. The goon says the next stop is the big museum. Is that the Philadelphia Museum of Art?"

Gina shakes her head up and down. "Oh, for sure. No question about that. It's ginormous and known for all its steps from the Rocky movie."

I snap my fingers. "That's right, I think I heard some of the crew talking about that while we were flying here."

"What are you guys going to do with stoogie here? I don't think you can drag him all the way to the art museum, it's far from here. And no, I'm not calling you by your real name, you don't deserve that," Gina says, leering at him.

It's a good question. Making him come with us would be a pain, but on the other hand if we let him go, he could easily figure out a way to warn One-Eyed Barnacle we are on our way.

"Can we dump him somewhere?" Lea asks.

Dave gasps. "Dump me! What did I ever do to you?"

Lea flushes. "Not like kill and dump you, I just mean, tie

you up somewhere so you can't keep bothering us or the city. We'd come back and let you go after everything's finished."

"If I had my Eastern State Penitentiary keys, we could lock him in one of the cells, but stupid Hallie stole them."

"Isn't there something like a citizen's arrest?" Lea asks.

I look over at Dave, whose eyes are wide, and then back at Lea. "That's a thing but it sometimes becomes dicey when I'm involved. It might hold us up."

"What if it's me? That might seem better, right? Just help me walk him over to the building, and I can take care of the rest," Gina says. "I'm sure the police are there by now."

"No! You can't rat me out. One-Eyed will kill me," Dave whines.

Lea gives Dave a condescending look. "Too bad. You should've thought of that before stealing these items!"

I think through the options. This could work and while he's being taken care of, Lea and I have the chance to stop One-Eyed Barnacle before he steals whatever is a part of his plan at the Philadelphia Museum of Art.

Making Dave move is the difficult part. I have super-strength that will hopefully work, so I can try that, but it's going to look really odd that I'm carrying around a grown man, unless we really play it up.

Lea comes over to me and whispers in my ear, "Jake, can you hoist him over your back and take him there?"

Is she reading my mind? If so, that's a scary thought because I don't want her to get creeped out about how much I'm starting to think about her.

Her breath is hot against my ear and I can smell a slight whiff of vanilla mixed with lavender.

"Worth a shot," I say, quickly pulling back before I think about her even more.

I take a deep breath, squat, and in one quick motion, heave Dave face first over my back. He's kicking his feet like a toddler who had a toy taken from them.

"Put me down! This is illegal. Help!" he yells.

Dave isn't too heavy, it's his squirming that's the problem.

"Gina and Lea, lead me to where the death mask belongs,"
I say, struggling to make sure he doesn't fall off my back.

CHAPTER TWENTY-THREE

LEA

I feel bad that Jake has to carry a wiggly Dave. He's flapping around like a fish out of water. I'm not sure how Jake's going to run with this guy on his back, but I hurry down the street to the Curtis Institute of Music as fast as I can. I sporadically take a quick peek behind me to see if Jake's still following us, and there he is, in all his superhero glory. If I hadn't already started to think he's attractive, now would be my *ah ha* moment. He single handedly picked up a slimy guy and slung him over his back without as much of a grunt. And he says his superhuman strength only shows up on occasion? It's worked almost every single time he's used it when I've been around.

The school's a block away but I stop in my tracks when I see red and blue lights spiraling in front of the library's entrance. Men in dark navy blue are running in and out. How are we going to get Dave close to the school without having to involve Jake?

Gina also halts beside me and chews her lip. "There are a lot more police than I expected." Her eyes look fearful.

"Hey, are you okay?" I ask, placing my hand on her shoulder. I can feel her shaking under my touch.

"Sorry, I thought I could do this. Let's just say I'm not the biggest fan of the police. I'd much rather trust Jake to catch a bad guy than them," she says, taking a deep breath in.

Jake's suddenly behind us. How did he catch up to us that fast with a man on his back? Is super speed also one of his strengths?

"Gina, I don't want to make you do anything that makes you uncomfortable. I'll go drop him off. The police don't always like me, but they can get over it," Jake says, a little out of breath. At least he's still a bit human.

Gina blows out the air she is holding in. "Really? Are you sure because …"

Before she can finish, he's already gone, jogging with Dave down the street.

"Wait, we have to bring back the death mask!" I say, motioning to Gina to follow me.

I watch the scene unfold as I'm approaching. The police stop in place for a second and shout, "Freeze!" And then that's the moment they draw their guns. My mouth becomes dry and my heart's beating a mile a minute. I've never seen a real gun, only on the TV.

Jake freezes like they ask, and with complete control of his voice says, "This man stole something valuable from this institution. I'm dropping him off in your care. Please make sure he doesn't get away. As soon as I put him on the ground, I need to go save the city so please don't shoot me. The woman behind me has the death mask that this man stole, so please treat her with the utmost care. She has done nothing wrong," he says, his head motioning back towards us. Gina's standing beside me, mouth agape.

Jake crouches and drops Dave on the street who curls up in a ball. He's shaking and crying at the same time. It makes you almost feel bad for him. *Almost.*

Jake backs away with his hands raised. "I have no lethal weapons; I'm just trying to save humanity. Thank you for your service." He keeps backing up until he's next to me. "Come on Lea, we should be in the clear now."

"How the hell did you pull that off?" Gina demands, raising her hand that's not holding the death mask. "That'd never work in my neighborhood."

Should my hands be raised? I don't even know if I can because they're shaking so hard.

Jake's eyes grow weary. "I know and I'm sorry. The police force in Philadelphia has been briefed that I'm here filming a movie, which is why they aren't putting up a bigger fight. I've also been trained on how to act and what to say around them although I still avoid them as much as I can."

I'm still not moving, just blinking my eyes.

"Are you okay?" he asks softly, pulling me into him for a side hug.

"I thought they were going to shoot you," I whisper. "I've never seen something like that before."

Gina's eyes flash for a second. "I have but it never ends like this."

I can't even imagine seeing something like this again.

"I'm so sorry," I say, pulling away from Jake. I'd give her a hug too, but I don't want to make any more sudden movements.

She straightens up and says, "I'll go return the death mask and answer the police's questions. I know what to say and can handle myself. Thank you for dealing with the hard part Jake, I owe you."

She leaves her one hand raised while she starts walking forward.

"You owe me nothing. I'm the one that should be apologizing that both of you are mixed up in this," Jake says.

"Are you kidding? This was going to happen either way.

You are trying to save my friends and the city. You can't take the blame for any of this," I protest.

"This has been the most interesting thing to happen to me since I've met Ashley, so at least there's that. You better get going before they steal something else," Gina says, continuing to stride forward, staring straight ahead at the police. "Ashley and I will meet you at the Philadelphia Museum of Art."

CHAPTER TWENTY-FOUR

JAKE

No wonder Rocky used the Philadelphia Museum of Art steps for his training. They're probably a beast to climb up for a normal person. I glance behind me, and Lea's breathing heavily and beads of sweat are dripping off her forehead.

"You okay back there?" I ask. She grunts.

"I need to get into better shape if I keep hanging around you."

She doesn't know what she's saying. My exercise routine is awful. Every morning before the sun rises, I'm at the gym, lifting weights and doing cardio exercises. Two hours of my life each day is dedicated to this routine with only Sundays as a day of rest. At first it was nice to see myself looking toned, but now it's monotonous. A means to an end I guess, although I'm not sure what the end is anymore.

As I reach the top and turn around, the city of Philadelphia comes into view. Straight ahead, behind a fountain and an elaborate monument with many statues, is a long parkway that leads straight to William Penn atop City Hall. Very full, green trees flank the parkway and to the right of City Hall are a couple of large skyscrapers, one standing out with a weird boxy roof.

Lea takes the final step to meet me at the top. "At least the view is worth the pain," she says, taking it all in.

If I knew where I stood with her, now would be the time I'd reach for her hand. But I don't want to make her uncomfortable. Or let myself get close.

"It's a great view," I say, sneaking a peek at her. She really is cute, with her blonde wind-swept hair and wide blue eyes. Even her pants with a hole in them give her character. The more I'm around her, the more I want to make sure she stays in my life. And she's so sweet. I'll never forget the moment she gave the homeless man half her cheesesteak. *Who does that?* I'm used to girls that only care about themselves and are with me to boost their own status. That's not Lea at all.

Even when I was alone with Dave, I found myself thinking about her more than necessary. Will having her taken away from me hurt worse than never getting closer to her? Or maybe I should choose to live in the moment and not worry about what could happen.

She glances over and smiles, showing her perfect teeth. "And no one I'd rather see this view with." She gazes up at me with the most heartfelt look and my stomach drops. *She's got to be feeling this too. It's not just me.* There has to be a way to keep her in my life.

Without any more thinking, I reach for her hand and interlace my fingers with hers. "Me too."

LEA

THE AMAZING BOY is holding my hand in the most intimate way possible. And not like before, to lead me somewhere, but because he wants to. I'm not going to lie; it feels nice and comforting. That someone cares about me, and we are in this together.

If today were a normal day, we could hang out at the art museum for fun and afterwards, have a nice dinner to learn more about each other. Instead, we have to go find some wanna-be pirate and save my friend who, the more I'm around Jake, I'm realizing really was selfish and didn't think about me as a person. Jake's kind and thoughtful, especially after how he handled that situation with the police and Gina.

He turns his head towards mine and whispers, "As much as I'm enjoying this, I don't want to lose One-Eyed Barnacle. We need to go inside."

I take one last look at the city view and nod.

"Yeah, you're right. Let's take this asshole down," I say, stamping my foot.

Jake gives a deep laugh. "That sounds like one of my one-liners. You're really starting to get the hang of this."

I smile back. "I learn from the best."

I don't know what we will find when we walk through the grand doors of the Philadelphia Museum of Art. Will the place be open to the public like the Mütter Museum, or closed like the Eastern State Penitentiary and the Museum of the American Revolution? There are a few people on the art museum steps but I figure that doesn't matter, they could be there sightseeing without visiting the actual museum.

Jake opens one of the humongous doors for me. Even the door handles are huge. If Jake wasn't super strong, I'm sure the door would be hard to open. Once I'm through the door, he sprints in front of me, probably to assess the situation. We've landed in a wide-open, sunny room, filled with the buzz of excitement. On the right side there are multiple ticketing counters with one very long line of people queued up. I look at Jake and say, "I don't get their logic. Why do sometimes they have the place closed and then sometimes it's open for anyone to see?"

Jake's lips are pierced. "I'm not sure. It means this time we have to wait to buy a ticket. We don't have time for this."

"That's stupid. Don't you have some kind of free pass that can get you in anywhere?" I ask.

"Wouldn't that be nice. Usually, the Agent and my crew make sure I'm able to just enter the museum. They either pay for me ahead of time or the museum gives me a comp pass. But since we gave them no advance notice, I don't want to spring anything on the staff."

We step in line and even though it's long, it's moving fairly fast. A few people turn around and gawk. I guess it's not every day you see two people, one being super famous, wearing capes visiting a renowned art museum unless maybe it's Night at the Museum, superhero addition.

"So, if we were here being actual visitors, what artwork would you want to see?" I ask, trying to pass the time.

Jake rubs his chin. "I need to look at a map to see my options, but this museum seems like it would have some classics, so that is probably where I'd go first. What about you?"

I perk up. "You're a classics man, huh. I can appreciate that. I'd want to see the American paintings and especially if there are any of the United States Presidents."

We're starting to get closer to the front and Jake's tapping his foot. "That sounds good. I think most art is great, except modern art. I don't think I'm smart enough to understand it."

"I haven't been around enough modern art to even tell if I like it or not. There are hardly any museums near where I live. Just a super tiny one that's only about the history of farming."

Jake gives a barking laugh. "Now that I want to see. All I've ever been to are big, over the top museums, nothing like that."

"One year our field trip was to the recycling plant. Only field trip of the year and that's where we go."

"Recycling is important and all but that's brutal."

I bring my shoulders up and down. "What can I say, I'm from the middle of nowhere, where a recycling plant and a farming museum are the big attractions."

"Next!" someone calls and that's when I realize there's no one in front of us. I could keep talking to Jake uninterrupted for hours but, until we stop the bad guys, that's not going to happen.

At the ticket counter Jake pulls out his wallet from one of his many pockets and pays for both of us. A machine prints out two tickets and a lady with gray hair and tight curls hands them over, giving us a stern look. "Kids these days don't understand how to dress to visit such an esteemed institution," she mutters under her breath, adjusting her dark-brown horn-rimmed glasses.

We wait until we leave her ticket counter to burst out laughing. "Yes, I chose to dress like this to come on a date to the museum," I say chuckling. As soon as it registers what I had said, I feel my face flush. *Why did I say we are on a date?*

"To be fair, I do dress like this on a regular basis, but never on a date. If this was a real date, you'd know it. I'd pull out all the stops," Jake says, with a serious look on his face.

My heart skips a beat and I blink my eyes. *I really do want to get to know him better, but what if the romantic stuff doesn't work?* With Jess, I knew her for so long that when our friendship turned to kissing, it just made sense and the attraction worked immediately. But after we broke up, I tried going on dates with people from random apps, and when they went to kiss me, I felt nothing. Not a single ounce of chemistry. *I don't want that to happen to Jake and hurt him.*

Maybe he can tell I'm in my own brain because he adds, "I'd love to be in my T-shirt and jeans right now."

"And don't forget that Yankees hat," I say.

We pass into the large hallway, and I gasp. The Great Stair Hall, as it's labeled, is unlike anything I've seen before. At the top is a golden statue of a nude woman holding a bow and arrow. Halfway up, the marble steps shoot off into two different directions.

"Now that's how you make an entrance," I say, spellbound.

Jake opens the map that we picked up when we bought the tickets and grimaces. "This place is huge. We better start looking now before One-Eyed Barnacle gets away." Jake slips on his special glasses. When he sees me staring at him, he explains, "Thought these might help me pick up One-Eyed Barnacle's imprint through the walls."

The glasses won't add any attention to our already ridiculous getup. Not at all. But if it helps us find One-Eyed Barnacle faster, I'm all for the over-the-top look.

We make our way up the grand staircase and many different galleries come into view.

"Which one?" I ask.

Jake consults the map and points straight ahead. "Here, European Art, Impressionism."

"I bet there are some classics in here!" But Jake doesn't respond. He's back in The Amazing Boy mode, also known as figure out the situation and jump into action.

I'm immediately surrounded by beautiful artwork. I don't know all that much about art, I'm more into historical artifacts and presidential history, but I can appreciate good art when I see it. I wish we actually had time to enjoy this place, there are so many cool, elaborate pieces. When we pass a painting with bright sunflowers, and I see the display name says Vincent van Gogh, I try to grab Jake's sleeve to point it out, but he's already out of my reach.

At the end of the gallery, Jake grumbles, "Okay, so we can check that off. I'm trying to think about what he would actually want here. Is he going to steal one of the valuable paintings? Or something else?"

"He wouldn't get very far with one of these large paintings," I say. "The antique frames they are in have to weigh a ton."

Jake rubs his chin. "Not sure why he would want them anyways, except for money. But it doesn't seem like what they have stolen so far is for the money. Dave said these items will help One-Eyed become the most powerful villain ever."

My eyes widen. "You got him to tell you that?"

Jake doesn't meet my eye. "Just for a little." He looks down at the map. "What about ..."

A shrill beeping interrupts him and I automatically cover my ears. White flashes of light erupt in the gallery.

"FIRE. FIRE. Please calmly walk to the closest exit and leave the building. Do not use the elevators," an automated voice says. They don't have to worry about me ever using an elevator again.

Jake meets my eyes, and I can see him mouth, "One-Eyed Barnacle."

I nod. This has to be his doing. His way of creating a diversion while he steals something. Jake waves for me to follow him and he slips into the men's bathroom. *Really? Another bathroom?*

Jake is gone for a moment and when he returns, he gives me the thumbs up sign.

"Can't you pick the women's room when we're going to have these meetings? They are so much cleaner," I complain.

Jake blushes. "Sorry, but I can't get myself to rush into the women's room unless someone is in trouble."

He does have a point. He is quite the gentleman. "How noble of you."

Jake holds the map up against the mirror and points near the top. "What I was trying to say before the alarm went off is there's an armory right there. I think that it could have some items that One-Eyed Barnacle might like, maybe a sword or something like that."

"An armory sounds so cool," I gush. "That's where I'd want to spend my time."

"Me too if we didn't need to save the city. Come on, let's go," Jake says, folding up the map and slipping it somewhere in his suit.

I linger, biting my lip. "If we do find One-Eyed Barnacle, what do we do?"

Jake gives me a questioning look. "What do you mean? We defeat him, get back all the stuff, and unfreeze everyone in the convention center."

"No, I get that, but how do we do all of that? How do you defeat an actual villain? We haven't even beat Hallie yet and now we're taking on a legit villain who is only trying to become more powerful."

Jake scratches his head. "We fight him."

"Right, but I don't know how to fight. I've never punched anyone in my life. I don't even get in emotional fights. Jess broke my heart, and we still talk."

Jake touches my shoulder. "Don't worry about it, let me handle that part. You can be there for backup."

I have to rely on someone else again. Jess always stood up for me and now here Jake is, doing all the heavy lifting, no pun intended. Why does he even need me if I can't take care of myself?

CHAPTER TWENTY-FIVE

JAKE

The clanking noise is what I hear first when we emerge from the bathroom. The sound is dim, and I almost miss it with the fire alarm still going at full blast, but there's a distinct metal sound, like a large robot on the move.

I grab Lea's hand. "Come on, I hear something."

We fly through the gallery, narrowly missing an individual stopped in front of a painting. *Don't they know the fire alarm is going off?*

"Excuse me, ma'am, you should exit the building," I say, motioning to the end of the gallery.

A woman with short, choppy brown hair wearing a bright multi-colored dress turns to me, pursing her lips. "I paid to see artwork. I only have a small window of time until I meet some friends for drinks, so until I smell smoke, I will not be leaving."

I shake my head and leave the lady to marvel at the

artwork. *I wish I had the time to see what she was looking at, but I don't have time.* There's never enough time.

"What should we do about her?" Lea asks, her brows creased.

"There's only so much we can do. If she won't leave, we can't make her. If the building somehow is on fire, I can come back and grab her. Come on, let's go track down that sound."

We're back at the grand staircase and the sound of clanging metal grows increasingly louder.

"Up these steps," I shout.

Dropping her hand, I take the steps two at a time. Lea, who I keep forgetting is shorter than me by a good six inches, struggles to keep up.

I turn around at the top of the steps and she motions for me to go ahead. "I'll be there in a second."

I hate to leave her, but One-Eyed Barnacle won't wait for anyone.

The metallic sound reverberates throughout the wide-open space. I use my glasses to see where he's at and I follow not only the noise but the heat radiance. I pass through a door and am surrounded by display cases of swords. I turn a corner and my mouth drops.

A full-blown knight and shining armor costume is stumbling towards me complete with a sword and flap cap or whatever the helmet thing is called. The figure, that I'm assuming is One-Eyed Barnacle, takes one large step in the bulky outfit. I can feel the floor vibrate when his foot hits the ground. He has the sword in both of his hands dragging it beside him. I have to hold in my laughter. *This is our supervillain?*

How did he even put that massive armor on? More importantly, how did he think he was going to get away with it? He seems even less threatening hidden behind the armor since he's got no control over it. If he can barely lift the sword, how does he expect to defend his prize?

"I don't think you thought this plan through," I say, holding back a chuckle.

I can just make out a pair of dark-brown eyes through the peephole of the helmet. They don't look pleased. *What happened to the eye patch?* "And you're not supposed to be around. That's why we froze everyone that could defeat us. That convention event made it so much easier since everyone that can beat us would be all in one spot."

I shrug. "That's what I get for using the elevator I guess."

One-Eyed Barnacle drops the sword on the floor, and it lands with a clank. He takes one of his armored hands and opens the eye guard so he can stare at me straight on.

"No. We were assured it would work on anyone in the building, no matter what floor or if they're in the elevator."

"You might want to get your money back on whatever you used. Lea was in the elevator with me, and she didn't get frozen either, so I think you're wrong about that theory."

I inch closer. I can keep him talking as a distraction. It's almost embarrassing how easy this is going to be.

"Something went wrong but I just can't figure ..."

I move forward and swiftly kick his legs out from under him.

"Ow! You're going to pay for that," he says as he topples over.

I push the sword aside with my foot. One-Eyed Barnacle keeps trying to rise off the floor, but the armor is too heavy, and he immediately falls back over, making so much commotion each time the armor hits the floor. Lea's behind me snorting and laughing at the same time.

"Looks like you got him; you didn't even need me. If all the stuff in the armory looks like that, it must be a pretty sweet exhibit."

One-Eyed Barnacle is now rolling around on the ground and stops for a second to say, "I wish I had more time to ogle all the magnificent armor, but I needed to take this quickly since Hallie made that distraction."

Oh no. Hallie's around somewhere. Clearly, after this ridiculous display, Hallie is the brains behind the operation. She must be the only one with actual powers because Dave certainly didn't have any and there's no way this man does either. Which leads me to a bigger question, is Hallie actually the supervillain we need to defeat?

"Where are you storing all the stuff you guys stole?" I ask him, my foot stepping on top of his armored chest. Every time he goes to get up, I push down harder. I want to interrogate him as much as I can before Hallie inevitably shows up.

He grunts. "Not telling you. Those are hard earned tokens to give to the Master." I whip off my glasses. My eyes shoot to Lea's and her brows are furrowed.

There's someone else involved? I didn't account for that. I really thought that up until now, One-Eyed Barnacle was the target. Why would the Agent, or someone else on my team, give me a mission card explaining that One-Eyed Barnacle is our MVP when there's some other person that's pulling all the strings? Someone who might also have some kind of powers.

"Who's the Master?" Lea asks, running up to One-Eyed Barnacle. "Is he able to unfreeze my friends at the convention center?"

One-Eyed Barnacle tries to turn his head towards Lea but fails. The flap keeps covering his eyes. He gives up and stays still. "Wouldn't you like to know."

Time to get into this guy's head. "Maybe you don't know. Maybe the Master doesn't tell you anything and only makes you do their dirty deeds, with none of the glory." I sneer down at him, my foot still firmly on his chest.

"The Master promised us after we get him all these items, we will all be well-rewarded and the most powerful villains, well, at least on the east coast. I'll even get to pick what powers I get!"

This guy's a complete joke. Just another stooge to whoever the Master is.

"That doesn't sound like a great deal," I say. "Especially when most of the villains live in LA. I'd really reconsider that offer."

I didn't tell One-Eyed Barnacle that if the plan goes well, most likely the Master would be the most powerful villain ever, and I doubt he or she would give this guy any powers at all. *When do supervillains ever live up to their end of the bargain?*

One-Eyed Barnacle is quiet for a bit. "That is true, I didn't think about that. I'm also feeling like something is wrong with this plan. I was explicitly told by the Master you were not going to be a problem. But here you are being a huge pain in my ass, along with that girl that's been following you around."

"I agree. They are getting on my last nerve and I'm not going to play nice anymore," a voice says. *Oh no.* I'd recognize that gravelly voice anywhere.

Hallie's in her true form, with her long black hair in a ponytail and her all-black getup. *Isn't that hot on a summer day? Or do shapeshifters not feel the heat?*

Before I can do anything to help, Hallie has Lea pushed up against a wall.

"Let him go and she doesn't get hurt," Hallie says to me. Lea's eyes are filled with terror. I don't see any weapons, but I can't take any chances. I don't know the full extent of Hallie's powers.

"You're not getting away this time," Hallie says, her eyes slanted. She pulls handcuffs out of her back pocket and roughly puts them on Lea.

How could I have let Lea get mixed up in this? What was I thinking? She isn't ready for a full-blown battle with a trained fighter like Hallie. Lea even tried to explain to me she has no idea what to do in a fight. Why didn't I listen to her? At least Hallie didn't use some kind of spell on her but I still feel awful.

I try and give Lea a reassuring look. She turns her head away from me but not before I see tears fall down her cheek. My heart drops. *How is she ever going to trust me now?* This is why the Agent said it's better to not have anyone close to me. They always get hurt.

Hallie squints her eyes and purses her lips, making her look even more deranged than usual. "Seems like we both have something the other wants. We should make a trade."

"No, Jake, don't do it," Lea pleads, sitting on the ground with her hands stuck behind her. "I already messed up enough as it is, I don't want to ruin anything else."

"This is not your fault," I reassure her. I really want to pull her into a hug, but I also don't want to let go of One-Eyed Barnacle.

Hallie shakes her head at Lea. "Actually, it is. The Amazing Boy is too good to be bothered with someone like you."

My blood begins to boil. *How dare she talk about Lea that way.*

"No you didn't, you witch!" Out of nowhere a woman's black dress shoe flies past my head and smacks Hallie square in the face. Hallie grabs her right eye. "Ow!"

Gina appears out of the shadows and says, "I have another one of those if you don't behave."

Hallie looks Gina up and down. "Ah, my Eastern State Penitentiary friend. Thanks for the keys and fedora, honey." Hallie changes her voice to sound like Meg.

Gina's eyes slit. "Don't talk to me like that. You are NOT my friend. I can't believe I fell for that. I even hugged you. Probably the most action you've gotten in a long time."

"Really funny, girl. I see plenty of action."

"Do you Hallie? It seems like you're always working,"

One-Eyed Barnacle volunteers from under my foot. He tries to adjust his body and I step down harder. "Ooof," he grumbles.

Gina and Hallie are still arguing. As they are doing so, I feel a gust of wind and a quick flash of something fly past the top of my head.

"Ahhhh," Hallie screams, grabbing her left arm as she falls to the floor. An arrow sticks grotesquely out of her left elbow.

Gina runs over and helps Lea up. "Go, hide somewhere quick. I'll look for the keys for the handcuffs."

Lea gives her a wounded look but complies with Gina's orders and runs deeper into the armory.

"Give me the keys," Gina demands, sticking out her hand in front of Hallie.

"What keys?" Hallie asks, grimacing. The arrow is still stuck in her elbow.

"All the keys. My keys to the Eastern State Penitentiary and the keys to open the handcuffs on Lea."

Hallie laughs and then winces in pain. "Hell, no."

Gina shrugs. "Have it your way. Ashley, another arrow please," Gina calls to nowhere in particular.

Hallie's eyes grow frantic. "No more arrows. This hurts worse than the time I had an ear infection." *I guess even supervillains get sick.*

She turns to One-Eyed Barnacle. "What should we do?"

I can hear a slight sigh come from the armor.

"He's going to be so disappointed in us," One-Eyed Barnacle says.

I peer down at him. "Then you should've learned to be a better villain."

Hallie tries to put her hands on her hips and winces. "I'm good at my job, but we were promised to be made better if we stole these items."

"By whom?" I ask.

"Someone who clearly lied to us," One-Eyed Barnacle says

dejectedly. "You must have had some kind of charm on you, so the spell didn't hit you."

How would I get that? And how would Lea have it too? That's when I remember Lea is hiding in the armory wearing handcuffs.

"Give me the keys," I say roughly to Hallie, closing the distance between us. One-Eyed Barnacle should be fine on the ground without me watching over him. It's not like he can go very far at the moment.

She rolls her eyes and places a single key in my outstretched hand.

"All of the keys," I prod.

"Fine. I never needed these to begin with," she says, throwing down a large, heavy key ring filled with rusty keys on the ground. "They just helped me not have to pick that decrepit lock."

Gina grabs the key ring before I can move to pick it up. "I'm never letting these out of my sight again. Now where's the fedora?"

Ashley appears, still in her business suit, behind a pillar with a pink bow and arrow raised. What a badass; she's like Kate Bishop, but in heels. I might not be the biggest Marvel fan, but I do know all my superheroes and their skill sets.

"Where's Einstein's brain?" she demands, the bow and arrow not wavering.

"And the rest of the loot you stole?" I add in.

Hallie's rubbing her elbow. "You might have thwarted our efforts in stealing the armor, but you're not getting the rest of our stuff."

"Well, actually we did. The death mask is already back with its rightful owners," Gina says, giving Hallie a triumphant smile.

Without warning, Hallie sprints out of the gallery. Ashley releases the arrow without hesitation. The arrow burrows itself in Hallie's right ankle and she gives a blood curdling scream and falls over, face first.

"Sorry, but I don't like that answer. I can't afford to be fired. Now where is everything else?" Ashley asks, standing over Hallie, impatiently waiting. Gina looks lovingly at her.

"That's my girl. She was a medal winning archer in high school. I tease her about it all the time because it's such a bougie sport but guess her random talent has finally paid off."

"Jake!" Lea's standing off to the side, her hands still cuffed behind her back. I rush over and place the key in the lock and wiggle around until it pops open. Lea brings her hands around to the front of her body and rubs them.

"Are you okay?" I ask. I want to hug her and tell her this is not her fault, but I don't want to get distracted.

Her smile that I've come to depend on is missing, replaced by a worried frown. "Just way out of my depth. You're better off without me."

"It happens to the best of us. Trust me, you don't see all the mistakes I've made on screen. Those get edited out."

Lea hangs her head. "I don't like letting people down."

I tip her head up towards me and look into her sky-blue eyes. Tears are threatening to spill over, and they are missing their spark. "Hey, you aren't doing that. You're so smart and like you tried to warn me, aren't trained for this. I've had thousands of hours of training. You'd be kicking butt if you had the same regiment as me."

Realization dawns on her face. "That many hours? I can't even imagine."

"Trust me, it's brutal. Another reason I have no life."

I want to keep talking to Lea, but I need to focus in case either of our hostages make a sudden move.

"Please don't be too hard on yourself. You're better at this than you give yourself credit for. Come on, let's return these cuffs to the rightful owner."

Hallie's still clutching her ankle when I reach her, blood dripping through her fingers. *Remind me to not get on Ashley's bad side.*

Hallie looks up at me and her free hand tries to push me away, but I easily grab it. If I really want to be mean I could pull the arrow out of her elbow or ankle but I'm not that kind of guy. Plus, I'd really prefer to not have to deal with even more blood spurting out everywhere. Lea wrangles to hold Hallie still while I slap on the handcuffs.

"Thank you, Hallie, I didn't even have to use my own handcuffs. I can save them for that one over there, if he ever gets out of the armor," I say, motioning to One-Eyed Barnacle, who's still rolling around on the ground trying to get up.

Lea looks over at him. "You really are a bad villain."

I kneel down in front of One-Eyed Barnacle. "Where are all the other goods stashed? If you tell us, we will help you up off the floor."

"Like I'm going to tell you," he groans.

Desperate times call for desperate measures. *Time to break out the big guns.*

I straighten up and say, "We can do this the easy way or the hard way."

Gina comes up next to me with her hands on her hips. "What, are you in movie mode or something? Why are you talking like that?"

"See, I'm glad I'm not the only one that thinks it's weird." Lea says, giving me an, *I told you so look.* "Apparently, there are cameras everywhere, so he has to be *on* during fighting scenes."

Ashley and Gina trade looks. "Are we going to be in this movie too?" Ashley asks. "I've always wanted to be an extra on a film."

They don't need to know the specifics, like that they won't even remember any of this or recognize themselves, so I'm not lying when I say, "Yep, all of this will be, I'm sure. But don't get too worried about what I'm about to do. It's perfectly safe."

Lea bites her lip. "It sounds worse if you use a disclaimer before doing something."

She does have a point. I'm not used to doing this in front of an audience. Well not a physical audience, only the people with their butts sitting in plushy movie theater seats after the fact.

It takes both of my hands, and a good heave to get off One-Eyed Barnacle's helmet. I set it gently down next to me. *Don't want to damage the artifact.* I rustle around in my pocket and find what I'm looking for.

Bending over One-Eyed Barnacle I say, "It's your last chance. Tell me where the stuff is stored."

He makes a sound deep in his throat, moves his mouth, and hocks out a huge wad of spit flying onto my face. Saliva drips down my brow, right into my eye.

"Gaw! That's so gross," I exclaim, blinking rapidly, trying to brush it off with my arm. "I'm so done with you."

I take my left hand to pry open his lips and slip a pill in and shut it. I clamp my hand over his mouth and wait until the disintegration process occurs. He's trying to move around, but conveniently can't. I can only hope more of the villains I have to defeat will be wearing armor.

"What are you doing to him?" Hallie shrieks. She tries to get off the ground but winces in pain after taking a step and collapses back on the floor.

"I have the same question. You better not have given something to kill him, or I'm going to lose my shit," Gina says, staring down at One-Eyed Barnacle, her eyes wide.

Lea and I trade looks. "If this is really like the movies, then he didn't. The Amazing Boy never kills anyone," Lea explains.

I smile at that. *How many of my movies has she seen?* "I try to save the world in the least violent ways possible. I'm going to test this out. One-Eyed Barnacle, where are the other items being stored?"

"I do not know. The Master hasn't told us yet," he replies in a monotone voice.

Hmmm. That could be the case, but I don't like the answer. "I need to try something else to see if this truth-telling pill is working yet."

"Truth-telling pill?" Ashley exclaims. "That exists? What a handy thing to have around. Before I found Gina, it would have been nice to give that to my dates to really weed out the toads," Ashley jokes, ribbing Gina in the side.

Gina rolls her eyes. "You'd leave such a good first impression, prying your date's mouth open and stuffing a pill in it."

"How can we get the people at the convention center unfrozen?" Lea chimes in. *Good one.*

"With a reversal spell or if you wait six hours, it will wear off," One-Eyed Barnacle says, without any inflection in his tone.

"Why does it wear off?" I wonder aloud, scratching my head.

"The Master thought everything would be accomplished before then," he says. "He didn't want them frozen forever."

"And we would have if The Amazing Boy wasn't involved," Hallie says, staring directly at me. I notice wisps of hair flying out of her ponytail and her black pants have a small hole in the knee, like Lea. "We were lied to. I wonder if it was by *him*?"

Lea rustles through her purse and finds her phone. "It's definitely been over six hours. I have to go see Jess."

"Go. We can take care of Hallie and One-Eyed Barnacle. If you see the Agent though, tell him I'm looking for him," I say. I pull out my phone, swipe through my camera app, and find a picture of him and I at my last movie premiere. His arm is tight around my shoulders and we're wearing matching smiles. As I'm putting it away Hallie says, "Wait, can I see that?"

I'm not usually in the business of complying to a villain's demands, but the way she says this makes me pause.

I turn my phone screen towards her, and she swears.

"Just as I suspected. Your agent is the Master. No wonder we were lied to. He must have given The Amazing Boy an antidote so he wouldn't feel the effects of the spell at the convention center."

"What are you talking about?" I say slowly.

They are working for the Agent?

CHAPTER TWENTY-SIX

LEA

Jake's face drains of color and his arm holding his phone begins to shake.

"Hey, it's okay, we can figure this out," I say to him, putting my hand on his arm.

Jake gave up his family and his whole life for this man, the true supervillain. I can't even imagine what he's feeling.

"Why would the Agent cross me like this?" Jake says, his eyes clouding over.

"Didn't you say he wanted you to keep being in superhero movies, but you weren't having it?" I ask.

Jake's eyes narrow. "There's no way he'd do this to force me into still being a superhero, right? He's not that terrible."

"Jake, he made your mom forget you. It can't get much worse than that," I say. I didn't want to tell him that, but it's true. *Who makes someone forget their family?*

"But that was for my own good," he whispers.

Jake sits down on the floor of the armory and leans against

a display case filled with ancient swords. I squat next to him. Some of his brown hair falls into his eyes as he looks down.

"I know you feel hurt and let down. He broke your trust and completely shattered everything you know," I say. I'm not speaking from experience or anything like that.

Jake leans into me. "He uprooted my whole life because it was, as he said, to *help me,* but clearly, he has other motives. Why would he cut the power and freeze an entire convention center? Or blow up the side of a museum for his own bene-fits?" Jake asks. "And like you said, make me cut out all my family and friends?"

"Don't pin the explosion on the Master, that was Dave being Dave. That wasn't supposed to happen. He wanted to try out a new spell the Master gave him and it didn't end well," Hallie scoffs. "We try not to leave a mess when we steal something. I excel at that, Dave does not."

"Is that why the case at the Mütter Museum didn't look broken into?" I ask.

Hallie straightens up, looking pleased with herself. "Maybe you are smarter than you look. I've learned how to pick locks. I just didn't want to waste time at the Eastern State Penitentiary, especially since the both of you were watching me like a hawk."

Since she's in a sharing mood, I'll try asking her some of my other burning questions.

"Maybe you can answer why some of the places were closed down and some were open today?" I ask. It's really going to bother me if I don't know.

Hallie closes her eyes for a second. When she reopens them, she says, "If I tell you, you have to promise you don't give me that truth-telling pill."

I exchange a look with Jake and he gives a quick nod. "You will answer her question and I have one of my own."

Hallie adjusts her legs on the floor. "We tried to close all the places, but the Philadelphia Museum of Art said no, without any reason. And then the Mütter Museum had some special exhibit going on today that people already bought tickets to, so we had to figure out some workarounds."

Ashley eyes up Hallie. "That's our cool new photography exhibit. The museum has over thirty-five thousand objects, many that can't see the light of day for too long, so a photographer took pictures of some of the more interesting ones and her work is on display right now."

"Oh, that's right, I've been wanting to see that. You need to get me tickets," Gina says to Ashley. "At least the pictures won't smell."

Jake's eyes raise to meet mine and I can almost physically feel the hurt they show. And I know that pain very well.

"How can I help?" I ask, nudging him.

He shakes his head. "I just need time to wrap my head around it, which I know we don't have right now."

Gina kneels next to both of us. "Speaking of time, didn't the drugged-up pirate say the people at the convention center should be unfrozen by now?"

I gasp. *Oh my gosh.* With all the commotion, I completely forgot. "Jess is probably wondering where I am! And she could be hurt."

Jake straightens up. "We should go there and check it out. It's where everything started. Maybe there will be some clues too where the Agent is hiding."

I jump up off the ground. "Yes! I need to get some things off my chest when I see Jess."

When Jess picked Olive over me, I thought I'd never recover from it. I let her get away with hurting me because I hate fighting with anyone. Why should she get off scot-free when I'm still trying to get over her? There's this literally *amazing* boy next to me and I'm thinking about Jess and how much she hurt me.

"We can come too," Gina offers.

"What about these two?" I say, motioning to One-Eyed

Barnacle and Hallie.

Hallie's still on the ground in handcuffs, an arrow stuck in both her arm and ankle and One-Eyed Barnacle's eyes are closed. I can't tell if his chest is rising and falling. As I bring my index and middle fingers to his neck, his eyes snap open. *Oh good, he's not dead.* I'm glad I didn't lie when I said there was no way Jake was going to kill him.

"Hallie, you owe me an answer to a question or else I'll give you a pill. Where do you meet up with the Agent, I mean the *Master*? If he's expecting you to show up with the armor, we can go to the drop-off location and take him by surprise," Jake says.

Hallie clears her throat. "Once we have the goods, he gives us an address to drop them off and one of his minions comes and gets them. We only saw him at the beginning of this mission when he recruited us."

The Master has more minions? *Not good.*

"So let me guess, since One-Eyed Barnacle bungled this mission, the Master won't send a drop-off location," Jake responds, crossing his arms.

Hallie shakes her head. "And don't even try to get us to send him a message that we have the items. I'm sure he already knows that we messed up. He always knows."

That's not creepy at all.

"Why did you join this mission in the first place?" I ask. What I really want to ask is, why did you decide to be an evil person and steal from museums, but I didn't want to offend her too much. She's actually being pretty agreeable, for a villain. Not that I have much experience confronting villains but she's not making fun of me anymore, so that's something.

"He says it will make us powerful. That these items have hidden magical powers and all of them together will unleash power that no one has ever known."

"That tracks with what Dave told me," Jake mutters, rubbing his chin.

"How do you know this Master is telling you the truth?" I ask.

Hallie sneers at me. "He gave us the freeze spell for the convention center and the one I used at the Mütter Museum. He has spells up his sleeve you'd never imagine, so yes, we believe him."

"But why did the power go out at the convention center?" I ask.

"It was a part of a special spell. The Master wanted to really make sure no one could go in and out of the convention center, including contacting the outside world. Cutting all the power was his backup plan in case something went wrong with freezing everyone. He never did a spell that complicated before."

"It sounds like he's some kind of magician," I blurt out. Everyone stares at me.

"That's the first smart thing I've heard you say all day," Hallie says. *So much for her being nice to me.*

Jake's eyes widen and he snaps his fingers. "That's it. That's what I've been trying to always figure out. Some of the stuff he's given me to use on people never seemed quite right. Like these truth-telling pills I gave Dave and One-Eyed Barnacle."

"He's got loads of different magic spells, and charms to ward them off. My guess is he protected you from the spell he put on the convention center," One-Eyed Barnacle offers. His eyes are focused on me and he's moving his lips back and forth. "What happened? Why does my mouth feel like it's bruised?"

"Then how did Lea not get affected?" Jake asks, ignoring One-Eyed Barnacle.

"Maybe that's where the elevator comes into play?" I pipe up.

Jake's brow furrows. "How so?"

"This is a total guess but what if this *charm* protects people in its vicinity and since we were in such close quarters, I was included in that."

Jake slowly nods. "That could make sense. See, there you are again, Lea, really helping us out."

I can feel my face grow warm. "Oh, that's nothing. And we don't even know if it's right."

"I agree with Jake, you're so smart. One person always needs to be the brains," Ashley says, her eyes sparkling.

"That's what I thought the Agent was, until now. You can be my new brain," Jake says, bumping me with his elbow in the side.

I want to believe them, I really do. But a little voice, that sounds suspiciously like Jess, keeps telling me that they don't really mean it. That I'm not really needed. It's the Jake show, always will be, always has been. Just like the whole time Jess didn't need me, even though she swore up and down she did. Until she decided she needed Olive more.

I try to shake off the thoughts but the commotion in my brain is louder than ever. I can feel my pulse in my fingertips and I grit my teeth. *Why did she have to go and ruin everything?*

"I need to go talk to Jess," I say.

I'm not going to be any good until I see if she's okay and if she is, let all these pent-up feelings out. "But what are we going to do with them?" I motion to Hallie and One-Eyed Barnacle.

"I'm sure the fire alarm alerted the police and fire company. Why don't we tip them off on our way out. Gina and Ashley, can you stay with these two until they get picked up?" Jake asks.

Gina crosses her arms. "Only because you asked nicely and Ashley is with me. These villains don't seem like great company."

Ashley looms over Hallie. "Don't you worry. I'll keep an eye on them and make sure they don't get away. I have plenty more arrows to go around."

Hallie involuntarily flinches. "No more arrows."

CHAPTER TWENTY-SEVEN

LEA

Nothing ever prepares you for seeing your ex, even when you are literally searching for them. As soon as we set foot in the convention center, out of the thousands of people milling about, I zero in on Jess walking hand-in-hand with Olive pointing at a merch stand. She twirls a strand of her long, dark curly hair and her light laugh hits my ears.

I ball my hands into fists. I can barely see with the blinding red rage encompassing my body. There's a little relief mixed in that she appears to be okay, but it is so small compared to the almost all-encompassing anger.

"It's as if nothing ever happened," Jake says, his mouth open.

He isn't kidding. Everyone's walking around like it's completely normal to lose six hours of your life. Jess is picking up a POP figurine. Even from here I can tell it's Brown Recluse.

Seeing her with Olive, so happy and carefree, makes me want to throw something against the wall. I also can't help the rush of memories that come over me, like a montage of my time with Jess.

————

JESS and I were friends forever, the kind of friends where we hung out almost all the time, and when we weren't together, we were texting or on the phone. She lives right down the road from me, so we'd always be at each other's houses. Her mom never minded setting an extra place for dinner and was always making something delicious; her homemade tamales were my favorite. Olive eventually moved into our neighborhood and then we all became one big friend group.

I wasn't very popular at school; history nerds usually aren't. I was the kind of person that flew under the radar most of the time, hiding in some corner reading a book, but if anyone said one bad thing about me, they had to deal with Jess. Same with Olive. When they came out as non-binary, Jess shut down any haters immediately, and even started a Genders & Sexualities Alliance club at our high school for the three of us. Eventually other people started to join, feeling like they finally found a safe place. Say what you will about Jess, but she does stick up for the people she cares about. She also knows how to let them down.

Two years ago is when things changed between us. Olive joined the lacrosse team and the nights they had practice it was just the two of us. Jess was out as pan to some people, but I was still finding myself. We started to spend more time at my house, unsupervised. At first it was just the casual flirty tones between each other, and then more *accidental* touching, like her grabbing a pen out of my hand with her hand lingering longer than normal.

I knew something felt different with Jess, but I couldn't put my finger on it. When we got into a tickle fight one night at my house and she had me pinned to the floor, my stomach began fluttering. That's when I knew there was something more going on.

She leaned down hesitantly, questions in her eyes, and I rose up to meet her lips. It felt right, like yeah of course, this is what we should always be doing. And so that's what we did. So whenever Olive wasn't around, we made out, and more. Whenever I was around Jess, I felt like all was right with the world. That she'd take care of me and that we would be together, eventually. I thought her not defining us as an official couple was because she didn't want to put labels on things. I realized the hard way that no, it was because she was doing the exact same thing with Olive. And Olive ultimately must have been better than me.

———

I SHAKE the memory out of my head. I need to focus on the moment and finally tell Jess how I'm feeling, once and for all. I point over to her.

"There's Jess and her partner. I'm going to go talk to her."

Before Jake can say anything, I march over and tap Jess on the shoulder. She turns and her face lights up. That smile used to bring me to my knees. Now it only heightens my anger.

"There you are! We thought we lost you. Where have you been?"

"Where have I been? I've been searching for a way to save you! And then you don't even message me when you're back to let me know you're okay?" I demand.

Jess raises her eyebrow. "What are you talking about? We haven't gone anywhere. You're the one that's been missing. I thought you needed alone time when you went to the bathroom. You never returned, so I left you be."

"Alone time? Is that all I need to get over the fact you

broke my heart? That you were with Olive and I at the same time and you didn't care one bit how I felt. How can you stand her?" I turn towards Olive.

Olive's eyes narrow and look accusingly at Jess.

"You said that Lea was obsessed with you, but you didn't say the two of you had been together at some point. When did this happen?"

Are you kidding me? Jess is worse than I thought.

I laugh. "Is that what she's telling you? We were together for the past two years until I walked in on the two of you. She can lie all she wants but I know the truth. And it's that she's the worst and you can't trust her at all."

Olive drops Jess's hand. "It makes way more sense now why Lea was so upset. How could you do that to us? We're all friends."

"And I still care about both of you for some stupid reason. So much so I fought a pirate and a shapeshifter to make sure you'd come unfrozen," I say, my voice rising. I'm still clenching my fists and every muscle in my body feels tense.

"Unfrozen? And a pirate and a shapeshifter? Did you smoke weed when you went to the bathroom? I mean, it doesn't seem like something you'd do, but I feel like I don't even know you anymore." Jess peers into my eyes.

I feel Jake's shoulder pressing against me. He whispers, "Lea, let's not get into the details. They don't need to know everything. They're safe now, and Jess seems about as terrible as you described so we should start looking for the Agent."

I know he's right and I've said my peace with Jess, whose eyes are currently about to fall out of her face. "Lea, you're hanging out with The Amazing Boy? And you told him I'm terrible?" I guess whispering isn't one of Jake's super skills.

"If the shoe fits," I say, glaring.

"We never promised each other anything. It was all a bit of fun," Jess says, crossing her arms. A dark, curly strand of hair hangs down in front of her eyes. I used to be the one that would move it out of her face before kissing her. Never again.

"It wasn't a bit of fun to me. I was in love with you!" I yell.

The area around us grows quiet with onlookers stopping to stare.

Jess's hand covers her mouth. "You never told me that. How was I supposed to know?"

"I didn't get the chance. I found you with Olive and then before I knew it, you two were officially together," I explain.

Olive takes a deep breath. "So that's why you asked me out so quickly," they say, turning to Jess.

"No, it wasn't like that," Jess says, her voice faltering.

"You're even worse than I thought. You didn't even tell Olive the truth about us. Olive, I'm sorry for treating you like crap. I thought you knew."

Olive's face is stone cold, and I even get chills catching a glimpse at their expression. "This is ridiculous. You don't mess around with two of your friends at the same time. You just don't."

Jess opens her mouth and Olive says, "Don't even bother. I'm going to find a flight that leaves tonight so I don't have to share a room with you."

Olive turns to me, adjusting their Commander Hero hat. "Sorry that you were hurt, I never meant to do that."

I reach for Olive's hand. "No, I know that now. I shouldn't have assumed that Jess told you the truth, since lying seems to be a part of her MO. I hope we can still be friends after all of this."

Olive nods and gives me a hug. "You deserve better than her," Olive whispers in my ear. They pull away and walk off into the sea of people dressed in cosplay. *Olive's right, of course. I deserve someone who only wants me.*

Jess starts to say *I'm sorry,* but I interrupt her before she can continue. "I don't want to hear any of your stupid excuses. You hurt me and it's going to be hard to come back from that. Enjoy WizCon by yourself."

I turn to Jake and say, "I'm ready. Let's find your agent and kick some magician butt."

CHAPTER TWENTY-EIGHT

JAKE

If I hadn't already had a crush on Lea, the word vomit she shot at her ex would have helped seal the deal. It's impressive and sexy, unlike the actual vomit I spewed on her earlier today.

It's also messed up what Jess did to Lea and Olive. I know I'm supposed to be some heartbreaker or something, but even my Jake Johnson persona wouldn't do that. Any girl that the Agent picks for me knows right from the beginning what they're getting into. Usually, their mind is erased at some point anyways, so I don't have to be with them for very long, it's only for the paparazzi.

With Lea, I want more. I want the fire in her eyes to disappear and to be replaced with her infectious laugh. And I want to be the one to do it if she'll have me. But there's no time for that now. We have to find the Agent before any more chaos ensues.

"Let's first check my dressing room to see if there are any

clues of where to find the Agent," I say. I hold out my hand, praying she'll take it. She clasps hers against mine and gives me a half smile. Maybe once this is all finished, the full smile will be back in action.

We weave throughout the convention center floor. The Agent must have integrated some kind of memory thing into the spell that Hallie and company cast.

The exit doors are in sight when all the sudden a large man dressed as a Roman centurion blocks our path. *Did he also steal his armor from the art museum?*

The difference with this man and One-Eyed Barnacle is he can walk in it, and it doesn't cover his whole body. In fact, the armor barely covers his waist, and peeking underneath it, I can see a toga. His legs and arms are completely exposed, although his head is covered in a helmet with bright red feathers on top. I've always wondered how the Romans had epic battles in their heavy gear and lack of clothing. Didn't they realize that it makes them more susceptible to getting stabbed?

"I can't let you do that," he says, jutting his palm out, inches away from my body.

"Why not?" I challenge. The door is so close, if I charge around him, I can make it but not with Lea attached to me. And I'm not going to leave her.

He gives me a toothy grin. "It's my mission from the Agent," he says, with an emphasis on Agent for maximum impact.

I gasp. It's like he punched me in the gut. I know by now that the Agent is against me, but it's one thing thinking it and another thing hearing it aloud from some stranger in a toga.

"I guess the Agent is done hiding behind his henchmen and letting you tell me what's actually going on," I say to this half-dressed goon. I eye him up. He's got about a hundred pounds on me, all of it pure muscle.

His face scrunches up. "I dunno. I just read what was on the mission card."

"Can't think for yourself then?" Lea asks. I'm still holding her hand, trying to come up with the next move.

"What? I think for myself," the man sneers down at her.

"Clearly not if you're following some dumb cue card for words. What else does it say?" Lea asks.

"I was going to continue but you interrupted me and now I forget," he says, putting his finger on his lips.

I motion with my head to the other set of doors down the hallway and Lea nods in understanding. I sprint towards them, still hand-in-hand with Lea.

"Come back here!" the Roman centurion yells. I turn my head and he's gaining on us. I see an inflatable version of myself at a vendor and throw the blow-up Amazing Boy right at the guy's head.

"Sorry, I'll pay for that later!" I promise the vendor as we fly by.

I open the double exit doors with my free left hand, and we pass through to a mob of people circulating throughout the hallway.

"Come on, we're taking the escalator," I say, dropping Lea's hand, even though I wish more than anything we can get a few moments alone, uninterrupted by any other unwelcome guests.

"I couldn't agree more," Lea says.

We take the escalator that I should've taken six hours ago. *But then I never would have met Lea.*

We're running down the escalator steps and I keep apologizing as I push people out of the way. "Sorry, we have pressing superhero business," I say. I don't even have to use my canned one-liners anymore since the Agent and I are history. *He's not making any more money off me.*

We're almost to my dressing room when I hear the thud of

another pair of footsteps behind me. Ones that are way louder than the two of ours combined.

I swipe my badge and this time there's a beep and a green light appears. "Quick, in here. I'm pretty sure the Roman guy is still following us."

"Won't we be cornered though?" Lea asks, biting her lip.

I shake my head. "I don't think we'll be able to outrun him for long so we can hold him off a little bit while we come up with a plan. And maybe he'll have the Agent come to us."

My dressing room is exactly how I left it. Even my street clothes are balled up in the middle of the floor. Maybe the Agent isn't at the convention center and that mission report the Roman dude is talking about was created ages ago and only triggered in case I figured out the Agent's true mission. Which means the Agent can see every single step we take and every word we say. I mean I kind of knew that was happening, but not to the extent that he would activate someone to eliminate me.

I shut the door, lock it, and shove a large brown comfy chair in front of it.

"That should hold him for a little," I say.

"Open up! I know you're in there!" the guy screams. We hear pounding against the door. He keeps going at it. After a few more seconds, he stops. I hold my breath and wait for it. I know what's coming next because I've been there before and done this retrieval. Done the Agent's dirty work that he never does himself.

A large thud sounds against the door.

"Woah." Lea clasps her hand over her mouth. "Is the chair going to hold him back?"

"For now," I say. "Let's go to the other side of the room and arm ourselves."

Lea sinks down on a leather couch on the far wall. "Arm myself? I don't know how to fight. You saw me at the art museum. I'm a liability."

"You can learn how to fight, that's a teachable skill. Being smart isn't, and you have that," I say, perching on the couch next to her. "I have plenty of gadgets to protect you in my suit. You can help me look." I unzip my shirt.

Having a zippered shirt is much easier and safer to remove than pulling it over my head. You never want to be in a half state of undress, with your shirt over your eyes, if there's a possibility of being attacked.

That's when it sinks in what I said. It doesn't help that Lea's turning bright red.

"Uh, I meant look through my gadgets to see what you want. Not look through my clothes while they are on me. Sorry," I say, tripping over my words and trying not to turn the color of the exit sign.

Lea lightly laughs. "No, it's okay. Someday in the future I can help you look."

I stop unzipping and look at her. "What do you mean?"

"I think I'd look through your clothes to find gadgets, someday in the future," she says, giving me a shy smile.

If that isn't a sign, I don't know what is.

I scooch close to her on the couch, so our legs are pressing against each other.

"Really?" I study her face and her wide, blue eyes stare earnestly back up at me.

She nods, playing with her bracelets. "I like hanging out with you. And want to keep hanging around you to see what happens."

I blink. "I'd like that too." What I really want to do is kiss her right now, but I can tell by her body language and what she just said that she wouldn't want that yet. I don't want to ruin any of the trust that's building.

I'd wait for her. She's the kind of girl that I'd be an idiot not to wait for. I just need to defeat the Agent unscathed and keep her memory intact.

A loud thud and then the sound of wood splitting interrupts our moment.

I straighten up and look towards the noise. A sneakered foot emerges from the middle of the door, wood dropping to the ground. *I guess even Roman centurions need comfortable footwear.*

"If he slams himself into the door one more time he's going to break through. Quick, take this syringe," I say, pulling it out of an inside pocket and zipping myself back up.

Lea holds it at the very top, away from her body, like it's covered in germs.

"What am I supposed to do with this?" she asks, giving me a horrified expression.

"If he gets anywhere near you, inject him with all of it," I instruct.

Lea bites on her fingernail. "How am I supposed to do that?"

"Don't think, just jab. But only use it if necessary."

She takes her finger out of her mouth and nods. She opens her mouth to say more but before she can, the Roman guy splinters his way through the door and lands face first into the plush chair.

CHAPTER TWENTY-NINE

LEA

I've never stared at death in the face before and I don't intend to start today. The man in the brown chair is flailing around, like one of those inflatables at a used car dealership. His legs are going a mile a minute. His feathered helmet slips off and lands on the ground with a clunk.

I know Jake said to use this syringe with a mystery substance only if I need it but now's the perfect time while the guy is confused and down for the count. Once he's back on his feet, the chances of Jake and I winning against him are slim to none. Don't get me wrong, Jake is super strong when his powers work, but I bet that this man will be strong all the time. I don't want Jake to get hurt protecting me.

Before I can second guess myself, I fling myself on the chair and stab the man in his arm with the syringe. I don't have to worry about not hitting skin since he's barely wearing anything.

"Lea, what are you doing? That's for emergencies only!" Jake yells behind me.

I push down on the plunger and inject the man with the unknown substance.

"Do we know what this does to him?" I say, my voice shaking. *Maybe I should have asked that before injecting him.*

He continues to flail around, groaning and bucking at the same time. I hold onto his shoulders so I don't fall off the chair. After a few more seconds he becomes deathly still. A cold feeling overcomes my whole body.

"Oh no, Jake. I really hope I didn't just kill him." I put my fingers up to his neck and breathe a sigh of relief. His pulse is there. Faint but there. "He's alive, for now," I say, crawling off of the guy.

Jake runs next to me and holds me steady. "What were you thinking, Lea? You could've gotten yourself killed."

"I don't know. He was distracted and it seemed like the right thing to do."

Jake lets me go and looks me in the eyes. "That was really stupid but I'm also really proud of you. Can you imagine doing that six hours ago? Or even an hour ago?"

My eyes widen. No, no I cannot. Six hours ago, I didn't even know weird things like magic and superheroes existed. And even an hour ago I couldn't be in a fight without being caught in handcuffs. And now I'm injecting some large, almost naked man with a foreign substance, so he doesn't hurt the guy I care about.

"I'm finally free of Jess," I say, flinging my arms around him.

Jake returns my hug but after a second, he straightens up. "I hate to break this up, but that injection was a sedative, and given this dude's size, it might not last long on him. Let's quickly look around to see if there are any clues to where the Agent is before we head out."

Jake walks over to a table attached to a large mirror with lights. There are papers and cosmetics strewn all over including a tube of mascara. I go over and pick it up. It's a brand I never even heard of. Probably some heavy-duty expensive one.

"Before you say anything, yes I wear makeup for my guest appearances and when I'm about to fight a villain," Jake says, rustling through the papers. "My makeup team hadn't put it on me yet before we got stuck in the elevator."

I put the mascara back. "Real superheroes wear makeup."

The man behind me groans.

"We better find something fast," Jake says. He looks at a paper in his hand and drops it on the floor. It swirls like a snowflake from the sky. "This is just the itinerary for the weekend, which clearly has been blown to bits."

As he's shuffling the papers, something laminated peeks out from under the stack.

"What's this?" I ask, pulling it out. It's attached to a red lanyard that has *COMCAST* written in black letters all over. On the front is a picture of Jake looking half asleep in a baseball hat and his name *JAKE JOHNSON, Comcast Center*.

"This has to be it. Good job Lea, once again you're saving the day!" He picks me up and swings me around.

"What'd ya do to me," I hear behind me.

Jake puts me down and yells, "Run, Lea!"

He doesn't have to tell me twice.

CHAPTER THIRTY

JAKE

I'd have to add a Roman centurion to the list of villains I've thwarted, well I guess in this case, that Lea helped me thwart. This guy is huge in all aspects, and I don't need him blocking us in right when we have found our next move.

Lea jumps over him in some kind of sweet ninja move that only makes her more of a badass. Before clearing him, she reaches down and puts something into the guy's exposed shoulder.

"Woah, where did you learn that move?" I call after her.

Lea looks at me, baffled. "I honestly have no idea. I'm usually pretty clumsy. Maybe I've seen too many Marvel movies," she responds with a devious smile.

I groan. "You need to find better stuff to watch than that Marvel trash."

Lea rolls her eyes. "Hurry up, I don't want you to get stuck in there."

I try and pull the same move Lea did but I'm taller than her so it's harder for my legs to go over the man. It also doesn't help that the giant's arm pops up and grabs my left leg at the last second right before I would've been in the clear.

"Ahhhhh," I scream as I tumble backwards into the room.

"Not so fast," the dude says, rising from the chair. As he's straightening up, he grimaces in pain.

"Owwwww," he howls, holding his shoulder. He turns around towards Lea and growls. *What does he think he is, a werewolf?*

I want to get out of this room before I'm officially boxed in, but I also don't want him running after Lea. She's gotten lucky but that can only last so long. I do a quick scan and find what I'm looking for.

"Prepare to meet your maker!" I say as I toss a brick at him. It's hard not to use my canned one-liners.

Okay, so it's not a real brick, I'm not that cruel. It's about the same weight as a textbook and made of rubber. I used it for a photoshoot earlier in the day to *show my superstrength* but since photoshoots go on forever, they gave me the fake brick so it wouldn't be as annoying to hold above my head for an extended period.

I'm hoping that even though it's not a real brick it can still do some damage, or at least distract him. It seems like I threw it pretty hard by the way it hit him. The smack reverberates throughout the room. He groans and slides to the floor, holding his head. I slip past him and slam the door shut before he can rise again.

"Are you okay?" I ask, running over to Lea.

She nods. "I was so worried for you. That guy is ridiculous."

"What did you do to him to make his shoulder hurt so much?" I ask.

She shrugs. "I still had the syringe in my hand, so I stuck it in him."

I nod my head. "Smart thinking."

"That'll teach him to at least wear something with

sleeves." Lea looks back at the room where we left the guy. "That brick looks like it distracted him."

"It's not real, by the way, it's a prop brick, but I guess I just threw it at him pretty hard."

"I figured it was a fake when blood didn't spurt out of his head. I like that line you used, *Prepare to meet your maker.*"

My face warms. "I'm so used to saying cheesy lines, that it flew out of my mouth. After hearing you say it, I want to retract that from your memory."

Lea's eyebrows bunch together. "Is that the only thing you want to take from my memory?"

I pull her close. I can feel her heartbeat thumping hard against me. "I don't want you to ever forget me."

She whispers, "Good because I couldn't stand it if I had to. Today's the best day of my life."

I become motionless. Having villains come after her and her friends makes this the best day of her life? There were so many close calls too. What if the Roman dude woke up a little earlier and threw a punch at her? Maybe this is why they say not to mix business and pleasure. She's starting to become a liability because I care about her too much.

We pull away and she reaches for the lanyard dangling from my arm.

"Do you know what this is for?" she asks.

"It has to be the Comcast Center right in town. As soon as I saw this, I remembered the Agent mentioning it's the second tallest building in Philadelphia and owned by Comcast, who also happens to own the rights to The Amazing Boy. I guess later on I was supposed to take a tour of the building or something."

Lea smooths down her hair. "Do you think he's hiding out there?"

Why didn't I think of this sooner? "If you were a villain, wouldn't you want to go to one of the tallest buildings in the city? He has to be there but what floor is the big question."

Lea nods. "This really will make a good movie someday. Your agent has it all scripted out, doesn't he?"

Too much so. He really played me. Not only will he make money off this iteration of my franchise but he's also trying to become super powerful all at the same time. I can't let him get away with it.

"Gina gave me her number before we left the art museum. I'm going to tell her and Ashley to meet us there. We're going to need all the help we can get," she says.

I agree with her there. I need to make sure the Agent doesn't hurt her and having Gina and Ashley as backup will be helpful, especially with Ashley's archery skills.

"Deal. Make sure Ashley brings her bow and arrows."

The door to my dressing room opens. Lea keeps distracting me. I should've suggested we run far away before figuring out our next step.

"We have to go, now! Run up those steps and I'll be right behind you," I say, gazing over my shoulder. The Roman guy is coming at us full force.

She slips her phone back in her purse, nods, and takes the steps as quickly as she can, and I follow behind her. If the Roman centurion is going to throw a punch, I want it to be me that's on the receiving end of the blow.

CHAPTER THIRTY-ONE

LEA

I'm not sure how the Comcast Center didn't show up on the list I googled as a lair for an evil villain in Philadelphia, because Jake's right, it makes perfect sense for the Agent's home base to be set up here.

My face turns upwards as I try to take in the whole structure with its many windows. The building keeps going and going up into the sky.

"So how do we figure out what floor he's on?" I ask. "There are so many."

We'd finally lost the half-naked man after we left the convention center. Jake kept suggesting turning down different alleyways until we almost literally ran into a taxi, which we hopped in and it took us straight here.

Jake's already walking full speed ahead. "I have an idea that might work, it's just a little risky. Follow my lead," Jake says, heading through a rotating door.

"Wait, what's the plan?" I call after him.

He turns back around and his eyes sparkle. "You'll see."

Irritation prickles against my brain. *Great, so now he doesn't trust me again to tell me what the plan is?*

I burst in after him through the front entrance and gasp. There are TV screens plastered all over the walls of the entrance. Each screen has a different clip playing. A TV that really catches my attention is the one on the left-hand corner playing a scene from one of The Amazing Boy films. It's at a part where he's saving some hot girl from a burning building.

We sure have come to the right spot.

I approach Jake, who's casually leaning on the security counter. As casually as one can wearing a superhero outfit.

"Sure, you're The Amazing Boy. Do you know how many times just today we've had people claiming they're him?" the security guard grunts.

Jake pulls out the lanyard with his ID. "Did any of the other guys have this?"

The security guard grabs the lanyard out of his hand and studies it. "I'll admit, this does look legit, but I have to call up to verify."

Jake shrugs, taking back his ID. "That's fine."

I try not to yell out, "No, don't do that," but I need to trust Jake, even if he's frozen me out of his new plan.

The security guard takes a phone off its hook and presses a few buttons. As he does this, Jake leans over the counter and grabs the phone out of the man's hand.

"Hey!" the security guard yells. "What did you do that for?"

Jake throws the phone on the counter. "Sorry, man. Changed my mind. You're right. I'm not the real The Amazing Boy, I don't want to bother anyone. We'll get out of your building now."

Before the security guard can say anything, Jake takes my hand and drags me outside.

"What was that?" I ask.

"Trying to see what floor we need to focus on. Floor number twenty-five is our key. Let's go find a side entrance."

"Won't your Agent now know you're here?" I ask.

Jake shrugs. "He probably already does. I'm sure there are cameras all over. At least now we have a lead on which floor to go to instead of blindly guessing."

I point to a sign nearby that says *The Concourse at the Comcast Center has it all. Dinner, drinks, shopping, and fun.* "What if we act like we're going to eat at one of these places and then try and find some emergency stairs?"

Jake ponders my idea then nods. "I like it."

"If you would've told me your plan from the beginning, we could've talked this out already and been on our way," I huff.

Jake looks sheepish. "Sorry, I wasn't even sure if my plan would work so I didn't want to tell you if it didn't."

I put my hands on my hips. "If we're going to be spending more time together, we have to tell each other things."

Jake wraps his arm around me, and I lean my head onto his shoulder. "I know. I'm just not used to this dynamic. I'm used to being a lone wolf."

"It's us against your Agent now, so that line of thinking needs to shift," I say gently.

He runs his hand through his hair. "It might take me a little to get used to it, but I'll get there, eventually."

I lift my head off his shoulder and smile. "Now let's go find your evil agent."

CHAPTER THIRTY-TWO

JAKE

Yes, I need to let Lea in, but it's hard when a part of my brain is still telling me not to get close. That she'll be ripped away from me like everyone else I've ever cared about. If that happens, it will hurt me about as much as me realizing the Agent betrayed me. *He made my own mother forget I exist.*

I close my eyes to curb the swell of sadness. It's always been my way of trying to overcome the pain about my mom, but sometimes it works better than others. Today isn't one of those days.

I feel a touch on my arm and my eyes snap open.

"Hey, what's wrong?" Lea asks, her concerned blue eyes staring intensely at me.

I had told her I'd be honest with her, so I better not break that promise.

"I miss my mom. I always tell myself that it's better this way, but the pain never gets better, only worse."

Lea squeezes my arm. "Maybe she's the first person you can see after we bring down your Agent."

I blink back the tears. "But she won't even know who I am," my voice catches.

"There has to be a way to reverse the memory spell," Lea suggests.

That's a good point. I always believed what the Agent told me, that my mom not remembering me is the best move for everyone. But I never asked about a reversal, not like he would tell me. But it could be worth a shot.

I gaze at Lea. How did I go this long without her? *Maybe, if we do defeat the Agent, there is a way to keep Lea in my life and also make my mom remember me.*

"You're right. There has to be something he can do."

For the first time in years, there's a new feeling in my chest. *Is it hope?*

"When we were inside, I saw steps leading downstairs. That might be where the food is," Lea suggests.

"Good thinking, we just have to make sure the front desk attendant I was talking to doesn't see us."

Lea's typing away on her phone. She looks up and says, "I'm letting Gina know our plan. She said earlier they are heading our way, and before you ask, the bow and arrows are also coming along."

This whole working with other people thing is new for me but it does make me feel better knowing backup is coming in case something goes drastically wrong. "Let's do this."

I search for a front desk attendant. His head is down, watching the phone. I spot the steps leading downstairs that Lea had mentioned. There are a few other people emerging from the steps, so it must be open to the public.

"Let's go while he's distracted." I try to walk as casually as I can in a fancy business building wearing my ridiculous superhero suit. This is when I wish I was back in my civilian clothes, instead of my bright red and yellow spandex costume. I'm impossible to miss, especially since there is an

Amazing Boy movie playing on the largest TV I've ever seen above our heads.

We reach the steps and hurry down them. A few teens coming up the other way whisper to each other and point at me.

"Come on, we need to find the emergency steps as soon as we can," I call back to Lea.

There are more people milling around the food court than I expected on a late Saturday afternoon in a building that is probably primarily used for offices. It has the typical fast food places you'd expect like Burger King, Chipotle, some cheesesteak place, and a chain pizza place that's only ever available in a food court or rest stop. A sit down, classy Italian restaurant is situated in the corner. The smell of fries, meat, cheese, and grease reaches my nose. I wouldn't doubt it if the people upstairs could hear the gurgling sound my stomach is making. Even though it wasn't that long ago since we had those cheesesteaks, my mouth is watering.

"Do you need to eat something?" Lea asks, looking down at my grumbling stomach.

"There's no time. How about after this is all over, I take you out to a nice dinner, anywhere you want?"

Lea gives me the breathtaking smile I'm already falling for. When she smiles, her whole face brightens. I want that smile to never leave her face.

"Like a real date?" she breathes.

"Absolutely like a real date," I say. I'd have to see if we could find some secluded dark place so no one would recognize me. That has to be doable in Philly.

I didn't think it was possible, but her grin grows a little wider. "I'd love that. If that's the case, let's hurry and get this over with so we can have more time together."

I'm hung up on the *so we can have more time together*. It's as if she already knows we have a limited life span. *Do we?* I stare over at Lea and take in her blonde hair and blue eyes.

I've got to at least try. What really do I have to lose? It's not like I have anything else at this point.

A crowd of chattering teens is forming nearby. Phones are pointed in my direction. I can only assume we're being live streamed on social media. It's not ideal if we don't want the Agent to know our exact location.

"We need to get away from all these people."

Lea turns to glare at the mob of teens. "This has to get old. I've only been around you for about seven hours now and I want to knock everyone's phone out of their hands."

"It's something they don't teach in high school, how to evade star struck fans. I've had to learn on the job, and the best way is to hide. Let's go." I grab her hand and we make a run for it.

———

LEA

WE'RE RUNNING out of the food court and Jake is trying to open doors. Each one he tries is locked. Near the end of the hallway he points. "There's an emergency exit. Let's pray we'll be able to access all the floors."

Jake opens the door handle, and it springs open to show stark white steps with fluorescent lighting. I close my eyes to try and get adjusted. When I reopen them, I check behind me. There is still a trail of teens following. I slam the door shut.

"We need to go up fast, or else your legions of fans will be here before we know it," I say.

Jake sighs. "I have to give it to them. They don't give up easily."

We begin running up the steps. Jake takes some of them two at a time. My legs aren't long enough for that. We reach another landing and a sign saying GROUND FLOOR is displayed on the door.

"That's clearly the main entrance. Let's go see what the next door says," Jake advises.

We sprint up the next set of steps and find the door with a large number two. Jake tries to open it, but it won't budge.

I point to the keycard reader next to it. "This floor has key card access only."

Jake frowns. "I'm sure all the rest do as well. My badge will probably get us in the twenty-fifth floor but that also means we won't have much time before the Agent knows exactly where we are."

I check my phone. "Gina and Ashley are here. I'll let them know where we're at."

Jake's frowning looking up at the endless steps. "Tell them they need to hurry up so we can all go in together."

I convey the urgency of the situation as much as possible in the text to them; lots of exclamation points and words in all caps. I hear a text ping and a cough behind me, and I jump.

I spin around seeing Ashley and Gina, grinning ear to ear.

"How is that possible? I just texted you," I say, my mouth dropping.

"We thought like you guys, and I guess we were right," Gina says. She motions up the steps. "Don't we have a bad guy to find?"

CHAPTER THIRTY-THREE

JAKE

I've been up many flights of steps before in my life. It's the part they don't ever show in the movies because it doesn't make for good entertainment, unless it's a chase scene. Villains, for some stupid reason, love to take over large buildings. Probably an ego thing and makes them feel important, towering over the whole city with everyone else having to cower below them. Either way, it always gives me a workout, but I'm used to it by now. The rest of the crew are not.

Yes, Gina and Ashley found us pretty quickly, despite the magnitude of the building. But with the speed they are taking the steps, I'm second guessing myself letting Lea have them come to help us.

By floor ten Ashley calls out, "Break time? Please?"

I sigh and turn around. "It's only fifteen more floors. You can do it," I say, trying to be as supportive as one can when the world is in danger.

Ashley is hunched over, grabbing her sides.

"I don't care. I need a break," she huffs.

Lea is also breathing heavily. "We don't have a superhero training routine like you," she says.

"Be glad for that," I mutter under my breath.

Gina's leaning against the railing. "At least I ditched my heels and picked up some cheap sneakers at a thrift store on the way over," she says, pointing down to her off-white sneakers. "I dressed this morning thinking I'd be running an event, not running for my life!"

"Are you guys ready yet?" I ask, looking at my watch. I guess you can call it a watch or maybe a smart watch, but not in the sense it tracks your exercise, and you can read your texts on it. No, this one helps me out in a pinch by not only providing me the time, but also by shooting out lasers. And that's just one of its many tricks, although I have to be careful where to aim it, I don't want to hurt anyone too badly.

I'm worried because there must be a larger plan here at play, especially now that One-Eyed Barnacle, Hallie, and Dave are locked up. The Agent's probably already plotting how to get them out and we need to stop him before that happens. At least he won't be able to get the armor from the Philadelphia Museum of Art or the death mask that he needs. That's two setbacks in his plan to world domination.

"Sorry, we're not all like you, in amazing shape. Get it, Amazing Boy?" Ashley says laughing at her own joke.

"Yea, you're full of great lines, hon." Gina turns to me. "I'm fine if we want to keep going."

I look at Lea and she nods, her breathing not as heavy as before. I take the last fifteen floors as fast as I can. I wait a couple minutes until everyone else shows up. Once they are all accounted for, I say, "While you're all catching your breath, let's go over a plan of action."

Gina rolls her eyes, but everyone keeps their mouth shut.

"As soon as I use my access card, the Agent will know I'm here. He might not know about everyone else, but we should be prepared just in case he does. Ashley, always have your bow and arrow ready. Gina, what can you do?"

She pulls a bright pink taser out of her bag. "I've got this."

Lea takes a step back. "Woah, why do you have that?"

"You're not from around here. Philadelphia has some really rough areas, including where I go to school. I have to protect myself," she says, shrugging.

"I don't have much in my purse out of the ordinary, except for maybe snacks, which I'm sure isn't useful." Lea bites her lip.

"If they were poisoned, they could be," I say, trying to make her feel helpful.

Gina pulls another bright pink object out of her bag. "Here, have this."

Lea holds the object, which looks like mace, away from her body. "How do I use it?"

Gina smiles gently at Lea's reaction. "Just make sure the part with the hole is pointed towards the bad guy, not at you, and then squeeze. They'll be in a world of pain."

I'm glad Gina has some devices that aren't difficult to use. I'm not about to offer Lea my dagger. I barely even use that thing, only in life threatening situations. "Thanks for having us covered, Gina. I'll go ahead of everyone with my glasses to see where I can sense heat. Then we can storm the Agent in his office, hopefully quick enough before he has a chance to hatch any sort of plan."

I look around at our rag tag team. Ashley with her pink bow in one hand and her quiver slung over her shoulder. Gina and her taser are at the ready. And Lea, sweet Lea, has the mace out in front of her with a fierce look on her face. We make quite the squad.

"Okay, it's time." I swipe the badge on the security pad next to the door. There's a single beep, and the red light turns green. I try the door and it opens effortlessly. I put my index finger to my lips and go through the door as quietly as possible. I slip on my glasses and scan the hallway. No heat sensors in the first couple of rooms but near the end I pick up four bodies.

I point down the hallway and hold up four fingers, hoping they understand my reference. I lead the way and whisper, "Let's storm the door now and catch them off guard. I'll get the Agent and the rest of you distract the minions."

Everyone nods. I pray this works and I am not leading my new friends into the worst decision of my life.

CHAPTER THIRTY-FOUR

JAKE

I burst through the door and immediately feel an impact on my chest. I try and keep myself upright, but topple over, my glasses bouncing off the floor beside me. I attempt to suck in my breath, but the wind is knocked out of me.

"I'm flattered. You needed to acquire three sidekicks when you don't have my help," the Agent says, swiveling around in a black, oversized chair. He looks more menacing than I remember, although it doesn't help that he's pulling a Steve Jobs by donning all black. He's even wearing a turtleneck even though it's the summer. His dark hair is slicked back and dark glasses are covering his eyes, very similar to my own.

Surveillance screens line the wall behind him and the entire room. Screens upon screens. I can vaguely make out the ground floor of the building on one of the screens.

I have been delusional to think we could surprise the Agent. He always has the upper hand, no matter how hard anyone tries.

"You don't know how good that felt," a feminine voice

says. I turn to my left and recoil. Hallie. *How did she get out of jail already?*

"Surprised to see me, my dear Amazing Boy? We're not as bad at being villains as you might think." She pushes the heel of her boot into my side, and I groan.

"That's for the arrows," she hisses. "Thankfully, the Master healed my wounds and I'm back to my normal, kickass self."

The Agent rips off his dark glasses, exposing his unforgiving brown eyes. "Who are you kidding Hallie, you're terrible at being a villain. I always have to patch you up or give you some spell to use. Your shapeshifting can only go so far," his booming voice says.

Hallie grunts. "Not everyone is blessed with the ability to do your spells. At least I can make myself look attractive."

"I can do that too but that doesn't matter to me, unlike you. You're always worried about how you look, and you don't even use your original form anymore. Such a waste of time and effort." The Agent rolls his eyes. "And don't even get me started on Dave and One-Eyed Barnacle. I'm constantly having to rescue your asses. Get the rest of these kids and keep an eye on them. I can't have any of them preventing the final plan," the Agent says, in a menacing voice.

I hear an arrow whiz ahead of me and a voice gives off a low wail.

The Agent sighs. "This is exactly what I'm talking about. Come on Dave, you worthless slug. It's just an arrow shot by some girl. Take them down!"

Dave's back too? That can also only mean that the fourth heat sensor I felt is my favorite pirate lookalike.

I turn my head to the left to get a glimpse of the other figure in the room. The knight helmet confirms my fears. The whole gang's here, armor included, which means there's a ninety-nine percent chance that the Agent has all the pieces he's looking for, including the death mask.

"How did this happen?" Lea asks, her voice trembling.

"Oh, you dear girl. You have so much to learn. How did you ever think you could be a superhero?" The Agent gives her a cold stare. "I'm surprised Jake didn't figure out that something was wrong. I'm the one that taught him you can't always trust appearances."

Gina and Lea exchange glances. *Was he always this patronizing?*

"What's going on? We handed all these people over to the police! I know because I was there both times," Gina exclaims.

The left side of the Agent's mouth turns up, making him look even more like an evil villain. "They might have looked like the police, but police uniforms are easy to replicate."

Gina gasps. "They acted like the police. There is no way they work for you," she says, shaking her head.

"It's okay, Gina. He fooled us all. I didn't think he would stoop that low and mimic law enforcement. What happened to you?" I ask, still struggling to get away from Hallie's boot. The Agent knows me so well and must have told her that my superstrength is all in my arms, which are currently trapped under my body.

The Agent made a gesture to Hallie, and she pulls her foot off my chest.

I jump up and rise to meet the Agent's gaze. He's taller and has about fifty pounds on me, but I can take him, at least I hope so.

He made me who I am today but when it comes down to it, I'm a movie star with no friends or family. People would kill for what I have but I'm here to tell you, it's freaking lonely. I'd give anything to hug my mom or be able to go on a date with Lea without any superhero madness overshadowing me. Not having to constantly worry that someone's going to pop out of the shadows and kidnap her.

Who am I kidding? I'm entrenched too deep to have a real life. But at least I can take the Agent down from his evil plan, whatever it may be.

"I'm impressed. I didn't know you had this in you," I say, making myself as tall as I possibly can.

The Agent narrows his eyes. "Flattery won't help you or your friends. It's not too late Jake. I'm about to become the most sought-after wizard on Earth after these artifacts mold to become one."

"Oh, so that's what you are. We thought you were a magician," I say.

He grimaces. "Magicians are child's play. I'm the real deal."

"So, you're like Doctor Strange?" Lea pipes up.

The Agent's eyes reduce to slits as he shoots her a death glare. "Dr. Strange is supposed to be a sorcerer, not a wizard but he's not actually real like me. It's a travesty the Marvel writers have him make fun of wizards in his first movie. Gives me a bad rap."

"What will the artifacts do?" I ask. I'm genuinely curious, but also trying to kill some time. Getting the Agent to talk always helps sidetrack him. I used to do that when I wanted something from him. It's just bigger stakes now, like saving the world but you know, no pressure or anything.

The Agent walks towards a table covered by a black velvet sheet. He's always one for theatrics. He takes his right hand and grabs the sheet to uncover a table filled with items that look extremely valuable. I do a quick scan and see a musket, the fedora, the death mask, a sword, and then some other things that I've never seen before, including a large key. There are also a few other items that look strangely like valuable pieces that appeared in my other movies. *But how can that be, I thought we returned them all?*

"One-Eyed Barnacle, bring me the armor. It's about time we show everyone what we will really be able to do."

The Agent turns to me. "When these sought-after relics are bonded together, whoever possesses the weapon it becomes is rumored to become the most illustrious supervillain of all time."

I scratch my head. "How did you know these were the artifacts? They make no sense. I mean the death mask of a dead composer? Will Schubert's music bore people to death?"

The Agent grits his teeth. "I'll have you know, classical composers are highly revered in the wizarding world."

"Guess Marvel forgot to add that detail in during the Dr. Strange origin movie," I quip back.

The Agent gives a low growl. "I told you, he's not a wizard!"

Two can play this game. I know how much the Agent hates Marvel. That's how I became brainwashed about Marvel's lameness. Now that I think about it, some of their movies are pretty sweet. Even more so than mine. When there's a guy that is an actual God that has biceps bigger than my entire head, how can you not be impressed?

"Don't make me list out all of the reasons why Marvel is the bane of my existence," the Agent snarls.

"Feel free to tell us, I have no other pressing business," I say, leaning back on my heels.

The Agent steps closer to me. "Enough of this talk. You're stronger than I thought but distracting me isn't going to make me forget my mission."

Even the way his face looks cold and evil makes me angry. *How could he turn on me?*

"Why did you have me become a superhero if in reality you're a villain? I don't get it," I say. "Wouldn't it always end with me fighting you?"

"Don't they always say hide in plain sight? No one would suspect a hero's agent. It's also a great way to earn some money. I've got to be able to pay my staff," he says, pointing to his minions.

"What about The Amazing Boy staff?" I ask.

The Agent shrugs. "They're not a part of my plan. I couldn't tell everyone, especially since they're so loyal to you. They *accidentally* all got stuck at the convention center."

I bet I'll hear from them soon since everyone there is unfrozen. They are probably frantic that I'm missing.

"You really were on your own except for that one mission card of mine, to throw you off my scent, until you found this group of miscreants. Couldn't you at least find people that have some skills?" the Agent asks, motioning to my squad behind me.

"You're one to talk. Look at your ridiculous team." I turn back to my crew. They still have their weapons ready. "They may be new at this, but I'd take them any day over someone who betrays me," I sneer.

The Agent's lip curls. "Sorry kid. No hard feelings but I've had to make a living." He folds his arms and walks over to the table of loot. "Enough of this talk. It's time to start the bonding process. Bring me the last piece One-Eyed!"

One-Eyed Barnacle grunts as he waddles over to the table of artifacts, still wearing the armor. *Guess he's learned how to walk with it on, or the Agent has him under some kind of spell.*

A feminine voice above us announces, "All of the artifacts are complete."

"Woah, who's that?" Gina asks, her head swiveling around.

"Is that like how Iron Man has Jarvis?" Lea says, looking up at the ceiling.

Oh, he's really not going to like that.

"My Jarvis is way more intelligent than Iron Man's," the Agent snaps.

"Do you have a name for it?" Ashley asks.

The Agent glares. "None of your business."

"He probably just named her computer, or something lame like that. It would be his MO. Hi computer, can you shut off?" I ask.

The voice responds, "Voice not detected."

"So, I was right. An unoriginal name made by an unoriginal villain," I taunt him.

The Agent says, "But who has the upper hand? Computer, prepare the bonding process."

"Wait, you're not going to do the process with One-Eyed Barnacle wearing the costume, are you?" Hallie asks, her eyebrows furrowed.

The Agent shrugs. "Spoils of war, am I right?"

One-Eyed Barnacle grunts. "What? This wasn't part of the plan!" He takes a large step to leave the area and a red laser light surrounds the artifacts, him included. He screams as he runs into the laser and falls onto the floor, armor clattering, very still.

Hallie runs over to the laser light and looks down at him. "One-Eyed, are you okay?"

He's silent and doesn't move.

The Agent waves his hand. "Oh, he'll be fine. And if not, I can conjure some spell to make him okay."

The robotic voice calls out, "Bonding process beginning."

No. I can't let this happen.

I frantically glance around. I nod at Lea, Gina, and Ashley. I hope that they understand I'm about to go all Amazing Boy on this joint.

"Bonding process prepared. Push the red button after the countdown," the voice says.

The Agent's hand hovers over a ridiculously large red button at his control station. *Why is it always a red button?*

I make a break for it, and before Hallie can react, I pick up the first item I can reach on the table, the musket. I know it's pretty stupid going right into the circle of death, especially after seeing One-Eyed Barnacle get knocked out by the laser, but I'll take my chances. Fire and lasers haven't stopped me before.

I quickly pull my hand back and inspect myself. Nothing seems out of place. I don't feel different. The musket is easy to carry so it's probably not even loaded, but at least I have the items separated.

The Agent growls. "Computer, I thought you said this laser would stop anyone."

"Bonding process has been interrupted. I have miscalculated The Amazing Boy's characteristics," the robotic voice says.

The Agent steps closer to me. "Put that musket back right now."

"Sorry, no can do. Not part of my code of conduct. I'm supposed to help save the world, not destroy it."

The Agent sighs. "I don't want to have to do this, but you forced my hand. If you don't put that artifact back, I'll blow up the convention center."

Lea gasps. "No, you wouldn't do that. Jess and all of those other people are in there!"

And so is my entire Amazing Boy team.

"I don't want to, but your boyfriend here decided to make a stupid decision."

I didn't correct him that I'm not Lea's boyfriend, well not yet anyways. We have bigger problems to deal with at the moment.

"You wouldn't do that. You're not that evil," I say. *But I've miscalculated him before.*

The Agent's hand moves to display a screen. "Here's the convention center." He hovers his hand over a slightly smaller green button.

"All it takes is for me to push this and BOOM, they'll be gone."

"Shouldn't a blow-up button be red? And the bonding

process button be green? Green for go?" Ashley asks, raising her right eyebrow.

The Agent grits his teeth while taking a deep breath in. "I'm about done with every single one of you. Now I'm going to have to cut a lot of dialogue from this part for the movie."

"What, don't want to be made a fool of by this *group of miscreants*?" Gina says sarcastically.

Lea's eyes are frantic. I can't let her ex-girlfriend die, even if she's a super selfish person. Lea would never forgive me. But not giving him the musket could help prevent future deaths. *Another impossible choice.*

I crouch down and slowly begin sliding the musket towards him using my foot. While his eyes are trained to the floor, I motion to Ashley with a nod of my head and an arrow hits the Agent directly in the neck, but unfortunately for us, he's wearing a turtleneck. The arrow somehow bounces off his shirt and falls to the floor. While he's distracted, I fly at his arm and direct it towards the wall rather than the destruction button.

I will my superstrength to kick in. So far so good. I'm able to hold his arm in place, which really means my powers are working overtime because the Agent's biceps are only a tiny bit smaller than Thor's. *How had I never noticed that before?* I guess there weren't really many instances I've been this up close and personal with him.

"Get off me, Jonah," the Agent snarls.

I falter, which causes me to lighten my grip. He pushes my arms off him and lunges for the musket behind me. *The Agent knew saying my real name would catch me off guard.*

I push him out of the way into his command desk. I take a quick peek at everyone in the rest of the room and see Lea's trying to fend off Dave. Lea catches my gaze and says, "Jonah?"

Dave takes that moment to push Lea to the ground. She screams and squirts the mace into his eyes. He howls and rolls off her, clawing his face. Hallie and Ashley are in a wrestling match on the floor, Ashley's arrows flung past her reach. One-Eyed Barnacle is circling Gina and her pink taser is out in front of her. He must have come to and been able to escape after the bonding process stopped.

"You come near me, you creep, and I'll press this somewhere that's really going to hurt," she threatens, shaking the taser in front of her.

He laughs. "Good luck trying to find an open spot through this armor."

This is madness. None of them are trained fighters. They aren't going to last long against the person they are matched up with. I need this to stop, for their sake and humanity's.

I pounce on top of the musket and the Agent grabs my feet to drag me off it.

"Jonah, you don't want to do this. You're making me really angry," he threatens.

I kick my feet as hard as I can and hear a grunt and a thud. I whip around and the Agent is holding his chin. *Got him.*

"That's for calling me Jonah," I say.

"You ungrateful fool! How can you not be on my side for all of this? All that I've ever done for you? I made you a superstar! People would kill to be you."

I shake my head. "I never asked for any of this. You ruined my life. I don't even know who I am anymore." I try pushing an SOS button on my watch but nothing happens. Usually a red flashing light appears to show it's working. *He must have somehow blocked me from using it.*

The Agent's still rubbing his chin. "You were a nobody before I found you. An extra on a TV show no one's ever heard of. Now you're worth watching. But since you don't want to cooperate, I'll make you do as I say. This is going to end my way."

He closes his eyes and begins muttering words under his breath.

I might have been a nobody, and still sometimes feel that way, but it's up to me to save the world against this monster. He isn't going to control me, or anyone else, anymore.

I slam my body against his, and as he falls over, he smacks his head against the tiled floor. I lean down and push against his chest as hard as I can. He moans and says, "You're going to regret that. What are the rest of you idiots doing? Why is The Amazing Boy still fighting me?"

"We're a little busy, boss!" Hallie yells. Ashley somehow retrieved her arrows and has them pointed directly at Hallie, whose hands are high in the air.

"Computer, call 911," I yell.

"Voice not detected," the computer states.

It was worth a shot.

The Agent keeps trying to get up and failing miserably. I need to figure out a way to detain all of them until the authorities, the real authorities this time, can take them away.

Lea must have used the mace on Dave again because he's on the floor rolling around crying. She's got her phone out and raises it to her ear.

"Stop!" The Agent screams. "I didn't want to do this, but you leave me no choice."

Lea freezes. "What do you mean?"

"Computer, make the girl appear."

A square in the tiled floor opens and a chair rises out of the ground. A girl that looks slightly familiar appears. Her dark curly hair is sticking up all over the place and her whole body is tied to the chair. She's trying to say something, but it's muffled since there's tape over her mouth.

"Jess!" Lea screams and runs to her. A laser field appears, and Lea stops herself at the last minute, an inch from the laser.

I focus my gaze on Jess. Her eyes are darting around the room, terrified. I'm not the biggest fan of this girl but no one deserves this kind of treatment.

"What are you doing?" I ask the Agent. "You kidnap people now?" I press down on his chest even more. He wheezes and says, "Only when things don't go my way. If you don't put the musket back, I'll have the computer drop her a couple of floors."

That doesn't sound too bad, right?

"Without the chair."

Okay, yeah this isn't good.

CHAPTER THIRTY-FIVE

LEA

Pure terror strikes my heart seeing Jess, wide-eyed, tied to a chair. I want to do all in my power to help her. Yes, she literally screwed me over, but I still care about her and don't want her to fall twenty-five floors to her death. The Agent might be lying but I don't want to take that chance.

"Jake, we have to help her," I plead.

His eyes are sad. "I know," he says. Jake blinks a couple of times, probably going through all the options in his head. Jake might be able to get through the laser to untie her but that would leave the Agent free to grab the musket and/or blow up the convention center. The Agent also seems to be the only one that can talk to the computer, so that can also pose a problem.

I wish Jake, or should I say Jonah, and I were on the level of being able to read each other's thoughts. I want to be able to talk this through with him and get his take on what to do next. Instead, I'm stuck here lost in my own mind.

"If I put the musket back, will you release her from the chair?" Jake asks, peering down at the Agent.

"Yes, you have my word."

Jake looks back at me and gives the smallest nod, one that you can only see if you were carefully assessing him. He's got a plan. I don't know what it is but it's time for me to go with the flow. I really hope the Agent isn't lying when he says he'll free Jess.

Jake takes his weight off the Agent and drops the musket back on the pile of artifacts. One-Eyed Barnacle reluctantly slogs over to the circle and the laser appears.

"Bonding process re-configuring," the computer announces.

The Agent scrambles off the floor and his hand once again hovers over the red button.

"What about Jess?" I say.

He rolls his eyes and says, "Right, your lover. Do you see how much she cares about this girl, Jonah? How do you think there's room for you in her life?"

Jake flinches. I'm not sure if it's from hearing the name Jonah or that Jess is my lover, which she's not.

"I want whatever makes Lea happy," he says.

The Agent laughs. "You say that now. But soon you'll never even remember her anyways and she'll be back with her precious girlfriend. Computer, release the girl."

The chair and laser disappear into thin air and Jess crumbles to the ground, all the rope jumbled on the floor next to her and her mouth free to talk. I rush over and wrap my arms around her.

"Are you okay?" I ask, smoothing down her haphazard hair. I know she'd be really upset if she saw her disheveled state. She's always concerned about her looks.

"I think so. What's going on?" she asks, her brown eyes wide.

"It's a long story but let's get you off to the side of the room." I help her up and she curls her arm around my shoulders. Streaks of mascara are dried on her cheek. I get her over to the wall and help her sit down.

"Where's Olive?" I ask, rubbing her back.

Jess sniffles. "I don't know. I haven't seen Olive since they left the convention center. Probably already at the airport. I was still in the convention center when that jerk over there found me. He said you were in trouble and he needed my help. As soon as I stepped into a large SUV with him, I knew something was off. That's the last thing I remember because then I woke up here, tied to that chair."

I keep rubbing her back. "Okay, at least Olive is probably okay and you're safe now."

Jess's tear-filled eyes bore into me.

"I didn't mean to hurt you. I just wasn't ready for us to become a thing. I was scared. I'm sorry."

My hand freezes on her back.

"But you weren't scared with Olive," I spit.

"Lea, you're my best friend. Olive's my friend too, but not like you. I didn't want to lose that if we dated."

"But you lost me anyway when you picked them," I point out.

Jess hangs her head. "I didn't expect you to find out that way. I was trying to figure out how to tell you and not lose your friendship at the same time. But now you hate me."

I shake my head. "I don't hate you, I'm just not happy how everything went down. You made me question myself. I kept thinking why Olive and not me."

Jess's face crumbles. "I'm so sorry, Lea. I didn't mean to do that. I cared about you too much to let it ruin us."

"Why didn't you just tell me how you were feeling? Instead of just being love struck with Olive? I'm the third wheel and it sucks."

"After you found me with Olive, you froze me out. I couldn't talk to you even if I wanted to. This trip's the first time we've hung out in ages," Jess explains.

"But Olive's here too, well at least they were. And you're all over them."

Jess bites her lip. "I know, I've been overcompensating. Olive's great, but honestly, I'm starting to wonder if I'm in love with you. It's just not the same. Not having you in my life is the worst."

It's what I've wanted to hear for ages now but that was before today. Before I knew I could live without Jess and before I knew I could fight off villains. And before I met Jake.

"Jess, I don't think I'll ever be able to fully trust you again and I've moved on, just like I thought you did. But maybe someday we can work up to becoming friends again," I say, removing my hand from her back.

Jess sighs. "I know. I royally screwed us up. I can even tell you don't need me anymore." She leans closer to me. "What is going on with you and The Amazing Boy? Even those couple of seconds I saw you guys together, it seemed like you care about each other."

I give a small smile. "I never thought I'd find a guy like him."

Jess shrugs. "Life's weird. You never know who you're going to fall for. I just wish I didn't figure it out too late." Jess motions over to Jake. "Speaking of The Amazing Boy, I think he probably still needs some help."

Jake's got the Agent pinned against a wall. *When did that happen?*

"Stay here. Take my mace and spray anyone that comes after you."

Jess opens her hands and accepts it.

"But what will you use?" she asks.

I know exactly what I'm going to do.

CHAPTER THIRTY-SIX

JAKE

Last I see, Lea's crouched against the far side wall consoling Jess. It's hard not to feel jealous. How can I compete with someone that's been her best friend forever? And someone that offers more stability.

But I'll have to worry about that later. The more distracted I am, the more my superstrength doesn't work. My whole body is pressed against the Agent. I can feel the Agent struggling under my weight and I know I won't be able to hold him forever. I need a new plan, fast.

"Hey stupid," Lea says, and I see a black shoe hit the Agent square in his face.

"Ow!" he groans.

It's the opening I need to go grab the musket again. Lea throws her other shoe, and it lands right on the Agent's mouth. Perfect timing, because by the time I'm back to the Agent with the musket, he still hasn't moved and is rubbing his lips. I press my arms against him again. Lea's scrambling to put her shoes back on her bare feet.

"We can't do this all day; you're going to inevitably get

tired. Although it's putting on a good show for the audience," he whispers so only I can hear.

For the first time since we burst into this room, fear seizes me. I know I'm always being filmed because they use bits and pieces of me being The Amazing Boy for the movies, but this time something feels really different. Everything just feels a little too easy. *Is this a set-up?* I stare, wide-eyed into the Agent's face. He winks at me and says, "See you on the other side."

What does that mean?

I'm trying to keep him in place but it's not helping anymore. It's like he's gaining his own superstrength at rapid speed.

"Bonding process de-configured," the computer announces.

"Lea, what can you get me? I need something to subdue him," I say, my voice a higher pitch than I knew was possible.

"Too bad we had some good times together, Jonah, but I'm going to have to put a stop to all of this so it fits the end of the movie. Nice working with you," the Agent says quietly.

Wait, what?

His eyes are closed as he mumbles a few incoherent words under his breath. Before I can stop him, his eyes shoot open. They're cold and hard, offering no forgiveness.

"What are you going to do?" I ask, afraid to hear the answer.

"Ending this storyline, once and for all," he says, pushing me off of him. I land on the floor with a thud.

When my superstrength is at its fullest, like now, no one's been able to defeat me. *What just happened? And why didn't he do that sooner?*

I turn my head towards Lea, and she's frozen in place. For a second I thought the Agent put a spell on her but then her eyes blink. No, she's just frozen in fear.

The Agent reaches down, picks up the musket, and

gingerly places it back in the circle. As he backs away the computer announces, "Bonding process re-configured."

No! He can't do this!

I try to put my hands behind me to help me spring back on my feet, but I can't move a single inch. I'm stuck on the floor.

"What did you do to me?"

The Agent's eyes gleam. "Now you know what it's like to be incapacitated, The Amazing Boy. This time is different, you're not going to win. It's time for you to say goodbye."

Goodbye? What is he going to do?

Lea still looks frozen. "Jake, what's happening? I can't move."

Oh no, she really is having the same issue as me.

"I don't know, but we'll figure it out, I promise." *At least I hope we will.*

Before I know it, the Agent's hand is hovering over the red button.

"Now's the moment we've all been waiting for. The day where I single handedly defeat The Amazing Boy and become the most revered supervillain of all time," he says in a menacing voice.

"Hey, boss. Don't forget about us, we helped too," One-Eyed Barnacle says from the artifact table. "This isn't going to hurt, is it?"

If looks really can kill, One-Eyed Barnacle would have died a horrible death.

"Shut up, you're ruining this scene!" the Agent hisses.

"But we never get any credit!" Hallie exclaims.

"SILENCE!" the Agent screams, waving his hand. It works, nothing else can be heard except the hum of the laser around the goods.

"The world will soon know me as the villain who took down The Amazing Boy, the true hero. I'll become The Agent of Truth!"

What a stupid name. He's the exact opposite of the truth. Everything he's ever told me is a lie. I attempt to say what I'm thinking but when I try, nothing comes out. He really did make all of us lose our voices. *How strong is he?*

"Computer, please do the honors with the countdown."

"Bonding process will be completed in three … two … one, please push the button."

The Agent makes a show out of hovering his hand over the button, giving us a horrifying smile and then his entire palm slams down.

I see him whisper and shimmery smoke immediately fills the room. I hear coughing behind me. At least I'm not affected by smoke, but I feel bad for everyone else.

All the artifacts, including One-Eyed Barnacle, are still in the same spot, but illuminated by a spotlight in the ceiling. The Agent stands in front of the items, now wearing a ridiculous black cape and a golden staff in his hand. His dark sunglasses have somehow reappeared on his face, along with a golden crown on his head.

He raises the staff in front of him with both of his arms. "I am now The Agent of Truth, and no one can defeat me! The Amazing Boy's reign has ended, as did all my naysayers. It's time for a new dawn of time, when I'll be running the show. These artifacts that once possessed powers above anyone's imagination have now transferred all their energy to me! Let's see anyone stand in my way now!" He gives a wicked laugh.

Talk about an overdone plot line. What is he doing?

He brings down his arms and drops the staff to the floor with a clang. He claps his hands. "Okay everyone, that's a wrap! I think I got everything I need for this movie! It's bound to be a hit," he says, removing the cape. It flutters to the floor, next to his staff. A bunch of people I don't recognize wearing black burst through the door to the room. One pats down the Agent's face with a towel and another has a huge fan pointed to where the smoke is still dense.

"Sorry about that, I can never seem to conjure up the right amount of smoke for scenes like this. I know it's a bit over-powering for most humans," the Agent says, removing his dark glasses and wiping them on his shirt.

I open my mouth and words can finally come out.

"What the hell?"

The Agent waves off the person toweling his face and he looms over me, a shadow overcasting his face.

"That's a wrap on The Amazing Boy franchise. I'm no longer in need of your service. You did your job, for the most part. But your contract has ended."

There's finally feeling coming back to my body. I straighten up and try to make myself as tall as possible, which is hard since the Agent has to be over six five.

"What's going on? What about the bonding process? Aren't you some supervillain now, you seem the same to me." *Same filthy liar.*

The Agent gives a hearty laugh. "You are so gullible. That's why it's been incredibly easy to fool you into *saving the world*. There isn't any supervillain weapon or *bonding process*. It's all a part of the movie. I thought it would make it more realistic if you thought I was gone and you were on your own to battle the villains, and for the surprise twist, that your agent was actually the one pulling the strings since day one. And it can lead to an opening to my next series, starring me."

I stare up at him, barely blinking. "You're not actually bonding together some items to become a supervillain?"

The Agent shakes his head. "Jonah, Jonah, Jonah. Think closely about the words you just said. It's the perfect plot from a superhero movie, right? Who wouldn't want to watch it? Besides, I'm already a strong supervillain, being a wizard and all. I don't need a weapon to get people to do my bidding. I can do that stuff already. All those items combined are worth a chunk of change on the black market and I can use the money to help fund my new movie trilogy."

It's hard to understand everything going on right now. It's like my whole reality has been shaken. *This is how Lea must have felt when she found out superheroes are real.*

"You betrayed us!" Hallie screeches, her arms crossed and lips pursed.

At least I wasn't the only one he deceived.

The Agent frowns. "Come on, how did you guys actually believe that?"

"You always planned for this movie to be the last one in the franchise?" I ask, still trying to sort everything out.

"You got it, kid. I thought if you really believed you were on your own, the movie would be even better quality and boy was I right. This final showdown battle was great. I could never have scripted it."

I take a deep breath, getting a huge whiff of the smoke that hasn't yet cleared. "How will this lead to your spinoff series?" I ask.

"I won and have defeated The Amazing Boy. I'll infer that you died during the bonding process, the spoils of war, but not actually kill you. That's even too far for me."

"Gee, thanks. How nice of you." I scratch my head. "Who will be trying to defeat you in these new movies?"

The Agent smirks. "Oh no, this will all be focused on my pillaging, but I'll be a Robin Hood of sorts. Rob the rich and sell them to help the poor, or some shit like that."

I cross my arms. "So, you'll glorify stealing?"

The Agent rolls his eyes. "You're such a Boy Scout. It's just a movie, I have to keep people entertained."

"But in reality, you're just stealing precious objects to fund your extreme wizarding lifestyle and movie ventures."

The Agent snaps his fingers. "You've got it! About time you finally figured it out. Too bad I had to spell it out for you. I have some great footage from today and you and your naive friends played right into my trap. I just have to dub in some of the dialogue to take out the boring parts. Now all we need to do is return you back to where you came from and I'll be rid of you once and for all."

I start pacing the room. Sometimes walking helps me best think things through.

"But I don't want to return to where I came from. Besides, my mom doesn't even remember me. Unless you can tell me where she is and get her to know who I am," I say, trailing off, a spark of hope coming alive inside of me. I look at him expectantly.

The Agent rubs his chin. "I don't think you want to know."

I stamp my foot. "You can't do this one thing for me? I've made you millions of dollars and you can't tell me where she is and make her remember me?" I say, my voice rising. I didn't realize how angry I was until this moment.

"She was my whole family. My only family. And I lost her. I thought you were my new family, and it turns out you're just some asshole using me for money."

I'm seething with anger and start massaging my temples. *How dare he make me feel like an idiot. That everything that we accomplished today was for nothing except to film this movie.*

"I was your family, kid. You didn't need her; she was collateral damage. She would've gotten in your way," he says.

I run to push him but he mumbles a word and I'm frozen again. I scream, "Stop it! Don't you dare talk about my mother that way. She's not collateral damage!"

At least I can still talk this time.

"Are we remembering the same person? She was all about you getting famous, no matter what. She would've wanted this for you."

"You don't know that because she doesn't even know who I am. Tell me how to find her!" I scream.

The Agent steps closer to me. "About time you grow some balls. You never actually wanted to hurt anyone or destroy valuable property, that's why your superstrength didn't always work. You blamed it on your powers being finicky, but I know that's not true. You just didn't have it in you to hurt anyone or anything and made us do the heavy lifting."

How can that be the case? I've always told myself there's something wrong with me, that my superstrength was something that couldn't be relied on, but was that really it? Here with the Agent, I had no issues at all.

"Why didn't you tell me?"

"I didn't figure it out until today, when your strength has been on point almost the entire time. It finally all adds up. You can be a killer if you want to. But only with motivation. That's what was lacking in all our adventures together. You had no personal reasons to do anything. But now you're helping your little girlfriend and hoping to see your mom, so you're more likely to not overthink your superstrength."

He's really starting to piss me off.

"Tell me how to make my mom remember me," I shout. I can feel tears running out of my eyes. I'm starting to not be able to see clearly. *How can everything I know just be a lie?*

"I don't know why he did that. I'm a pretty terrible person but I wouldn't make a mother forget her kid," Hallie says behind us. "Although it seems like all he does is lie to everyone. I thought I'd be some powerful villain right now, but instead I got duped into fighting off you kids all day."

Gina, Ashley, and Jess are all sitting on the floor with Hallie aiming the bow and arrow at them. *How did she get control of Ashley's gear?*

Lea's the only one that's free right now and she inches towards Hallie.

"Do you know how Jake's mom can remember him?" she asks.

Hallie's eyes dart to a set of office drawers. "You know how he has a pill to make people forget things? I bet there's some kind of pill that can reverse it," she suggests. "The

Master always has some kind of reversing spell or charm as a backup plan."

"What are you doing?" the Agent hisses. "Am I going to have to get you to stop speaking again?"

Hallie moves her body to point the arrow at him. "You lied to me. Why should I hide your secrets anymore?"

The Agent grasps his hands together. "Hallie, you don't want him to discover his mother's identity. You're not going to like what he finds."

"What are you saying?" I ask. Feeling is returning to my body, and I turn to Hallie as if I'm seeing her for the first time. She's also eyeing me up, her eyebrows knitted.

"Kid, you've asked for it. Meet your mother. Well, not in this form, but in one of her other forms, she's your mother. Hallie, here's your son." The Agent makes an introductory motion back and forth.

This time I can't help it. All feeling is gone from my body, not from a spell, but from shock. I drop to the cold, tiled floor.

"No. No no no no. I can't have a kid. There's no way," Hallie says, bringing the bow and arrow down to her side. They drop to the floor with a clatter. She grabs her head and keeps muttering words under her breath.

This is just great. Not only does my mother not remember me, but she's been working all this time for my arch nemesis. *Can it get any worse?*

"I should know, I'm the one that made you forget him," the Agent says.

"She doesn't look like my mom," I whisper. My brain is fuzzy and I'm feeling light-headed.

Lea runs over and says, "Jake, it's okay."

I bury my face in my hands and let Lea wrap herself around me.

CHAPTER THIRTY-SEVEN

I've been dreaming of seeing my mom for years, but this vile black-haired woman cannot be my mother. There's no way. In this form, she looks to be about ten years older than me and is about as nurturing as a snake; most snakes abandon their babies once they are born.

"Why would you keep this from me?" Hallie screams at the Agent.

The Agent still has a ridiculous grin on his face.

"When you remembered being his mom, you wanted to help Jake out as much as possible, and this was the perfect way, especially with your rare shapeshifting abilities. You're an asset, most of the time, when you aren't being a pain in my ass."

How did I not know my own mother was a shapeshifter? That only makes me have more questions.

I unwrap myself from Lea's arms and stand between Hallie and the Agent. Her gray eyes are filled with anger.

"Who's my dad?" I call back to the Agent, my eyes never leaving Hallie's. "And please don't say it's you." That would be the icing on the cake, a trope that is way overdone. *Star Wars anyone?*

Hallie chokes. "It better not be. I'd really start to wonder about my sanity if I slept with *him*."

"No, she refused to tell me before she lost her memories. She wanted to protect your dad," the Agent scoffs.

Protect him. Why did she want to protect him?

"Couldn't you have used one of your mind spells to make her tell you?"

"I didn't care that much. If he was out of the picture, then it didn't matter who sired you, just as long as he didn't come back and try to take any of my, I mean our, money."

The whole explanation seems suspicious but I'm not sure what else to ask about my dad if no one in the room knows a single thing about him.

I scrutinize Hallie. "Why am I not a shapeshifter like you?" I ask, squinting my eyes.

We're now circling each other, still unsure if the other one is going to attack.

Hallie scoffs. "Hell if I know. Maybe you inherited your abilities from your unknown father."

I bet that's why Hallie, before her memory was erased, didn't reveal the name of my dad. I bet he has superhero abilities like me. Maybe he's also trying to save the world.

CHAPTER THIRTY-EIGHT

Everyone seems to have forgotten that I exist. That's okay, I'm used to it.

Hallie's attention is only on Jake and the Agent. I catch Jess's eye and motion my head towards the door. She raises her eyebrow and whispers to Ashley and Gina. They all give me an *are you sure* look and I nod. At this point, with the Agent's powers, they are all liabilities. I need to think like Jake and even though I have been around him less than twenty-four hours, I'm pretty sure he would tell me that there's no way we can defeat the Agent without a new plan, especially with all these extra people around. My friends, or *civilians*, need to get out of here before anyone gets hurt. I'll stay around and see if I'm needed, but my friends need to go.

The movie crew members are either watching the showdown between Jake, Hallie, and the Agent, or they are doing some random cleanup tasks around the room, like packing up the artifacts or removing hidden mics. I can't believe we were on a set of a movie and hadn't even realized it. My heart races thinking about what is going to happen to those priceless items. They really need to go back to their rightful owners but there's no way we can grab them. Jake's a superhero, but no match for a *wizard* who can shoot spells out at any second.

My friends are moving on their tiptoes to the door. I need to make myself useful while everyone else is distracted. *How can I help the most?*

Jake wants his mom, who somehow is Hallie, to remember him. I inch closer to the office drawers that Hallie talked about. There has to be something of use in them.

One-Eyed Barnacle and Dave are talking to the new crew members that came into the room. A few of them are attempting to tear the armor off One-Eyed Barnacle, causing a lot of noise. *Perfect distraction.* I start to back up, keeping my eyes trained on everyone in the room. I open one of the drawers as quietly as I can and stuff as many pill bottles as possible that will fit into my purse.

I'm not going to waste my time looking to see what the pills are. And if I help at least one person not get forced to take a memory pill in the process, so be it.

Gina makes it to the closed door but now's the tricky part. Most doors don't cooperate and make a noise at the very last moment, right when you think you got away with being sneaky. This time's no different. A loud creak sounds and everyone turns towards them.

"RUN!" I scream.

Gina pushes the door the whole way open and sprints through. Ashley and Jess run after her and at the last moment Jess slams the door shut.

"Go after them!" the Agent roars. "We haven't erased their memory!"

No one moves. "What are you waiting for? Hallie, One-Eyed, even Dave, go get them!"

Dave folds his arms. "Sorry, boss. I'm off the clock. And pretty tired of the way you treat me. You never told us this was all part of a movie. This isn't what I signed up for. I thought I'd be a supervillain by now with some cool powers, like being able to control someone's mind."

One-Eyed Barnacle grunts in agreement. He's out of the armor and standing in the middle of the room in a white undershirt and blue boxers decorated with parrots. *There's the parrot we've been looking for.* His hair's sweatily matted down to his head. Even his eye patch is still missing. I quickly turn away. *That's a sight that will always be burned in my memory.* He just looks like some regular creepy middle-aged man in his underwear.

"You also promised me that I'd be able to have superpowers. All of that was a lie?" One-Eyed Barnacle whines.

The Agent doesn't answer him right away. Jake catches my eye and then looks at the door. Is he telling me to leave? Isn't that what I just did to Gina, Ashley, and Jess?

It hurts a little that he doesn't want my help. I don't want to leave him here, but he probably is making the same assessment I did. I'm a burden. What can I really do here to help him? I would probably create more issues, and he'll just be worried about me. I have to trust he knows what he's doing and that he'll be okay.

The Agent is saying something back to One-Eyed Barnacle, but I can't hear him. My ears are ringing too hard from fear. It's now or never.

I hug my purse close to my chest like a prized stuffed animal I won at an arcade and make a run for it. While I'm running you can hear the clinking of all the unknown pills. I swing open the door and dash down the hallway. I turn behind me and no one is following me, yet. *No turning back now.*

CHAPTER THIRTY-NINE

JAKE

I can tell by Lea's eyes she's not happy that I asked her to leave but I will never be able to forgive myself if something happens to her. I'm starting to care too much and there is really nothing she can do in this room. I'm even out of options myself. *How can I defeat the one person that taught me everything I know?*

The Agent stomps his foot. "Dammit! Now another one got away while you're arguing with me about semantics! Just get those girls and I'll make it all up to you. That last one sounds like she stole some of our pills from all that rattling in her purse."

"I'm not going anywhere wearing this," One-Eyed Barnacle states, not moving.

The Agent mumbles a couple of words and One-Eyed Barnacle is back in his pirate gear, complete with the eye patch.

"There, what about now?"

One-Eyed Barnacle looks down at himself. "That's better, but I need to know that you'll reward me."

The Agent showily rolls his eyes. "Is that all you care about? What's in it for you?"

I'm ready to burst at this moment. "You're one to talk. *I'm a selfish asshole* should be etched on your gravestone. Who are you to lecture any of us on what is right or wrong? Nothing you told any of us is true. What happened to you to make you this way?"

The Agent steps closer to me and pokes me in the chest. "Listen here, kid. You have no idea what I've been through to get to where I am today. I grew up like you, but my parents actually didn't want me because of my powers. They thought there was something wrong with me and that I was too hard to handle. I had to fend for myself at some run-down orphanage where I was always getting in trouble. When my mentor found me, I was at my lowest point, barely able to get up in the morning. He taught me how to hone my powers to manipulate people, not only through spells, but also by using normal tactics, like acting personable. He made me realize I could have the life of my dreams."

I shake my head. "What kind of way is that to live? I'm sorry you had a hard life, but that still doesn't mean you couldn't have chosen to be good and actually help people with your abilities, instead of manufacturing movies based on lies and stealing."

The Agent laughs. "All of humanity is out for themselves, whether you admit to it or not. I just want what I'm owed. And with this new franchise and selling off these items, I'll get to be the hero with more money than anyone has ever seen! If I have to lie to get it, too bad. This movie became way more interesting when the stakes were so high."

He turns toward his minions. "I'll give you a portion of all the money the movies make. Ten percent."

I shake my head. "Don't say yes. It's the worst deal I've ever heard. What about all the goods you are going to sell on the black market? Your staff doesn't get a cut of that even though they are the ones that stole the items for you?"

The Agent takes a deep breath and walks over to the office drawers.

"I've had enough of your talking. Those girls will be easy targets to find, so let's get you out of the way first."

He opens the top drawer and swears. "That little girl-friend of yours cleaned us out of *all* our pill bottles!"

Dave says, "Since you're so powerful, can you just say a spell and erase his memories that way?"

The Agent looks like he's going to strangle someone, with his face turning the same color as the *bonding* button that apparently was only for show and didn't do a single thing.

"No, you idiot. You still don't understand how my powers work. If I need to erase a lot of memories and want it to hold for a longer period, I need to make the spell into pill form, especially a strong dosage, if it needs to last forever. I had a "forget me" pill right here with Jonah's name on it and it's gone!"

Now's my chance. If the pill disappeared, he really might not let me leave or even live. I know too much.

"It's been nice learning how you betrayed me, but time to go find my friends. I'm sure I'll be seeing you later," I say, dashing out the door that Lea left open. I know the Agent will be hot on my heels but at least I'm faster than him. I'm more worried about the roadblocks he might summon to make me not leave the building.

I head for the stairs. As much as I don't feel like running down twenty-five flights of steps, it's better than getting stuck in the elevator without Lea to keep me company. The Agent probably controls every single section of this building and there'd be no way he would let me leave the elevator. Hopefully, he doesn't have the ability to lock the doors from afar.

I have to be careful not to take the steps too fast. I don't want to fall and break my neck. It would be the lamest way for a superhero to die.

"You'll never be able to hide from me, I have cameras all over the city," the Agent calls from the stairwell.

Is this true? I really have no idea, but I'll take my chances. I don't want to lose all my memories.

I hear multiple footsteps running behind me, so it isn't just the Agent following me. Hopefully, it's just One-Eyed Barnacle or Dave, the ones that probably can't even catch their own shadows, and not Hallie, aka my *mother*.

I rush past the sign that says Floor Two. One more set of steps. Had it only been less than an hour ago that Lea and I were at this door on our way to see the Agent? Before I found out Hallie is my mother?

Then I hear some words echoing in the stairwell that don't make sense. The Agent must be doing some kind of spell. I have to get to the door before he can finish.

I'm taking the steps two at a time and the black door in front of me says Ground Floor with a red exit sign above it. I try to rip it open and I stumble back. It won't even budge. Instead of wasting my time, and my superstrength, trying to open it, I have one more idea.

I take another flight of steps down to the basement where we originally started and instead of trying to pull the door open, I slam my whole body into it and spill out on the tiled floor. Either the Agent only had time to lock the ground floor door or my superstrength is really on point. I don't have much time to think about it because the thudding of footsteps behind me grows louder.

I pick myself off the floor and sprint through the food court, apologizing to a few people I almost take out. I dash up the steps that lead to the ground floor. I wish I wasn't wearing this ridiculous costume. I'm a marked man.

At the entryway, my eyes dart to the check-in desk. The man I originally spoke to is on the phone. He sees me and yells, "Stop!" Out of the corner of my eye I notice two imposing figures running my way.

There are still people scattered about the entrance, even though it is now evening. The last sliver of sunlight peers through the enormous floor to ceiling windows. Many of the individuals are staring up at one of the many TV screens. It's playing one of my favorite parts in the last Amazing Boy movie. The one where I saved the Hope Diamond. I'm guessing that also was fake since I'm pretty sure I saw the real Hope Diamond sitting upstairs in that pile of artifacts.

Revolving doors are up ahead, with people swirling around laughing. *Will I ever be like that?* I jump into the next open door and push as hard as I can. The door spins so fast it doesn't leave me any time to leap outside and now I'm back in the building. A man in the slot in front of me turns back at me, his eyes wide.

"Woah, you're him," he breathes.

"Sorry, just trying to get out of here really fast but guess that worked against me," I say, not even in my Amazing Boy persona. *No need for that anymore.* I don't push as hard this time and when there's an opening outside, I jump.

I have no clue where Lea, Gina, and Ashley might be, but I'm really hoping they are somewhere close by. *Why didn't I ever give them my cell phone number?*

That's when I feel a tug on my arm and look down. Lea's scared blue eyes stare back.

"Follow me," she says, dragging me down the street.

CHAPTER FORTY

LEA

I lead him to some weird named street called Cuthbert. It's not a busy area so we're less likely to run into anyone from the Comcast Center. We sprint to the end of the road where there's an Irish looking sign that reads, *The Irish Pub*.

Not a very original title, but at least you know what you're getting.

Never thought the first time I'd set foot in a bar I'd be wearing a cape and gold spandex pants with a hole in the knee, but there's a first for everything. I open the door and let Jake in first and I bring up the rear. The bar is very low lit but has sort of a homey feel. Guinness signs are plastered all over the wall and pictures of castles that I'm assuming are from Ireland.

"What are we doing here?" Jake asks. "I don't have my fake ID."

I can barely hear him over all the noise. "What do you mean, you have lots of fake IDs."

Jake gives me a sheepish look. "I mean, I don't have the fake ID where it says I'm twenty-one. The ridiculous number of fake IDs I own would make my wallet weigh a ton, so I left some of them at my condo in Hollywood."

I blink a couple of times. *He really did live a completely different life than me.* "Why wouldn't all of them make you twenty-one?"

Jake brushes his hair out of his eyes. "My boyish looks might make people suspicious. Usually when I'm entering a bar it's dark, and people can't get a good look at me, so I reserve that one for occasions like this one."

The podium where a waitstaff member would normally stand is empty and I motion towards it. "Guess we don't have to worry about getting carded right now anyways. Come on, Gina texted me that they are here in some back room."

We weave through the crowd of people surrounding a large, wooden bar. Guys are chugging a dark liquid left and right and I can't even hear myself think. There are even people in superhero costumes; it's the perfect place to hide.

We keep going deeper and deeper into the pub, passing a room with a lit fireplace and string musicians playing some Irish jig. *This place seems legit, as if I've been transported to Ireland.* I wish I could sit down, grab a drink, and enjoy the atmosphere with Jake, but sadly that's not an option. *Maybe if we get this all sorted out ASAP.*

We're winding around tons of different private rooms when I hear, "Psst, Lea. Over here!"

I peek into a low-lit room, and Gina sticks her head out of a wooden booth and waves. I approach the booth and wince; it's clearly meant for four people. I squish next to Ashley and Gina, which leaves a spot open next to Jess. Jake looks at the empty seat and sinks into it. I'm sure my ex is the last person he wants to sit next to, but I really don't feel like being beside her either.

"Who are you supposed to be?" he asks her, raising an eyebrow.

She folds her arms. "The best superhero ever, Brown Recluse."

Jake scoffs. "You know she's not a real superhero, right? You'd think the writers could have thought of something better than having her only powers be poisoning people with her long fingernails. What if she breaks them? Then what?"

Jess narrows her eyes. "It's at least a more original superpower, unlike superstrength."

This is awkward. I need to get them to stop talking before things turn ugly.

"We should probably come up with a plan, right?" I say pointedly at Jake.

Jake props his arms on the wooden table. "Agreed and fast. We don't have much time until the Agent finds us," he says.

"What are you thinking?" Gina asks, her arm tightly around Ashley's waist.

He looks over at me. "I'm not sure. The Agent is stronger than all of us combined. I really underestimated him. I'm just glad none of you were hurt."

I heave my orange purse onto the table and empty its contents. Pill containers fly every which way. Jake's arm flies out, stopping a few from falling onto the floor. While he's occupied, I grab the tampons that also escaped and stuff them back in my purse before he notices. Not that he'd care, I'm just not on that level with him yet.

"Do you think any of these will help?" I ask.

"Did you rob a CVS?" Gina asks, her eyes wide. "I thought you said stealing those scooters was only a one-time thing."

I stuff my wallet, granola bar, and strawberry lip gloss back into my purse. "We returned those scooters; we were only borrowing them. I took the pills from the Agent. They were just lying around in an office drawer."

Jake digs through the pill bottles like a rodent trying to

burrow. "Lea, these pills are priceless! How did you manage to steal all of them?"

I shrug. "I'm just lucky my purse is big. See, Jess, this orange purse you hate is good for something." I glare at her.

She shrinks down in her seat. "Sorry."

I try to hide my smile. I'm not used to her being the one apologizing. The tides are turning.

"This also means the Agent really is going to search high and low for us," Jake says, still rooting through the stash. He finds what he's searching for and holds up a pill container and points to the name *Jonah Williams* on the side. "Ah ha. The forget me pill that was originally meant for me. Maybe if we somehow give this to the Agent, he'll forget who he is and his purpose in life. It might be the only way to get him to stop shooting out spells."

Now I know his full name. One item checked off on the list of question marks about who Jake, or Jonah, really is.

Gina's eyebrows are scrunched. "How do you suggest we do that? It's not like we can just stuff it down his mouth."

Jake rubs his chin. "I might be able to. You saw me give a pill to One-Eyed Barnacle. We just have to make sure he doesn't put any spells on us before I can get it to disintegrate."

I look at Jake nervously. "One-Eyed Barnacle was incapacitated and has no superpowers. Your Agent is literally a wizard. It seems hard and risky."

"Unfortunately, that's what being a superhero is," he says looking intently at the pill container. "We should go somewhere more out in the open though, so none of these civilians get caught in the crossfire."

"Civilians? Why are you calling them civilians?" Jess asks, giving Jake a wild-eyed look.

He sighs and is probably holding back rolling his eyes. "That's what we call people that don't have powers and are not involved in the mission. People that can get injured and aren't able to defend themselves."

Jess buries her head in her hands. "What the heck is going on? How can you actually have powers and your agent, or whoever he is, be able to use spells on people?"

Jake glances down at his watch impatiently. I know we've been here too long, but I do feel for Jess. It is a lot to comprehend, especially since she was kidnapped on top of everything else.

I'm about to respond when Ashley says, "Hey, I know it's a lot to take in, I'm still trying to figure it out too, but right now we need to just get through it until Jake's agent isn't after us anymore."

Jess peeks through her fingers and nods. "Okay. I'll try."

A brunette waitress in pigtails wearing a short plaid green skirt and low-cut white T-shirt stops by the table and cocks her head. "There is no way you kids are twenty-one. You need to get up to make room for paying customers."

"Ashley and I will be next year," Gina says, under her breath.

The waitress doesn't have to tell me twice. I throw all the pill bottles back into my purse in record speed.

"We were just leaving." Jake steps out of the booth. The waitress's mouth drops.

"Wait, are you The Amazing Boy? Like the actual one? We've had a lot of costumed people today, but none that look as real as you," she comments, scratching her head.

"You can be the judge of that," he says, and keeps moving towards the entrance.

"Now you'll never know if you kicked a movie star out of your bar or not," Gina says sarcastically behind me.

"Wait, I'm sorry! Can I get a selfie? None of my friends will believe me!" the woman calls after us.

Jess catches up to me and pulls on my arm. "Is it always like this around him?"

I remove myself from her grasp. "Yep. At least this one didn't have time to ask him out on a date."

Once we're all outside the bar, my eyes dart around trying to see if I spot anything suspicious.

"So where to next?" Ashley says. She has her quiver slung over her shoulders.

"You rescued your bow and arrows," I exclaim.

She smiles. "Hallie dropped them on the floor during all the commotion. I couldn't leave my babies there with those evil people."

Jake looks at her appraisingly. "Good, we're going to need them for my plan. If I googled correctly, there's a park around here that will work perfectly for my idea. Let's get there first before the Agent and his henchmen come find us unprepared."

CHAPTER FORTY-ONE

JAKE

If this raw footage ever gets made into a movie, this one should be the final reckoning scene, not the lame one at the Comcast Center with the Agent winning. This will be the one scene that's the make it or break it and I've been through enough to know I don't want to fail. I want the Agent to be put into jail and all those priceless items to go back to where they belong. And I'd like my life back, even if it means that Hallie is my mother.

We make it to the park down the street before anyone catches us. People are taking selfies next to a sculpture that says LOVE. I sneak a look at Lea. If only I could be here with her, on a proper date, showing her around the sites of Philadelphia. Instead, we have to fight for our lives to make sure we aren't forced to forget the memories of today, or in my case, my entire existence.

I explained my plan on the way to the park. It will be a miracle if it works but it's better than not putting up a fight. I'm going to try and take the brunt of everything that happens and hope for the best. I really don't want any of these civilians to get hurt, especially Lea, but none of them had wanted to leave. Trust me, I kept trying to get them to. I don't want any of their blood on my hands.

"Okay, get into the positions we talked about," I instruct.

"You got it, The Amazing Boy," Gina says, giving me a salute.

Everyone else nods. They are trying to put on a brave face but Lea's biting her fingernail, Gina's eyes are darting around, Ashley's tapping her foot, and Jess keeps blinking. Is it because she's trying not to cry?

Lea looks at each one of us and says, "In case something happens, I want to say it's been great knowing everyone. I didn't even want to come on this trip but now I'm so glad I did."

Ashley shudders. "Okay, that's morbid. I hope we'll all see each other again."

I take Lea's hand. "Everything will be okay; I'll make sure of it."

Hopefully, it's a promise I can keep.

"We need to get to our places, right now," I direct.

We scatter and I inspect the tree I'm about to climb. It might be an oak or maple tree. Who am I kidding? I have no clue what it is. All I know is it's not as sturdy as I'd like but it'll have to do. It's not like the city of Philadelphia thought about the best kind of tree to plant to catch an evil villain.

I start to climb when no one is watching and take it one branch at a time. I look down on occasion to see if the Agent has appeared. He hasn't and luckily for us, the park is starting to clear out since the sun is starting to set.

I keep scanning the area when I see him. He blends in with his all-black clothes, but his menacing manner is hard to miss. He's near the LOVE sign with One-Eyed Barnacle and Dave in tow, no Hallie to be seen, which means nothing since she can impersonate anyone. *It's showtime.*

Gina struts up to the Agent and starts talking. That girl

certainly has guts. He squints and looks around, probably trying to see if he can find me.

Come on Gina, lead him my way.

I can just make out what she's saying. I put a device in my ear that gives me super hearing. Comes in handy in times like this. Gina is saying, "He's around here somewhere, I swear I just saw him."

"Why should I believe you're helping us now?" the Agent asks.

"My girlfriend and I didn't want to get mixed up in all of this. I'm hoping if I help you, you'll return our stuff to our museums, so we don't get in trouble."

They are getting closer to my tree. Just a little bit more now.

"I'll consider it. What if I give you replicas to return and some of the money after I sell the originals?"

Gina cocks her head. "That could work, depending on how much."

Gina's a decent liar, a quality that makes someone a good actor. If I keep up with my acting career after all this is over, I'll have to see if she wants to make another appearance in any future movies.

"Don't get too greedy. Let's see if you actually take us to The Amazing Boy and his little girlfriend."

The Agent is finally where I need him. I can do this. The fate of my memory, and Lea's, depends on it. I pull out the pill container and stick the pill meant for me in the palm of my hand and make a tight fist. I can't lose this. I take a deep breath, look down at my target, and jump. I land right on the Agent's back and bring him down on the ground.

He swears at the top of his lungs and breaks his fall with his hands. He's trying to get up, but I'm stuck on him, like a monkey on his back. Luckily my superstrength is working pretty well because he's having trouble pushing me off. He's twisting himself side to side like a bull trying to throw its rider but I'm hanging on for dear life. My right hand reaches for his mouth to shove the pill inside, but I'm having trouble seeing where his mouth is. My left hand keeps digging into his shoulder but it's a lot harder to hang on one-handed.

"You think you can beat me at my own game? You better think again," the Agent scoffs.

I hear a scream behind me that sounds like Dave.

"Why the arrows?" he moans.

Yes! Ashley found one target. Hopefully, she or Gina can take out One-Eyed Barnacle next before he tries and helps the Agent.

My hand finds his mouth and I attempt to slip the pill in but before I can do that, he bites down hard on my fingers.

I scream. I almost forgot what true pain feels like. Normally when I'm fighting villains, I don't get that hurt. The production crew would come to my rescue if things got too dire and help me out. But this time, except for Lea and company, I'm mainly on my own.

He keeps biting down on my fingers and not letting go. In the process, the pill falls out of my hand onto the ground. I dig the fingers of my left hand into his neck as hard as I can to see if he can release my fingers and thankfully it works. I swing off his back and bring my fingers to my face and inspect them. He's broken the skin, and the metallic smell of blood reaches my nose. The blood's dripping down my hand onto the sidewalk.

The sidewalk … where did that pill go?

I drop to the ground and begin to feel around with my uninjured hand. The dusk night is not helping. I'm not having any luck and I can sense the Agent cowering behind me. I might need a new plan but what? I spring off the ground and turn around to face the Agent.

"You thought you could beat me?" the Agent says, pushing me backward. I stumble but catch myself before I fall over. "Think again. You and your friends are going to have to come with me. I can't have you running around with everything that you know."

I see from behind him that Gina's next to One-Eyed Barnacle, not moving. *Why isn't she trying to fight him?* Her eyes are frantic. That's when I notice One-Eyed Barnacle has her pink taser pressed up against her side. *Oh no.*

At least Lea, Ashley, and Jess are hidden somewhere. Dave's on the ground holding his bloodied arm and an arrow next to him. The Agent grabs my shoulder and starts muttering. I know what will happen next if I don't somehow stop him. I have one last option. I hate to do this, especially to someone who at one point I thought of as a father figure, but he leaves me no choice.

I push a button on my watch and a red laser shoots out of it and brushes the side of the Agent's arm. He groans and drops his grasp on me.

"So now you want to fight dirty," he growls. "Dave, get up and start searching for his little girlfriend. Bet you'll not be as risky if her life is in danger."

"He doesn't have to search, I'm right here," Lea says, appearing out of the shadows, hands on her hips, eyes narrowed. Her blonde hair and gold cape are blowing behind her. Goosebumps appear on my arms. She truly looks like a superhero.

I gasp. "Lea, what are you doing? Get out of here!"

She shakes her head. "I'm tired of always hiding in the background. I need to help."

The Agent gives a menacing laugh. "You stupid girl, you aren't cut out for a life with Jonah. What can you really do anyways?"

That is really below the belt and uncalled for.

"She isn't a traitor, like you." I point my watch to his leg and press a button. He howls in pain and hobbles around on his other foot. I need to keep doing this to try and distract him from using any spells.

I hear a shriek behind me, and I turn. One-Eyed Barnacle is on the ground, an arrow sticking out of his shoulder.

"I should've kept on the armor," he cries, turning his head towards the arrow. When he sees it, a scream erupts from his mouth. Gina reaches down and grabs the taser out of his hand.

"That, you stupid pirate, belongs to me!"

Gina runs over to Lea, and they are whispering furiously. *I wonder what plan they are hatching?* Then out of nowhere, the Agent's arm punches me in the side, and I double over.

Such a rookie mistake. I took my eye off the villain. I need to get up, but my side is throbbing.

I try to lift my head and see through my squinted eyes that the Agent is giving me a sad smile. "Sorry, kid. This pains me as much as it hurts you. I've started to become fond of you, but as they say, all good things must come to an end."

I rub my side and try to push through the agony. "But it doesn't have to be like this. You don't have to steal things and be evil. We've made some incredible movies together; why do you need more than that?"

The Agent's eyes narrow. "I have bigger plans for myself than just being your *agent* and overseeing your life. I want to be the star, the one getting all the attention. The person everyone reveres but fears at the same time."

I pull myself upright and wince. "Being famous is not all it's cracked up to be. I'm sorry you had a crappy childhood, but this isn't the way to fix it. You could help other kids that are in a similar position as you were."

The Agent shakes his head. "You don't understand. I can help them when I'm super rich and famous. I'll buy my own orphanage and make sure they don't have a childhood like mine. That's why I'll be like Robin Hood."

"But you can still do that, without the stealing."

"You're too much of a do-gooder to ever understand.

Sorry Jonah, but ... OWWW," he screeches, grabbing his behind.

I peer over his shoulder and an arrow is sticking straight out of his butt, like a pointed tail, just like the devil he is. I try to hold in my snicker, but it's too hard not to.

"You're laughing now but wait until you can't remember anything. Then I'll get the last laugh," he hisses.

Lea's waving her hands and I catch up to her while the Agent's grappling with the arrow. Her shoulder's pressing up against me as she whispers in my ear. "I found more forget me pills. The bottle doesn't say who they are for, so maybe they are just generic ones?" She flashes me an orange bottle.

"I could hug you right now, but I can't get distracted," I say back.

She smiles, showing her perfect teeth. "Gina and I were thinking each one of us should keep a pill, in case we have the opportunity to give it to him."

I nod. "Good idea. Quick, slip me one."

She's got her hand on the bottle cap when she gasps. "Behind you!"

I turn around and the Agent is muttering, his eyes closed. Before I can think, I take a running leap and push him as hard as I can. He smacks his head right into the tree I had just jumped from and sinks to the ground.

"Hurry, let's give one to him now!" I call to Lea. She's opening the pill bottle when I notice Dave running at her full force.

"Watch out, Lea!" She looks up at the last moment and gives a yelp as Dave connects with her. She drops to the ground with Dave stuck on top of her, but she doesn't spill the pill container. Gina sinks the taser into Dave's back. He squeals and rolls off Lea, his body shaking uncontrollably.

Then I remember the Agent slumped against the tree; I can't take my eyes off him again. I whirl back around and he's already on his feet, his right hand clasping an asp. *Where did he get that?*

"You may be stronger than me, but I still have the upper hand. I know all your weaknesses. Your superstrength works with your upper body, but not other places."

He takes the asp and aims for my legs. I jump out of the way at the last moment. I'm not used to my opponent having so much information about me. Most of them always play into what I need them to do, hitting me up top. I can easily duck and return the hit with a wallop. But when my legs are involved, it's a bit trickier.

He laughs as I stumble backwards. "This is even better than putting a spell on you, I can see you sweat."

The Agent keeps aiming for my legs and I leap out of his way at the last moment but I'm only getting lucky. He's bound to hit me there eventually and that asp looks like it could do some serious damage. I frantically look around to see what I can use to help me out. In the meantime, I use the laser again but miss him, and almost hit a civilian. *I need to be more careful.*

In my state of panic, I'm getting clumsy. Almost hurting an innocent bystander is not at all my MO. I'm just going to have to rely on something that isn't the laser.

We're moving towards the bright red LOVE sculpture, and I yell at all the civilians to get out of our way. Gina, Lea, and Jess are streaming behind us clearing the crowd. *When did Jess appear? I told her to stay hidden.* Another liability I have to worry about.

I bump into the sculpture and am cornered. I may not be able to go backwards, but I can go up. I apologize under my breath to the city of Philadelphia and climb on the sculpture. It's harder for the Agent to reach me, but now he's muttering something under his breath.

That's when an idea hits me. It might not work as well as the tree plan, but I'm really limited in options. I take my right hand and place it on the *L* of LOVE and pull as hard as I can, with my left hand holding me steady on the *O*. The letter snaps free easier than I expect, especially since my fingers are still throbbing from where the Agent bit me. I balance myself on a metal bar between the *V* and *E*. I hate destroying artwork, but I'm out of options. I'm going to have to send money to the city to repair it.

I'm surprised the Agent hasn't hit me with a spell yet, but I look down to see that he's wrestling with an arrow stuck in his left arm. *Now's the time.* I catch Lea's eye and make a pointing motion to the Agent's throat, and she nods.

I throw the *L* and it hooks around the Agent's neck, bringing him down on the ground, with me straddling him. I keep a firm grasp on the *L* while Gina and Jess go on either side of his face and attempt to pry open his mouth. Lea's behind his head and as soon as she sees an opening, she drops a couple of white pills in his mouth. Gina and Jess clamp his mouth shut and I pull the *L* upwards so he's sitting up. If they are similar to the truth-telling pills, they will work better when they disintegrate, rather than swallowed. They hold his mouth shut even though he's struggling to open it. I didn't think Lea was going to give him more than one. Hopefully, they don't kill him.

"When do we know it worked?" Lea calls to me.

"When he stops struggling." His arms are flailing all over, almost taking out Lea's eye, but she ducks at the last moment, scrambling to hold down his limbs.

While I'm still gripping onto the *L*, I notice Ashley's walking towards us, her quiver empty. Behind her, Dave's still passed out on the ground, with a few people bending down to help him.

That's when the Agent closes his eyes and becomes limp like a rag doll. *Please don't die.* Lea's eyes are full of terror.

"What did you do to him?" One-Eyed Barnacle demands,

running up to the Agent's side. The arrow is gone, and blood is dripping down One-Eyed's shoulder.

"We're just giving him a taste of his own medicine," I say bitterly.

After a few more tense moments, the Agent's eyes fly open, cloudy, and confused.

"What's going on? Who are all of you?" he asks, his voice a different timbre.

"Be on guard, he could be faking it," I warn.

One-Eyed Barnacle looks at us incredulously, with his one eye. "He doesn't remember anything? Like at all?"

"It's too early to tell what he remembers or doesn't. What's your name?" I ask. That's when I realize I have no clue what his real name is so I wouldn't be able to even confirm if it's right or not.

"I don't know. Why don't I know my name? What's wrong with me?" he asks, his voice increasingly getting louder.

I am keeping my eye on One-Eyed Barnacle. He's starting to look a bit too happy for my liking. He's probably already plotting how to take over the Agent's business.

"Where's Hallie?" I ask him.

"Don't you mean your mother?" he replies, smirking.

I really want to wipe that smug smile off his face, but that would mean letting go of the Agent and I'm still not convinced he lost his memory. "We don't know that for sure. Where did she go?"

One-Eyed Barnacle shrugs. "We haven't seen her since she stormed out of the Master's office. Guess she was pretty mad that he erased her memory."

"Who wouldn't be? And it's all your fault!" Gina squints her eyes at the Agent.

"What do you mean? What did I do? And what's around my neck?" he asks, looking down at the *L* still hooked to him. His eyes are wild.

One-Eyed Barnacle begins to back away. Ashley, who has been sneaking up quietly behind him, takes her quiver and hits him over the head. He groans and rubs the spot she hit. Ashley grabs an abandoned arrow off the ground, probably the one that had been stuck in the Agent's butt and shoves it in One-Eyed Barnacle's face.

"You want this to go in your other shoulder? If not, you better not leave."

Gina looks at her proudly. "That's my girl!"

Now's the time for the real police to come and help. Not the Agent's fake ones. I release my hold on the *L* with my right hand and push the SOS button on my watch. This time the red light starts to flash like a heartbeat and I inwardly smile. *We've got you.*

CHAPTER FORTY-TWO

LEA

I never thought I'd be in another situation on the same day where armed policemen ask me to freeze. Jake might be used to it, but I'm not. My hands shake as I raise them above my head. Everyone else, except Dave who still isn't moving, follows suit. Even the clueless Agent does as he's told.

Everything happens at whirlwind speed. A policewoman demands to know what happened and before I can say anything, Jess speaks up. "I filmed almost everything that went down, if you want to see it."

The policewoman nods and lets Jess pull up the video on her phone. All the police officers crowd around to watch. "Are you really The Amazing Boy?" one of them asks, turning to Jake. "We heard you were shooting a movie in town but didn't realize such an amateur would be filming it."

Jess puts her free hand on her hip. "This isn't part of the movie. His agent, the guy that looks like Gru from *Despicable Me* but with more hair, turned on him!"

The police still look very confused, and I don't blame them. I think all of us are, except Jake.

One of the policemen turns to Jake. "We have to ask all of you to come down to the station while we get the facts straight. Your crew didn't mention in the briefing you'd be defacing public art."

Jake hangs his head. "Sorry about that, I'll pay to have it fixed. You should also go to the Comcast Center, floor twenty-five, last office on the right. There are a bunch of valuable items there that these men stole."

The policeman scratched his head. "What kind of items?"

"Like the musket from the Museum of the American Revolution that went missing this morning," I say.

"And items from the Eastern State Penitentiary and the Mütter Museum," Gina adds in.

The officers look skeptical but one says into his radio, "Send back-up to the Comcast Center to possibly retrieve stolen items."

He glares at us. "Now all of you need to get into our police cars right now so we can hear the full story."

My hands are sweating. I rub them against my gold spandex pants. *What if they don't believe us? I've never been questioned by the police before.* If I'm this scared, I can't even imagine what everyone else feels like. Jess is biting her lip. Gina's face is devoid of all emotion and she's taking deep breaths in and out.

"Hon, it'll be okay. We're all in this together," Ashley whispers, squeezing Gina's hand.

She nods. And if anything, we have Jake on our side.

———

JAKE WASN'T KIDDING when he said the police aren't his biggest fan. We went through some intense questioning, especially Jake. He kept getting grilled over ruining public property. In the end he had to sign some document saying that he'd pay back all the damages plus a steep fine. I guess even when you're a famous movie star and a real-life super-hero, you can't get out of everything. They did, however, clean up Jake's wounded fingers so they wouldn't get infected from whatever germs might have been in the Agent's disgusting mouth.

The police were also unsure why there was a man in their custody that had trouble remembering his name. Jake played it off as the Agent must have hit his head really hard when they were fighting. No one could find a single identity card on him either. *Maybe some things are better left unknown.*

Jake asked to have a phone call and was able to connect with a few of his crew members that hadn't turned on him. They brought some of the footage from the Comcast Center to show the police what really happened there and that's what finally convinced them we were telling the truth. The police were highly confused though about the Agent's *performance* before he lost his memory. Jake glossed over the part where the Agent could put spells on people, saying that was part of a movie scene. The police looked wary but I'm sure they weren't going to say anything different. Who would want to state aloud that they thought magic was real?

The police also put out a warrant for Hallie's arrest, but I highly doubt they will find her. She's probably already long gone, in some other form.

The policewoman that had originally brought us in walked all five of us out of the precinct.

"Can I get the box with the slides of Einstein's brain to take back to the Mütter Museum? My boss is probably frantic at this point," Ashley asks.

The policewoman shakes her head.

"Sorry, that's evidence. It'll be returned to the museum once it's approved to go back to its owners. If your boss has any questions, have them call us."

Ashley reluctantly nods. Gina whispers under her breath, "I guess that also goes for Al Capone's fedora."

The policewoman must have super hearing because she replies, "Yes, you're correct. All of you are cleared, for now, but we strongly encourage you not to leave the city over the next few days in case we need you to come back in for more questioning." She gives us a stern look.

Jess and I trade a worried glance and I bite the nail on my index finger. "Our flight back to Ohio is tomorrow."

The policewoman folds her arms. "Looks like you're going to have to change it."

"More time to tour Philadelphia, I guess," Jess says, shrugging.

"Just don't do any more damage to it," the policewoman responds, shaking her head as she walks back inside the police station.

The five of us stand there staring at each other.

"Is it really over?" Gina asks.

Ashley slings her right arm around her. "We got the bad guys! Well almost all of them. And somehow none of us got charged for anything."

"That really is a miracle. I was starting to worry a bit there," I say. "The police are so intimidating. I felt like I did something wrong even though I knew I didn't."

Gina purses her lips. "Sounds right. But thanks to Jake, we all made it out alright."

Jake ducks his head. "It wasn't just me. All of you helped. And Jess, having that footage really saved us. Good thinking."

Jess puffs out her chest. "Oh, uh, thanks." She turns to me. "What are we going to do about staying here?" Jess asks as she plays with her long, curly hair. I remember I used to love running my hands through it. Anything as a way to get closer to her.

I shrug. "It's not like my parents are going to care. I'll just move my flight to a couple of days later and see if I can find a cheap place to stay."

That's my not-so-subtle hint that she needs to do her own thing.

"Don't worry about that, I've got it covered," Jake says, casually slinging his arm around my shoulders.

"What about me?" Jess asks.

Jake sighs. "Fine. I can cover you too. What about your partner?"

Jess looks down. "I haven't heard from Olive since they yelled at me."

"That's because you didn't reach out," a voice says, coming out from beside the building.

Jess gasps. "Olive, what are you doing here? I thought you left."

"I couldn't find a flight until tomorrow morning, so it wasn't worth changing." Olive motions to me. "Lea texted me what happened to you guys. I didn't believe it at first but then I saw a video on social media about how The Amazing Boy and a gang of teenagers put his agent in jail, so I guess it's true."

Gina scoffs. "Who are they calling a teenager? I'm legal next year!"

Olive tentatively hugs Jess. "I'm still pissed at you, but why don't you come to our room tonight. We can talk things through."

Jess kicks a stone on the ground. "That sounds great. But I don't know what to do after that. The police don't want us to leave so I'm stuck in Philadelphia for a few more days."

Olive shrugs. "We can figure out what to do next. My parents probably have some extra hotel reward points that I can persuade them to let us use."

Jess's face lights up. "Thank you. I won't let you down again." She turns to me. "You'll be okay? You sure you don't want to come back with us? There are two beds."

I'd rather go back to the police station for more questioning.

I shake my head. "I'm good. Be safe and text me if you need us."

That's when it hits me, I said *us*. Am I already considering Jake and I a thing? Are we a thing?

Jess nods and trails behind Olive.

"You dodged a bullet there. That girl does not know what she wants," Gina says, shaking her head.

"It's funny, I always thought Jess was my soulmate. But it might have just been the idea of her. But now I think I really need someone who actually cares about me." As I say that I'm looking straight at Jake.

"I believe I owe you a real date," he says.

"Dinner?" I ask expectantly. My stomach is on empty; all this superhero fighting depleted the cheesesteak we ate hours ago.

"Absolutely."

CHAPTER FORTY-THREE

JAKE

Lea takes a bite out of a taco and a few black beans spill on her plate.

"This is mind numbingly good. I was so hungry I was about to faint, and this time it would have been for real," Lea says.

I take a huge gulp of my water. I'm not used to doing all this superhero work without my crew. Normally, we'd have breaks before I go find the next villain and can fuel up on water and electrolytes. But not today.

Gina gave us a restaurant suggestion in Old City Philadelphia before we said goodbye. The place isn't the swankiest restaurant but is dark and still serving food this late at night, so it's alright in my book. The joint has Día de los Muertos murals on the wall and I'm pretty sure the smell of jalapeno is permanently embedded in the red cloth covering the seats. It's a great first date spot; nothing too fancy but not a complete dive. I made sure to ask for a booth in the darkest corner. Hopefully, no fans or paparazzi see me.

I pick at my fajitas. I'm too tired and unsettled to put them together.

Lea stops and places her taco right in the fallen black beans on her bright blue plate.

"What's wrong?" she asks, her eyebrows scrunching.

"I thought I'd feel different after taking down the Agent. But I don't know, I still feel the same."

Lea reaches across the table and squeezes my hand.

"You're probably still processing. And need food and sleep."

Time to bite the bullet.

"Speaking of sleep, we still have that hostel room around here," I mention.

Lea bites her lip. "Yeah, I kind of figured that's why we are down in this area again."

"But I can get us two rooms if you want. I don't want to rush anything," I say quickly, stabbing a green pepper. "Or I could go back to my hotel that the Agent booked for me."

"One room is fine. I don't want to rush things either, but I trust you." She rubs my hand.

"But you barely know me," I say.

Lea gives me a small smile. "I know enough."

I return her smile, but then think about all the pills she swiped. I bet some of them could make Hallie remember me.

"I guess everything still feels unresolved because Hallie might be my mother but has disappeared from the face of the earth."

Lea's thumb continues to rub my hand. "That can be our next stop, after we're cleared to leave the city."

My eyes widen. "Really? You'd try and help me find her? And maybe we can look for my dad too?"

She nods. "Absolutely. You saved Jess and all those priceless artifacts. The least I can do is come help you find Hallie so we can figure out once and for all if she's actually your mom."

"Don't forget, you helped save Jess and those items too. You're the one that gave the Agent the forget me pills. We'd probably still be fighting him if you hadn't done that."

She turns red and looks down.

"Yeah, I guess."

"Don't ever sell yourself short. You're incredible and I couldn't have done any of this without you."

She chews on her fingernail. "It'll take me a bit to think that way, but okay. I'm not used to being the one doing something right."

"Well, you better get used to it."

Her eyes sparkle, her face still red.

"What about your parents? Won't they care if you aren't around this summer?" I ask.

Lea scoffs. "I'm the least of their worries. As long as I go off to college as planned, that's all they are concerned about. I'm a waitress at a diner, but I've got enough scholarships and savings to last me through the first year so I could quit."

I nod. "And, if this movie we just made ever comes out, you'd get some of the profits."

Lea's eyes widen. "Really?"

"Of course. How could you not? You helped us solve the case and were essential in taking down the villain."

"Now that your agent is out of the picture, what do you need to do for this to become a movie?" Lea asks.

I take that as a cue that Lea didn't want to talk about her parents anymore.

"I want to take a good look at the footage from today and see if any of it is salvageable."

"I still don't get how that works. Where are the cameras?" Lea's gaze ping pongs around the room.

I shrug. "I have no clue, but you saw the Agent's setup. He has some super elaborate city-wide recording system. I'm pretty sure he did that in every city we were in. He never would explain how he got all the footage, but it always came together somehow."

My stomach grumbles. *I guess I should actually eat some of this food.* I pick up a fajita tortilla, add some meat and veggies, and shove it in my mouth.

"That seems impossible, and very illegal. I bet all those people on camera never signed a release."

I hold up a finger while I finish chewing. "Oh, for sure. That's what the forget me pills are for. We'd also blur out background people so they wouldn't sue us for being in a movie they didn't agree to."

Lea pulls her hand away from mine and uses it to prop up her head. "That's so wrong. What will happen this time though now that I have all of the pills?"

I look up from my plate into Lea's blue eyes. "This will be the final chapter of The Amazing Boy and the Agent's movie franchise, going out with a final bang. We can try and contact people that show up clearly in the movie or continue blurring them out, but I don't want anyone else forgetting things that happened. I'm done with that."

"That sounds like a perfect way for it to end. Is The Amazing Boy going to retire?" Lea asks, a hint of sadness creeping in her voice.

"I don't think so. I want to help the world, but for real this time, without being manipulated by the Agent. I enjoy saving historical artifacts from villains, but this time, the artifacts would actually go back to their owners. I will be the producer and I'd donate a portion of the profits to people that want to adopt children but can't afford the cost. Everyone deserves to have a family. And I'd like you to be by my side, if possible," I say, still staring into her eyes.

Maybe someday I can become a real actor, but I think what I really wanted is to have something of my own. Something I can control, which is now possible without the Agent. I might as well do something useful with this gift I was given, for actual good this time.

"That sounds awesome, but I do have college soon," she says, trailing off.

"You can do both. You can even use your history degree to help us. I'd stay in my condo in Hollywood, and we'd kick some villain butt around that area with a camera crew following us around, and we'd make sure people sign off on consent forms. That way we're doing this the right way."

Lea scratches her head. "UCLA isn't too far from Hollywood," she says.

"Just think about it. We have time."

I didn't want to put pressure on her, but if she says no, I don't know if I would want to do this without her.

———

I'M PLACING my credit card on top of the bill when a gravelly voice says, "Make room for me."

My eyes dart to my left and I do a double take.

"Hallie? How did you find us?" My mouth grows dry and I take a quick swig of water. I know I had wanted to find her, but now that she's here, I'm not sure what to do.

She motions for me to move over, and I scoot as far as I can against the wall of the booth. What a great way to end our first date, a guest appearance from my supposed mother and the villain that has been putting Lea down since they met. Lea's eyes are watching Hallie like a hawk, her hand glued to her phone.

"Cool your jets, girl. I'm not going to try anything. I'm just here to have a conversation with my *son*," she says, using air quotes.

"You didn't answer my question. How did you find us?" I try as hard as I can to keep my voice from shaking.

"The Master keeps tabs on you through the tracking

device in your watch. He spilled that info at the Comcast Center when I made him tell me what the hell was going on. I stole his phone when I left earlier so I could find you."

No wonder the Agent always knew where I was but had trouble finding me in the park. Not only did he have cameras everywhere but tracking devices. I need to get rid of this watch ASAP. I look down at it and frown. It's got all the bells and whistles and has been with me since day one, but I guess it's time to start fresh.

"Don't you know that the police are looking for you?" Lea asks, her other hand squeezing the side of the table so hard that the tips of her fingers are bright red.

Hallie smirks. "That's the fun part of being a shapeshifter, sweetheart. I can turn into anyone, including you."

Lea pales. "Anyone? That's horrifying."

Hallie clears her throat. "Well, anyone that I can picture. I can't just shapeshift into someone I've never seen before."

I take another sip of water before I ask, "What's the probability you're my mother?"

Hallie rubs her chin. "My memories, up until a couple of years ago, are pretty blurry which aligns perfectly with when you became a movie star. I just thought maybe I did too many drugs in my younger years but apparently, it's from the Master's stupid memory spell. As much as I don't want to admit it, it's probably true."

I force myself to look into her cold gray eyes. They are lined with lots of black makeup. *How can this person be my mother?*

"What's that mean for us?" I am not really sure I want to hear her answer, but I have to know.

She shakes her head. "I don't want to be anyone's mother." My stomach twists and blood pounds against my temple. I had been preparing for her to say something like this but to hear it aloud is something else.

"I have some pills I stole that probably can reverse the

memory spell. What if you take one of those? I bet you would want to be Jake's mom then," Lea pipes up before I can say anything.

Hallie glares at her. "Just because I can't remember doesn't mean I want to. It's best to leave the past buried."

I was ninety-nine percent sure Hallie wouldn't want to take them, but I didn't realize how much it would hurt hearing her say it. It feels like the wind is knocked out of me, just like when the Agent punched me in the gut earlier today. I look away from both of them as I'm processing this information. I can shove a pill in her mouth but that just feels wrong. No one should force their mother to remember them.

"Then he's better off without you. Who knows, you might not even be his real mom. That could have been a lie that Jake's Agent came up with to throw him off his mom's real scent," Lea says.

Hallie's eyes narrow. "Then why are my memories so weird? As much as I hate it, I'm pretty sure I'm Jake's mom. It all makes sense."

I turn back to her, in more control of my emotions. "What do you really look like? The Agent said that this isn't your original form."

Hallie looks flustered. "I haven't been that shape in so long. I always revert to this form. My true shape is so old."

I stare her down. "It will tell us once and for all if you're my mother."

The waitress takes that moment to come over to see if we need anything else. She looks down at Hallie.

"Oh, you're new. Do you want anything?" she asks, pulling out a pad of paper from her black apron.

Hallie shakes her head. "No. I was just getting ready to leave."

The waitress shrugs and takes the bill and my credit card off the table. After she's out of earshot Hallie says, "I tracked you down because I wanted to tell you not to try and find me.

I'm going into hiding and not interested in any type of relationship."

I grit my teeth. "If that's the case, just show us what you really look like, and we'll leave you alone, once and for all."

Hallie looks around and no one's watching us now. She closes her eyes and instantly transforms. Her black hair is replaced by brown streaked with gray. Her cloudy gray eyes are now dark brown eyes staring directly at me. Ones like my own. She's wearing a flowery blouse and beige dress pants.

My mouth opens and no words come out.

"Woah. The resemblance is ridiculous," Lea breathes.

I can't stop staring at her. She looks exactly like I remember, just a little older.

My mom blinks. "I told you I was most likely your mother. That satisfy you?"

Her voice even sounds the same. I'd recognize it anywhere. I remember the countless bedtime stories she read to me with that voice until I fell asleep. I mutely nod, tears starting to form in the corners of my eyes. *My worst nightmare has come true. This heartless person really is my mother.*

"Turn back to your other form. I can't stand looking at you anymore, because even if you're my mother, you will never be her," I spit.

Hallie reverts to her all-black look, including her hair. I let out the breath I'm holding. At least now I know the truth and won't linger on some thread of hope that my real mom might be out there. I need to move on and figure out where I fit in this crazy world.

Hallie's staring straight at me, not able to see the flashing blue and red lights outside the window.

"You've made yourself very clear that you want nothing to do with me. But I don't think you'll be able to hide very long. I have a few new friends on speed dial that might have a couple of questions for you," I say in a monotone voice.

It's at that moment that the doors burst open, and three

policemen come barreling in the restaurant. "Police, everyone stay where you are!" Hallie's face pales. I have to do something before she shapeshifts.

"Over here, the one next to me," I say, pointing. Everyone's eyes are on us. It's too late for Hallie to do anything.

"You little bastard, you were stalling," she hisses.

I shrug. "You want nothing to do with me and trust me, the feeling is mutual. But I wouldn't be called The Amazing Boy if I let a dirty criminal get away, even if you are my mother."

Two policemen pull Hallie out of the booth. One reads Hallie her rights as the other one slaps handcuffs on her.

"And don't worry, I won't be visiting you in jail," I call as they lead her outside.

The last policeman lingers at our table. "Thanks for the tip, The Amazing Boy. You just saved the city a lot of time and resources."

I nod. "Hey, it's all part of my job. Happy to help."

He props himself against our table and asks, "Can I get a selfie with you? My kid loves all your movies, and it would make me seem cool in his eyes."

We get our selfie, and the place starts to clear out.

Lea keeps blinking a lot. "That was impressive. How did you get the police to come here so fast?"

I bring up my wrist to show off my fancy watch. "This thing has an SOS button on it. Once I push it, The Amazing Boy distress signal goes to the closest police station. I was hoping that this precinct would have talked to the one we went to, and I guess they did. That's also how I called the police at the park. But I need to get rid of it now that I know there's a tracking device installed."

"Maybe you can get someone to remove the tracking device?" Lea suggests, scratching her head.

"That'd be nice, but I think it's time to start over. Remove any trace of the Agent from me. That means I'll also need a new suit and glasses. It will be a good chance to rebrand myself," I say, getting into the idea as I'm saying it aloud.

The waitress chucks a pen, the receipt, and my credit card on the table and scampers away, biting her lip. If that isn't a sign that we need to leave, I don't know what is.

"This has to be the weirdest date ever," Lea says. She must realize how that sounds because she quickly adds, "Not that it's a bad thing. It keeps things interesting, that's for sure."

I pick up the pen, leave the tip, and sign my fake credit card name.

"If you keep hanging around me, this is what happens," I say in all seriousness. "Are you okay with that?" I catch her eye.

She vigorously nods her head. "Yes. Absolutely yes. I'm totally down for more weird, not boring dates."

I break into a huge smile. "Good."

CHAPTER FORTY-FOUR

LEA

And then there is one bed. It's not like Jake hasn't warned me about the one bed situation, I just conveniently made myself not think about it. I've shared a bed with Jess many times and that's when things usually got heated.

I'm still standing at the entrance of the room, stuck to the ground. Jake comes back to me and says, "I can take the floor."

I shake my head, "No, you don't have to do that. I'm fine."

Am I ready for this? And what is this? He's not the same Jake that's portrayed on the gossip sites. The one with a new girl every week. I'm not the flavor of the day, right? I mean he did invite me to Hollywood to fight bad guys with him. That has to mean something.

Jake lightly holds my hand and leads me into the room.

"I really care about you, but if this is too much, we can get separate rooms," he says, taking a piece of my hair stuck in my eyelashes and tucking it behind my ear. "Or I can leave."

I shake my head. "No, it's not you. It's just so hard to trust anything after Jess broke my heart," I confess.

His hand is still in mine and he squeezes. "We are getting to know each other first, so you can see I won't do that to you. We're both tired and had one of the longest days ever. We're just going to chill and sleep. That's it, I promise."

"That works for me." I let out the breath I've been holding in. "It also takes me some time to feel something, like in a sexual way." I look down at the ground. I haven't told many people I'm demisexual, and Jake didn't seem to care when I first met him, and hopefully he still doesn't.

Jake nods his head vigorously. "Absolutely. No pressure."

"What about our clothes?" I ask, chewing on the side of my finger.

He looks down at his costume. "What do you mean?"

"Neither of us have anything else to sleep in. My suitcase is with Jess and Olive."

He shrugs. "We can sleep in our costumes."

I really, really want to be free of the sweat-soaked material clinging to my body but what he says makes sense.

His cheeks are becoming red and he's rubbing his free hand on the side of his leg. "Honestly Lea, I really like you and want whatever this is between us to eventually become something more. And we can take all the time you need."

I smile. "I'd like that. Being with you makes me incredibly happy."

"Then that's all we need right now. And if more happens, that's great, if not, we at least have each other as friends," Jake says, staring down into my eyes. I don't know if it's a sixth sense, but I can tell he's telling me the truth.

"That sounds perfect."

AFTER WE BOTH have taken showers, we lay in bed wearing robes. I couldn't stand putting back on my dirty clothes so Jake made a quick phone call and these super plush white robes appeared. There's no way they came from the hostel. Even without the Agent, he's still able to pull some strings.

Jake and I turn to stare at each other, me into his dark brown eyes. They no longer have a sadness that I had at one point noticed.

"You seem more hopeful," I point out. "I'm not sure if you want to talk about it, but I was worried about that revelation with Hallie."

His smile disappears. "I've been having such a great time with you, it kind of left my mind."

I take his hand into mine. "I'm so sorry. I can't even imagine what you're feeling."

He gazes out the window and takes his time to reply. "For so long I had this dream that I'd see her again and once I explained everything, she'd want to remember me. I never imagined she'd be some villain teaming up against me."

I squeeze his hand. "What about your dad? You still have no idea who he is. What if we look for him?"

Jake turns and it's hard to look into his downcast brown eyes.

"Is it worth it? He might be like Hallie and not care if I even exist."

"But you won't know until you try. Isn't it better than never knowing?"

Jake scratches his head. "Where would I even start?"

"What about where you were born? That could be something."

"And you'd come with me?" He clears his throat.

"Absolutely. It sounds like a fun road trip."

Jake studies my face. "You seem happier."

"I am. I don't think I realized how much Jess was weighing me down. What she did to me was constantly on my mind. But now that she and I talked, I'm over her more than I realized. I had been missing the thought of her." I take a good look at Jake, with his kind eyes and infectious grin. "Now I have you. Someone I genuinely care for and want to learn more about. And you like me for who I am."

Jake puts his arm around me, and I lean my head on his chest.

"That's what I like to hear. Tomorrow we can figure out our plan to save the world from other criminals, but tonight we can just be here, together, and no one can take that away from us. Not even some supervillain or my dead-beat mom."

"Or a pirate," I add in.

We both laugh at the same time.

"He had to be the worst pirate known to mankind," I say.

"Hands down. He didn't even have a real parrot, only the ones on his boxers. I thought that was a pirate requirement."

Jake's quiet for a second and adds, "I want to see what happens next and help other people because now I know we will actually be assisting them, and I can do it on my own terms."

I trace my index finger along his hand. "I'd like to help others too. I only ever thought college was my next step, but if there is some other purpose I should be serving that I can do at the same time, I'd be open to it. And recovering historical artifacts is perfect for me. Our movies could be like Marvel meets National Treasure."

Jake squeezes me tighter. "But we'd be way cooler than any Marvel hero and Nicolas Cage. With my strength and your knowledge, we'd be the perfect match. The villains won't know what hit them."

I return his smile. He always knows how to make me feel special.

Jake yawns. "As much as I want to stay up talking all night, I need to get some sleep, otherwise I'll be useless."

My whole body feels heavy. "Same," I reply, covering my mouth with my hand as I also yawn.

"We can see what tomorrow brings. In the world of superheroes, things are always a surprise," Jake says, settling under the sheets and laying his head on the pillow.

No truer words have been spoken. Neither of us have the answers to what will come, but at least we have this moment together before we face the real world. And that is enough for me.

EPILOGUE

JAKE

I stand with my hands in my jean pockets outside of the house that supposedly belongs to my father. *Do I really want to do this? Do I want to be rejected again?*

Lea's there beside me, just like she has been the past couple of weeks. After we were cleared to leave Philadelphia, I took a flight home with her, Jess, and Olive. It wasn't as awkward as I thought it would be. Jess and Olive were back to dating each other and didn't really notice us. Lea was even able to switch seats with some random guy to be next to me.

Once we got to Ohio, I booked a room in one of those extended stay hotels for the week. I took a DNA test at Lea's suggestion and after only waiting a little over a week, a match came back to someone who has the DNA of my supposed father. *David Smith.* If that doesn't sound like a fake name, I don't know what is. And I should know, I have quite a few.

What was shocking to me is he's not living in the town I

grew up in, but in Grand Rapids, Michigan. Lea and I rented a car to go up there for a weekend, telling her parents she was going on a road trip to see a new state before she heads off to college in California.

When I asked their response, she shrugged. "As long as I don't come back pregnant, I don't think they care." As soon as those words escaped her mouth, her cheeks got all red.

"I didn't mean that you'd get me pregnant, I just mean ..." she trailed off.

I chuckled. "No, I got it."

After some sleuthing, we found the exact spot where my supposed father lives. It really isn't hard these days to track anyone down. What did people do without the internet? Probably live a quieter, less intrusive life.

It was a four-hour drive but it passed by like the blink of an eye with Lea. We laughed at all the random sites we came across like the *World's Largest Beer Can* and lost track of the number of cows.

And now is the moment of truth.

I walk up closer to my *father's* home. It's a two-story brick house with red shutters, a couple of bushes in the front, but not much else. I turn to look at Lea and she squeezes my hand. "I'm not going anywhere."

I shakily reach for the doorbell but before I can press it, the front door creaks open. I see a man taller and skinnier than me through the screen. He's wearing jeans, a T-shirt that might be from a local craft brewery, and a scruffy beard. He looks like the typical man you'd imagine would live in Michigan.

"You might as well come in," he says, opening the screen door towards us.

"Don't you want to know who I am?" I ask, staring into his brown eyes that look like mine. And I had thought Hallie looked just like me. This guy's entire face shape, even though its more shrunken, is an exact replica of my own.

"I know who you are, but you better get in here before anyone sees you. I have a reputation of being a loner to uphold." He quickly ushers us inside.

I stand frozen in the hallway. *How am I actually here, in my dad's house?* And he hasn't turned us away yet.

He shuts the door and locks the doorknob and two different sets of deadbolts. Lea looks at him, her eyebrows raised.

"You can never be too sure of anyone these days," he explains. "Now come sit at the kitchen table and I'll bring some pop."

Pop, what is pop?

Lea and I settle in at a small, wooden table that only sits four people in his small kitchen that's in desperate need of an update. The refrigerator is off-white, with nothing on it. Not even a magnet. Even the kitchen counters are pretty bare, except for a coffee pot and knife set.

He brings two sodas and sets them in front of us and grabs a beer for himself. Lea looks around and asks, "Coaster?"

He shrugs. "Don't worry about it. I got this table at Goodwill and it's probably older than you. I never know how long I'm going to stay at a place, so I don't invest in much."

I pop open the can, maybe that's why it's called pop, and take a swig. Too bad it isn't something stronger, I have a feeling I'm going to need it.

"I know Jonah, but who are you?" My dad turns to Lea. I wince at him saying my birth name.

"I'm here for moral support," Lea says, reaching over and rubbing my arm.

"And she's my partner in crime," I say proudly.

My dad nods.

I've had enough of this. There is so much I need to know. "How do you know who I am?" I ask.

He looks intently into my eyes. "How can I not? You're my son. I've been following your career."

My mouth falls. "Wait, what? I thought you deserted my mom and I when I was a baby," I say, thoroughly confused. "Why would you want to follow my career?"

My dad sighs. "That agent of yours lied to you. Your mom and I, well we never really did get along, so it was best if we lived separately from each other, but I still wanted to have some kind of relationship with you. But when you started acting and then were found by your agent, that all changed. I was cut off from you."

"The Agent had something to do with this?" I ask. "He said he had no idea who you were."

My dad shakes his head. "That's what he led you to believe but no, I was there. I tried to come get you, and have you live with me, but he slipped me one of those forget me pills in my whiskey. It didn't have the effect he wanted though. The next day I woke up with a nasty hangover, but still remembered everything, so he had a last-ditch resort."

"What do you mean?" I ask, pulling myself closer to the table.

"You and your mom were the ones that got the forget me pills that were meant for me."

Lea gasps. "No! But Jake remembers his mom."

"It was just intended for him to forget I ever existed, because there was no way I'd ever forget him, not with my special abilities. I guess your agent thought it would be too odd if you couldn't remember both your mom and dad, so he chose to completely erase me."

Silence hung in the air until I uttered, "Special abilities? Are you like me?"

My dad scratches his beard. "Not quite. I'm a telepath. Probably why the forget me pills wouldn't work."

My mouth opens and then shuts. *Does that mean he can hear*

what I am thinking right now? I better not think of anything I wouldn't want him to hear, like how hot Lea looks right now, with her determined expression.

My dad gives me a half smile. "I try not to use them to listen into people's heads unless I need to."

Does that mean he heard me or not?

"But why did you never come and find me? Or try and help me?"

My dad takes a long sip of his beer. "I wanted to, trust me, but your agent made it very clear that if I came near you, both you and I would pay a price. And from afar things didn't look too bad. You were a movie star; I could never give you that."

"But Mom's memory was wiped so I didn't have either parent!" I exclaim. "And apparently she was some minion of the Agent's."

My dad sighed. "I'm sorry. I should have tried harder, but I thought maybe forgetting about me was for the best. I usually cause people nothing but trouble. I took a DNA test a few months ago, under this alias, hoping that maybe you'll take one too someday, wanting to find me."

Lea gasps, "So you did want Jake to look for you."

My dad nods. "There isn't a day that goes by that I don't think about you. I saw on the news you apprehended your agent and I was getting ready to find you, but you beat me to the punch."

Lea tugs on my arm. "Jake, we have some remember me pills left. Maybe you should take one?"

Do I want to remember everything that I lost? Maybe Hallie, aka my mom, is right, that sometimes it's best to leave things forgotten.

I look over at my dad. His face is unreadable. "What do you think?" I ask him.

"It's up to you. I understand if you don't want to take it. You probably have a lot of issues with trust right now, but if you do take the pill and remember our times together, you might be surprised."

"What about Mom?" I ask.

My dad cocks his head. "What about her?"

"If I take the pill, will you and I go back to being a happy family without my mother?"

"Is she still calling herself Hallie and wearing all black?" he asks me, raising his eyebrows.

I nod. "Yep. She changed into Mom's original form for one quick second, so I know she's in there somewhere, but how do we reach her?"

He sighs. "There are some things in life you can change, and others you cannot. I think she's too far gone at this point. But if you're up for it, I'd like to make up for lost time."

I figured as much about Hallie, but it doesn't make it hurt any less. But maybe he's right. One parent is better than none, especially since I really am on my own right now, except for having Lea.

Lea reaches into her purse and pulls out an orange pill container. She gingerly places it on the table in front of me.

I quickly grab it, open the top, and throw one pill into my mouth before I have second thoughts. It strangely tastes like marshmallows. No wonder people that we give it to don't usually spit it out. It's just like candy. I wait for it to disintegrate. Lea and my dad both stare at me, barely blinking and not saying a word. *How long will this take?* I wonder.

After a minute, my head begins to pound, and I raise my hand to my temple. *Hopefully, it isn't a truth-telling pill or even worse, a kill pill.*

The headache just gets worse, so much so I have to close my eyes and put my head down on the table. I feel like I'm floating and am far away from everything in the world. *What did I do?*

Then I hear, "Jake. Jake, are you okay?" and a feeling of someone rubbing my back. I attempt to open my eyes and see

Lea peering worriedly at me. My dad has risen from his chair and has his phone in his hand, as if he's prepared to call 911.

I look at him and all the memories rush back. Each and every one of them burst into my head like a montage during the finale of a TV series. When he taught me how to ride a bike, the times we threw a football around, when I could hear him and my mom arguing about my future, and most importantly, when the Agent gave me some white pill, saying it would help me keep up my superstrength. That's the last memory to appear.

"You weren't lying," I whisper.

He shakes his head. I push myself out of the chair and slowly walk over to him. He opens his arms and I meet him and am enveloped into his hug. One I distinctly remember; he even smells the same, like fresh pine.

It's not the happy ending I am expecting but I don't care. Who knew that my dad is the one that would be waiting for me at the end. If this was still part of my movie, it's when everyone in the theater would either be in tears or groan at the cheesy ending. I'm not always a fan of cheesy, but this isn't the films, but my real life. I finally found what I've been looking for, when I am least expecting it.

I pull away and smile over at Lea. "Thank you for giving me my dad back," I say, wrapping my arm around her. "You're the one that got the pill for me. I'll always remember this moment."

She hugs me back and says, "And I'll always remember how you make me feel like I'm worth something, that I can do anything."

I give her the largest smile I've probably had in years, the kind that physically hurts you to make but you can't stop even if you try. Nothing with me is fake anymore, not my smile, not my personality, and not even my name. Bad boy, superficial Jake Johnson is gone forever. Time to be Jonah again but this time I can do whatever I want and not be scared someone's memory will be erased. Not only can I remember my past, but I still have all the newer memories that are equally important. Now I can move onto the next stage of my life and truly help the world. I'm going to become the best version of The Amazing Boy I can be, this time on my own terms.

ACKNOWLEDGMENTS

I can't believe I'm writing the acknowledgements for my second book. I had so much fun with this story, but it was also the hardest thing I've ever written and very much out of my comfort zone, so I'm grateful to everyone that helped me along the way.

Thank you to my wonderful team at Creative James Media. Staci, thank you for loving Lea and Jake's crazy adventure. Rachel, thank you for being my amazing editor; Stuart, thank you for being my sensitivity reader; and Jean, thanks for always believing in me and my work.

Thank you, Diana, from Triumph Covers, for my beautiful cover and thank you LGBTQ Reads/Dahlia for my exclusive cover reveal. I appreciate my beta readers Neil and Mariel. Your thoughts and wisdom were very helpful. Sierra, thank you for blurbing this book! It's been great getting to know you through our various author events.

Thank you to the amazing 2023 debut group. You've been such a support to me as I tried to finish this story while caring for a newborn and attempting to market my debut book *Does Love Always Win?*

Charley, thank you for always beta reading my books, including this one; your ideas are always so insightful. Someday soon we need to meet for tea.

Mariah, thank you for beta reading and providing a blurb for this book. It wouldn't be the way it is today without your help. I also love our daily voice memos to each other about writing and life; they always brighten my day.

Robin, thanks for your blurb and always being there to listen when I have writerly questions and inevitably face imposter syndrome. When I was unsure of *Superficial's* ending, you gave me advice that will always stay with me.

To my awesome street team, Bruce, Carmen, Kristina, Mariah, Robin, and Shannon, thank you for everything you have done to promote this book.

Heather, ever since we met back in sixth grade, you've always wanted to read my stories. Thank you for being a super early reader of *Superficial* and loving it.

To my family members and all my friends and co-workers. You are always championing my writing and having your support means so much to me.

Luke, I can't wait until you are old enough to read this book.

Thank you to my fantastic husband, Matt. You were the first person to ever read *Superficial* and I appreciate that you pushed me to keep going with the story. You always believe in me and make me a better person. I love you.

Lastly, thank you to all my readers. I love receiving your messages and hope you enjoy this new book.

ABOUT THE AUTHOR

Diane Billas lives in the suburbs of Philadelphia with her husband and son. When she's not writing she can be found reading multiple books at once, performing the French horn or piano, and dreaming of the next country she's going to visit. She is the author of the young adult sapphic romance *Does Love Always Win?* featured in *Parents* magazine, and the young adult queer superhero book *Superficial.* You can connect with Diane at dianebillas.com, on Twitter, TikTok, and Facebook @dianebillas, and on Instagram and Threads @dianebillaswrites.

www.ingramcontent.com/pod-product-compliance
Lightning Source LLC
Chambersburg PA
CBHW061644190726

48289CB00006B/1739